FUGITIVE FROM INJUSTICE

A County Wicklow Mystery

by Robert T. McMaster

UNQUOMONK PRESS
Williamsburg, Massachusetts
U. S. A.

FUGITIVE FROM INJUSTICE:
A County Wicklow Mystery

Copyright © 2023 by Robert T. McMaster

www.WicklowMysteries.com

Published by Unquomonk Press
Williamsburg, Massachusetts USA

ISBN 9798869031457

Dedicated to

Hannah Hughes McGurk

(1821 – 1884)

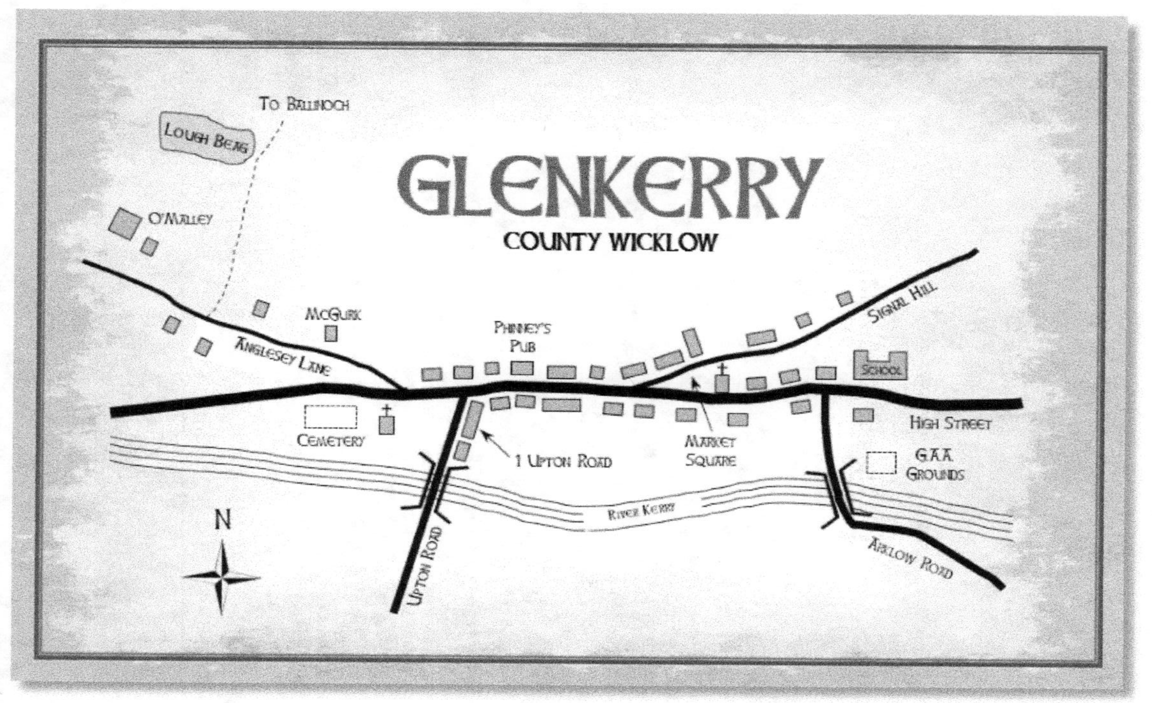

GLENKERRY
COUNTY WICKLOW
To Ballinoch
Lough Berg
O'Malley
McGurk
Anglesey Lane
Phinney's Pub
Signal Hill
School
Cemetery
1 Upton Road
Market Square
High Street
G.A.A. Grounds
Upton Road
River Kerry
Arklow Road
N

Contents

*'There are no strangers here,
only friends you haven't met yet.'*

William Butler Yeats

1 LOST CATS AND JUMBLE SALES

Cary McGurk and Rosie O'Malley stepped out of the Fishmonger on the High Street in Glenkerry carrying their takeaway supper in a brown paper bag. They walked together past a row of lime-washed storefronts–a launderette, a beauty salon, an estate agency–before entering a white two-storey stone building with black quoins at the intersection of High Street and Upton Road, the offices of the *Glenkerry Gazette*.

Cary's father, Patrick McGurk, had published the *Gazette* in that modest building for nearly three decades, beginning in the days of manual typesetting and offset printing. The information age was slow to invade Glenkerry–even in the early years of the new millennium Patrick resisted the inevitable process of computerization. But competition from online news and social networking proved too much for both man and newspaper. It was a sad occasion, some five years past, when the last issue of the *Gazette* went to press–sad for Patrick, sad for his family, and sad for the citizens of Glenkerry.

Then, just two months ago, the *Glenkerry Gazette* got a new lease on life. Twenty-one-year-old Ciaran McGurk, encouraged by his mother, by Rosie, and by many townspeople, decided to revive the newspaper. It seemed a fitting homage to his father who died in early June, just one day before Cary's graduation.

The ground floor of 1 Upton Road that housed the *Gazette* offices consisted of three small rooms furnished with a ragtag collection of desks, chairs, grey file cabinets, and several rickety bookshelves containing a few old reference books: the 2010 *World Almanac*, a 1980s edition of the *Oxford English Dictionary*, and a *Philip's World Atlas* that included a map of the U.S.S.R. and its fifteen Soviet Socialist Republics.

At the top of a steep, narrow flight of stairs was a small flat with a sitting room, bedroom, and kitchen, the place that Cary now called home. It too was furnished sparsely, largely with items Cary had purchased at used furniture shops in Bray and Dublin.

At the rear of the building a wooden table stood on a tiny patch of grass with a view of the River Kerry. There Cary and Rosie sat in the late afternoon sun, their fish, chips, and mushy peas spread on a serviette before them.

'So, you excited about your new job, Rosie?' asked Cary. He cast her a doubtful gaze, struggling to imagine Rosie O'Malley, the epitome of sweetness and light, in that particular role.

'Yeah, sure,' she replied confidently. 'I mean, I know the place, right? And I can ride my bike to work–that's a big plus.' She paused, munching on a chip. 'We'll see how it goes. Anyway, I can't just stay at home weeding the garden and feeding the chickens the rest of my life, can I? I need some regular income.'

Rosie was now the sole occupant of her family's home on Anglesey Lane, a short distance west of the centre of Glenkerry. Her father, Harry O'Malley, had died in July. Her mother, Mary O'Malley, was living in Galway now with Gerald Flaherty, an old flame from her school days. She had left Harry last spring after enduring his abuse and neglect for many years, leaving Rosie alone in the family homestead.

'What does your ma think about your new job? Have you told her?'

'I talked to her a bit last evening. She thinks it's a good idea.'

'She and Gerry doing okay?'

'Yep, just fine. They invited me to visit, maybe on Michaelmas weekend.'

'What about the house? Any news?'

Only after her father's death had Rosie learned that her parents had never been legally married. Harry, it turned out at the time of his death, was still married to a woman from Wexford. He left no will, but the nearly thirty years that Mary and Harry lived together seemed to leave the way clear for Mary to inherit the property.

Rosie shook her head. 'No, but she thinks it will be hers in just a few weeks, if the probate court approves. Then she says she'll sign it over to me and Buddy.'

Buddy O'Malley was Rosie's younger brother. Just nineteen, he was living with his girlfriend Danielle in Shankill and working in a garage in Dalkey. They had an older brother, now twenty-five, but Jimmy O'Malley was serving several sentences in a prison in Dublin for drugs offences and did not figure in his family's plans.

'So, is the next issue of the *Gazette* almost ready to go?' asked Rosie. She knew the weekly went to press on Tuesdays.

Cary shook his head. 'No, not nearly,' he groaned. 'I've got so much work to do. Plus the printer will be wanting to be paid, of course, and I'm skint–flat broke. My ma will lend me the cash, if I ask, but she's sunk so much into this place, and helped me with most of my August bills, so I hate to ask her again.'

'Well, you must have *some* income, right?' asked Rosie.

He picked distractedly at the last piece of battered monkfish. Rosie had noticed a certain darkening of Cary's mood in recent weeks. She had a feeling she had hit on the source of his gloom.

'Yeah, subscriptions and advertising, but they're all so slow. Meanwhile I gotta pay the printer, insurance, the electricity bill.'

He buried his head in his hands for a moment, as if trying to fend off all the bad news.

'My big mistake was that special offer for new subscribers, yeh know?' He spread both hands to suggest a banner headline: '*Get the first four issues free–then we'll bill you for a one-year subscription.*'

'But I thought you said you were surprised at the response.'

Cary nodded. 'Well, yeah. There were over six hundred takers–*for those four free weeks.*' He rolled his eyes to emphasise his point. 'But the subscription bills went out two weeks ago and so far I've received only a few dozen payments. What if that's it? Fewer than one hundred paid subscribers?'

He shuddered, then took a deep breath. 'A good story's what I need. Something other than lost cats and jumble sales. Something that will get people interested, make them want to buy the paper.' He paused, then added with a chuckle, 'Maybe even make a few subscribers feel obligated *to actually pay.*'

'It'll happen, Car. Everyone in Glenkerry wants the *Gazette* to succeed–they want *you* to succeed. They'll come through, I'm sure of it.'

She stood, took his hand, and led him out across the small patch of grass to that view of the river, its waters roiling as they passed beneath the Upton Road bridge. The distant hills were bathed in the late day sun, each pasture a different hue of green or gold, the sky beyond a stunning turquoise. She wrapped her arms around Cary's waist and kissed him.

'Trust me, they will,' she added.

Gazing into her green eyes, then at her plaits of auburn hair turned golden in the sunlight, he couldn't help but smile. 'Yeah, you're right–or at least I hope you are, else the *Glenkerry Gazette* and Cary McGurk are goin' down–hard.'

'Walk me up the hill?' she asked.

'You could stay here tonight, yeh know.'

She smiled shyly, holding one of his hands in hers and stroking it softly. 'Thank you, Car. I'd love to. But I got animals to feed. And I need a good night's sleep.'

'What, you're saying you wouldn't get a good night's sleep here?' he asked with an innocent grin.

'Yeah, well, we both know how that goes, eh?' She blushed. 'On the weekend–Friday night, Saturday night–I promise we can lie in all we want, okay?'

They walked up Anglesey Lane hand-in-hand, past Cary's mother's house, to the O'Malley farmhouse a short distance beyond. At Rosie's front door they said their final goodbyes.

'Oh, I'm running on the beach in the morning–early,' added Cary. 'Hope to get my head in a better place, yeh know?'

This is good, thought Rosie, *self-help–he knows he needs to pull himself out of this funk.*

'Okay, well, I'll stop by the office on my way 'ome, half-three or so–if I survive my first day, that is.'

Cary smiled. 'I hope everything goes well for you. Just remember my advice: don't so much as crack a smile for at least a month, Rosie.' She contorted her sweet smile into an ogrish glower. They both laughed.

'*Slán agat,*' said Cary.

'*Slán leat,*' replied Rosie.

The Black Castle

2 RUNNER'S HIGH

The placid waters of the Irish Sea shine dark green in the pre-dawn light as Cary descends the stone steps to the beach at Wicklow town the next morning. He's wearing tan gym shorts, a pair of well-worn runners, and a t-shirt sporting the profile of his idol, Irish songster Van Morrison.

He stands for several minutes taking in the scene before him. Sunrise is still a few minutes away, but the eastern horizon is already streaked with crimson, pink, and blue. High on a rocky promontory to the north stands Black Castle, waves heaving and ebbing at its base. According to archaeologists, the original fortress at that site dated back nearly a thousand years to Viking times. The structure was destroyed several times, then rebuilt on the same site. All that remains today are several sections of stone wall, the mortar holding them in place having been repaired many times.

To the south a long narrow strip of sand stretches into the distance. Cary kicks off his runners and leaves them in the sand, then begins his barefoot run along the beach. All is stillness but for the raucous calls of herring gulls soaring over the shallows, searching for a meal.

This beach holds a special place in Cary's childhood memories. Many were the times his father took him and his brother Aiden on early morning rambles here. The pungent smell of the salty air, the thunderous crash of the waves, and the warmth of his father's hand around his, those sensations feel just as fresh now as they did all those years ago.

Cary is missing his father these days. Patrick McGurk died suddenly after a series of strokes over two days back in June. The empty feeling Cary felt in his chest that day remains even now, a visceral reminder of his loss that all the sympathy he and his mother received, all those gifts of meat pie and aubergine lasagna, could not assuage. Revisiting this beach at sunrise is his way of calling up those memories, of holding them, examining them, reliving them.

For days he has wished for a break from his worries about the *Gazette*, for a chance to fill his lungs with fresh sea air and perhaps rejuvenate his flagging spirits. And right now a run at Travelhawk Beach feels like a remedy, a badly needed antidote, for his malaise.

He runs for nearly half an hour in the firm, moist sand just above the tideline, the wind at his back, only occasionally dodging small rafts of seaweed and the odd piece of driftwood lying partially buried in the sand. As he runs, he tries not to dwell on his worries and self-doubts. Instead he conjures up images of him and his brother wading gingerly in the shallows, then retreating hastily as a wave approaches, of his father picking up a crab, then wincing and releasing the many-legged creature with a loud 'ouch' when it pinches his finger, father and sons laughing together.

Finally he pauses and rests, gazing out at the rising sun and the thin line of the coast of Wales now visible to the east. He is thinking of Rosie, soon to be off to the first day at her new job on this September morning. And his mother, Catherine McGurk, kneeling in dew-soaked trousers, pulling weeds in her flower garden.

He turns, then begins his return run, now with an icy wind in his face that makes his eyes water. When he passes the Wicklow Head Lighthouse, he knows he is approaching his starting point.

Finally he arrives at the cove where he began his run, in the shadow of the Black Castle. He stops and bends forward, hands on knees, trying to catch his breath.

A good workout clears the brain, cleanses the body, lends a certain euphoria, he thinks. Which is precisely what he needs right now.

Finally he straightens, catches one last lungful of the briny air, one last glimpse of the sea, before climbing the steps.

But at that moment he spots something out of the ordinary at the base of the nearly vertical cliff beneath the Black Castle. It's on the beach, right at the water line. It looks very much like a mound of seaweed, except that it is a little too big and rises a little higher above the sand than a mere clot of seaweed. It is dark like seaweed except for a small patch of bright red at the seaward end.

He walks toward that bulk, blinking to sharpen his view. As he approaches, the patch of red resolves into a single shoe, a runner, nearly covered with kelp but for a bit of exposed canvas. Then there emerges a whitish-grey patch, then a broader expanse of grey, then a mass of hair, dark, wet, with deep red splotches that make his stomach churn. It's a body, a man's body, wrapped in seaweed like a mummy that has been prepared for a watery grave.

Cary stands several feet away, stunned. His first impulse is to flee, to separate himself from this thing. He looks around frantically to see if anyone else is nearby, someone, anyone who might help him to make sense of what he is seeing. There is no one.

He steps forward slowly until he is looking down on it. The head is awash in a dark sticky mass, hair matted against the skull, face pressed into the sand. One arm is stretched out as if reaching for a handhold against the surging tide. He leans down and touches the arm. The skin is cold, very cold, and stiff. He feels for a pulse–nothing.

As he watches, a crab scuttles over the body and a many-legged seaworm weaves among the hair. Suddenly Cary's breathing becomes laboured and he feels nauseated. He turns, walks a few steps away, bends over, and vomits forcefully and repeatedly into the water. He slumps down into the sand and sits for a moment, willing his stomach to settle.

Finally he reaches into his pocket, pulls out his mobile, and dials 9-9-9.

'Yeah, I–I need an ambulance, at Travelhawk Beach, the Black Castle. Right away. There's a man lying here, on the sand–I think he's dead.'

The emergency dispatcher asks a series of questions–his name, location, the time of the discovery, the appearance of the victim. Finally, the questions concluded, he is assured that help is already on its way. He is instructed to stay away from the victim and to keep his mobile on to help responders locate him.

He stands, still woozy, looking up toward the top of the steps, expecting at any moment to see gardaí or EMTs coming his way. Still there is no one in sight.

Then he turns and looks down at the man again. And in that instant his journalistic impulses kick in: he should take a photo. The very thought repulses him–the intrusion, the indecency, of photographing the dead. It feels like a violation, an invasion of privacy. Would he want his own bloodied corpse photographed, he asks himself?

At that moment a siren sounds in the distance. He looks up toward the headlands. Still seeing nothing, he turns back to the body and snaps a photo, one single photo. He slips his mobile into his pocket just as two gardaí appear at the top of the steps.

* * *

A half hour later Cary was sitting on the sand, a bright green gardaí poncho wrapped around him. An ambulance crew had departed after examining the body while two gardaí cordoned off the area with yellow tape. Several other officers stood at the top of the steps turning away walkers and rubberneckers.

A garda, Sergeant Farrell, was questioning him about his arrival time, his exact route from motorcycle to beach, the route of his run and the time. When exactly had he first noticed the body? Did he approach the body? Did he touch it? Had he seen anyone else in the vicinity? Had he heard anything out of the ordinary?

Yes, he replied, he had approached the man. He had reached down and touched his right arm, felt for a pulse. The man's arm was cold and stiff. But he had seen no one else–he had heard not a sound.

Then followed a series of questions about himself, his full name, address, date of birth, occupation, etc. And the bike? A Ducati purchased during the summer following his first year at uni. He showed the garda his driver's licence and motorcycle registration.

'So you say you're a newspaper editor. What paper?'

'The *Glenkerry Gazette*,' replied Cary.

'Uh-huh,' replied the sergeant as he scribbled on his notepad.

Finally the sergeant thanked him, handed Cary his card, then told him he could go.

'I don't suppose they know who he is–the victim?' asked Cary.

'Nope. No information on that yet. But the forensics team will be here soon from Dublin–they'll try to get an ID.'

Cary stood up.

'One more thing, Mr McGurk. Please don't share any details of the victim in your newspaper–understand? The Press Office will probably release a statement later today.'

Cary nodded. 'Yeah, sure. A course.'

* * *

When he returned to Glenkerry, Cary parked his motorcycle in his mother's drive. She smiled when he walked through the door, her pale blue eyes twinkling.

'Oh, love, I was just about to have a cuppa. Join me?'

He sat with her at the kitchen table and told her about his run on the beach.

'I bet you had the place to yerself, yeah?' she asked.

'Not exactly.' He sighed and buried his face in his hands.

'What's the matter, Car? What happened?'

Then he told her everything–the beach–the stillness–his memories of walking with his father and brother.

'It was all so beautiful. And I had a good run. I felt better than I have in days. Yeh know, runner's high?'

But then he got to the details of the body. He paused and swallowed, the emotions of that experience still washing over him. 'There were crabs climbing on 'im. It made me sick. I boked.'

'Oh, dear, that musta been awful, love. What did you do?'

He told her of his call to 9-9-9 and the long wait–at least it seemed long–for the first garda car to arrive.

'The tide was rising and I was thinking if they don't come soon he'll be carried off by the waves–maybe I should move him up the beach. But fortunately the gardaí showed up then.'

'What did they do?'

'They knelt over the guy for a minute–then talked into their radios. Then one of them, a Sergeant Farrell, took me back to the steps and we sat in the sand while he asked me some questions and wrote up some notes.'

'What kind of questions?'

'Like what time I arrived at the beach–how far I ran–why I didn't have any shoes on.'

'You took off your shoes?'

'Yeah, when I run on the beach I like to run barefoot. It feels good. I think it's easier on my feet and ankles sometimes.'

'So, the dead man–was he young? Old?'

'Maybe thirties or so. White with darkish hair.'

'So, how did he die? Did he go over the cliff onto the rocks? Or did he, yeh know, fall off a boat, drown, then wash ashore?'

Cary shook his head. 'I don't know, Ma. It looked like he hit–like something hit his–his head–I didn't look too closely.'

He paused and closed his eyes, as if trying to banish the image from his memory.

'What was he wearing?'

'He was mostly covered with seaweed, but he had on a black t-shirt, grey trousers, and red runners. Oh, and one hand was stretched out on the sand. He was wearing a ring.'

He paused, thinking about the ring.

'I almost forgot, I snapped a photo with my mobile.' He sighed. 'I don't know why–as soon as I took it I felt kinda weird, yeh know? Like a voyeur or something. Maybe I should delete it. I don't really wanna look at it.'

'May I see it, Car?'

Cary shook his head. 'Trust me, Ma, you don't wanna see it.'

'Did you show it to the garda?'

Cary thought for a moment. 'Nah. I forgot all about it. But what does it matter, anyway? Six or eight gardaí were there when I left–they've probably taken a million pictures.'

Back at 1 Upton Road, Cary climbed the stairs to his flat, then sat on his bed for several minutes thinking. Finally he dropped his shoes to the floor, flopped down on the bed, and pulled the covers up over his head.

3 YOUR WORST NIGHTMARE

Barely twenty kilometres from Dublin, the town of Glenkerry nestles among the verdant pasturelands of County Wicklow, its single main thoroughfare lined with modest buildings of granite, brick, and slate. To the casual visitor Glenkerry appears frozen in time, much like the agricultural centre it was a century ago. But a closer look reveals a subtle transformation. The shops on the High Street now include a day spa, an espresso stand, and a frozen yogurt vendor. Several of the many stone farmhouses scattered along narrow farm lanes outside of the village have been replaced by sprawling vacation homes belonging to wealthy urbanites, many of whom spend only a few days here a month.

And the people of Glenkerry bespeak change as well. On this September morning two women in flowing, brightly-coloured saris stroll along the footpath in the morning sun, then pause to greet an elderly gentleman in a turban just opening his shop. Further along the High Street three children with caramel skin and hair in delicate corn rows make their way along the footpath, their eyes wide in anticipation of the first day of the new school year.

Less than a kilometre down the road, the doors of *Coláiste Gaeilge*, Glenkerry's secondary school, have just opened for the first day of the new term. Students are shuffling into the art studio for the first lesson dressed in their school uniforms, blue-collared shirts, navy blue ties, and grey trousers for the boys, blue blouses and pleated tartan skirts for the girls. Most look bleary-eyed, unceremoniously dropping their bookbags onto desks, slumping into seats, and groaning loud enough to be heard by one and all.

But there are a few exceptions. Two sixth year girls are bright-eyed and enthusiastic as they enter. Both have taken Visual Arts previously. They were particularly fond of Ms Brogan, their art teacher, and are looking forward to seeing her once again.

Their teacher is standing with her back to the class writing on the white board: *Visual Arts, MWF 8:30-10:05.* She is just starting to write her name when the pair step up behind her.

'Hello, Ms Brogan. We're back!' says Gráinne Phinney cheerily.

'Did you miss us over the summer?' asks Eileen Keough.

The teacher turns and smiles at the pair. Their jaws drop simultaneously. 'Rosie?' they say in unison.

'Uh, it's Ms O'Malley now, I'm afraid,' replies their teacher with a wink.

'You gotta be kiddin', what are you doin' here?' asks Gráinne, her green eyes wide with amazement, her freckled face framed by long reddish-brown curls.

'Ms Brogan is on maternity leave. I'm her replacement, for three months.'

'I don't believe it, you're gonna be our art teacher?' giggles Gráinne, her eyes shining. She turns to Eileen. 'This is gonna be a hoot.'

'Oh, is that what you think?' replies Rosie. 'Beware, girls,' she says, casting an exaggerated stern glare at the pair, the same look she practised on Cary the previous evening. 'I may look like a softy, but I could turn out to be *your worst nightmare,*' the last three words spoken with a ghoulish vibrato.

Gráinne shoots an impish grin at Eileen. 'Soft-ee,' she mouths long and slow, making certain that Rosie can see.

Rosie smiles, then turns to Eileen. 'Your friend here seems to have forgotten that I was her babysitter when she was in nappies. But I would never embarrass her in front of her classmates by telling stories about little Gráinne now, would I?' Her gaze pivots back to Gráinne. 'And how she loved to run around the house naked?'

Gráinne's cheeks turn beet red. 'You wouldn't dare, Rosie–I mean Ms O'Malley.'

'Don't count on it, Gran, don't count on it.' They all laugh. 'Well, find seats you two. Class is about to start.'

* * *

Rosie distributed a course syllabus, then read the attendance roll, trying in this first class to attach a name to each unfamiliar face of the fifteen or so students seated before her. She was not entirely new to teaching; she taught several workshops for children at the arts centre in Wicklow one summer as well as a series of art classes for adults. But teaching a group of teens in a secondary school like *Coláiste Gaeilge*, this was a new challenge for her. She took a deep breath, then addressed the class slowly and clearly.

'My name is Ms O'Malley. I'm filling in for Ms Brogan until she returns from maternity leave.'

'Has she had her baby yet?' asked Eileen.

'No,' replied Rosie. 'But any day now.'

She reminded her students of the importance of being on time for class and about paying strict attention to her instructions. She discussed the school's policies–showing respect for one another and teachers–zero-tolerance for bullying and harassment, and all. Then she reviewed the new rules regarding mobiles. Students will be permitted to bring them to school, but they must remain turned off and out of sight while anywhere on school property, inside or out of doors. She heard some grumbling from several students.

'Listen, you lot, I know some of you may not like it, but it is school policy now. You know it, and your parents know it. And I will strictly enforce it in this room. Is that clear?' Again she put on that practised glare.

Next Rosie distributed pads of drawing paper, reminding her students that starting the following week they would need to bring their own art supplies to class. She had placed three tables near the windows. On one she had arranged four pieces of fruit–a pear, an apple, a banana, and a pomegranate–on another a vase with red, white, and yellow roses picked fresh from her garden that morning. On the third rested a pine bough with clusters of bright green needles and several cones with brown scales.

'Okay, well, for the first few weeks you'll have a chance to try out all sorts of media and techniques–drawing, painting, pen-and-ink, sculpting, printing. Later in the term you'll get to do a project using whichever medium you wish.' She pointed to the bulletin boards on two sides of the room. 'Those are examples of the final projects of some of Ms Brogan's students from last year.'

'Here's what I want you to do today. Just pick whichever subject interests you.' She walked along the row of tables by the windows gesturing to the different objects placed there. 'Fruit, flowers, or pine bough. Look them all over first before choosing. You'll find drawing pencils of different weights plus a few charcoal markers–take your pick. You can use more than one if you like. And before you start you should think about your point of view, the orientation of your subject on the paper, size, direction of light, shadow, texture, and so on. I'll come round to see how you're doing.'

After a few minutes of walking about and considering their choices, the students moved their chairs, then settled into their assignment.

Just then another student appeared at the classroom door, a short, slight girl with long, dark brown hair that partially hid her face. She stood warily as Rosie approached her, looking like a frightened deer that might turn and flee at any moment.

'And you are?' asked Rosie with a smile.

'Molly, Molly Boyle, miss.' She looked into Rosie's eyes only briefly, then averted her gaze.

'I don't see you on my printed roster, Molly.'

'I just registered yesterday,' explained the girl. 'The principal, Mr Forster, signed me up for Visual Arts.'

Rosie was looking at the updated class list on her tablet. 'Yep, yes, there you are. Well, Molly, my name is Ms O'Malley–welcome to *Coláiste Gaeilge*. You've just moved to Glenkerry, then?'

The girl nodded without looking up.

'Where'd you move from?' she asked, anxious to draw her out a little more.

'Cork.'

Rosie sensed that this particular student was not going to be easily engaged.

'Well, Molly, why don't you put your backpack on the table there, then grab a chair? I'll show you what we're doing this morning. Class, this is Molly Boyle. She's new. I hope you will make her feel welcome.'

For the next hour students worked at their drawings, some intently, others half-heartedly. Rosie walked among them, looking over shoulders, trying to find things about each drawing to praise while offering some advice about shading, texture, and technique.

At one point when Rosie was shuffling through the supply cupboard for more materials, two of the boys, Brendan and Noah, were leering at Gráinne and snickering.

'Hey, Gran,' whispered Brendan, 'I hear next week we'll be drawin' nudes. Why don't you volunteer to model?'

Gráinne had worked in her father's pub since she was thirteen and was experienced at putting rude young men in their places. She shot the boy a dismissive look: 'In your dreams, perv.'

'Oh, you are, Gran, ev'ry night, fer sure,' replied Brendan with a self-satisfied smirk. The two boys chuckled, but just then Rosie returned with additional supplies, finding everyone hard at work.

Eileen was struggling in an effort to capture the entire arrangement of roses. 'I suck at drawing,' she groaned. She looked up at Molly who was seated next to her, then down at the new girl's paper.

'Man, that is so good. How do you *do* that?'

Rosie heard Eileen's exclamation and came over to have a look. Molly had chosen to draw just one rose blossom and several unopened buds. She had used a sharp pencil to define the edges of the flowers, then added shading with a broader point on its side so that the blossoms appeared to rise right off the page.

'Oh, Molly, that is wonderful,' noted Rosie. 'Your shading is exquisite.'

Molly shrugged her shoulders. Several other students gathered around to admire Molly's work.

'Where did you learn to draw like that, Molly?' asked Gráinne.

'My mom mostly,' she replied softly.

When the class ended, Rosie reminded her students that they would be using coloured pencils and pastels on Wednesday. She invited anyone who wished to do so to bring a bouquet or a single flower or any other colourful object that they would like to draw.

As the other students were leaving Gráinne and Eileen hung back and spoke again to Rosie.

'You used ta play camogie, didn't you, Rosie–I mean Ms O'Malley?' asked Gráinne.

'Yup. I was on the Glenkerry community team for three years, but I wasn't very good. I guess I was never aggressive enough,' she said, remembering how many of her teammates approached the game with bloodlust. 'Why?'

'There's a new school camogie team this year,' replied Gráinne, her eyes shining. 'Eileen and me are both on it.'

'We're callin' ourselves the Hurley Girlies,' added Eileen with a chuckle.

'But we need a coach,' explained Gráinne. 'Hey, why don't you volunteer? It'd be brilliant having you as our coach.'

Rosie laughed. 'Eh, I don't think so. I really don't know much about the game, I mean, tactics–strategy–all that.'

'It's easy. We could teach you,' said Gráinne wide-eyed.

Rosie smiled. 'I don't think so. But thank you.'

'Well, at least come to our first practice after school–*please*?' begged Gráinne. 'Eileen's our captain so she's in charge until we have a proper coach. Mr Forster said it'd be okay, just for today.' She paused. 'Just so's we don't break any bones or anything,' she added, flashing a sheepish grin at Eileen.

Rosie smiled. 'I'll see if I can make it. I'm supposed to be at a meeting for new teachers, but maybe if I get out soon enough, I'll come by the pitch.'

Just then she noticed Molly standing in the hallway watching them through the open door.

'Hey, guys, that new girl, Molly, she probably doesn't know anyone in the school. Why don't you try to help her out–yeh know, show her round?'

'Oh, yeah, totally,' replied Gráinne.

'Who knows, maybe you can recruit her for the Hurley Girlies.'

The two girls exited while Rosie continued to rearrange the tables for the next class. But truthfully, she thought to herself, Molly Boyle–that timid wisp of a thing with a reluctant, almost fearful look in her eyes–she hardly seemed a likely candidate for the Hurley Girlies.

4 A DAY WITHOUT CAMOGIE

That afternoon as Rosie left school, she rode her bike past the camogie pitch. The players were seated around a young woman wearing a bright red t-shirt emblazoned with the words, *'A day without Camogie is like–just kidding–I HAVE NO IDEA!'*

Camogie is a Gaelic team sport for girls, much like men's hurling. And while camogie is a non-contact sport, it is lightning fast and very demanding on its players both physically and mentally. Nearly every Irish schoolgirl grows up with a hurley–a wooden camogie stick–in her hand and visions of greatness, of rising to the professional leagues, in her head.

Rosie couldn't see the woman's face, but she heard her voice. It was strong, authoritative–and strangely familiar. Just then a cheer rose up from the team. Rosie moved to where she could see the speaker's face–and immediately recognised her. It was Sabrina Selkirk.

Sabrina was a garda, formerly the Family Liaison Officer for Glenkerry. She had worked with Rosie and her brother Buddy when their mother went missing last spring. But she had recently been reassigned to the Wicklow garda station. She was tall with broad shoulders, sinewy arms and legs, olive brown skin, jet-black hair cut short, and eyes that were deep set and intense.

Rosie watched and listened as Sabrina addressed her team.

'The first thing I want you to understand is that camogie is all about the f-word. That's right, the f-word: *fundamentals*. Dribbling, lifting, passing, striking, hooking, blocking–those are the fundamentals of the sport. To be successful at camogie you have to focus on the fundamentals.'

She paused briefly, then continued. 'Don't worry about winning or losing–don't bother about championships, trophies, and all that. Focus on the fundamentals and the rest will take care of itself. Understand?'

She had the rapt attention of the group and they all nodded in unison. Then her serious expression turned into an impish grin.

'And, when you focus on the *fundamentals*, you also have *fun*. Right? *Fun* goes right along with *fund*amentals. See what I mean?' The girls all chuckled.

'So every day when you come to practice, whatta you gonna do?' She held a hand to her ear.

'*Focus on the fundamentals*,' came the unanimous and enthusiastic response.

She nodded her approval, then looked around at the crowd of shining faces, meeting the eyes of every single girl seated before her.

'Now, whatever else is on your mind today–family–friends–fellas...' She paused on the word 'fellas' for dramatic effect, then continued. 'Forget 'em all, at least for the next ninety minutes. Forget 'em all–and what?' Again she held her hand to her ear.

'*Focus on the fundamentals*,' they repeated in unison.

'Yeah,' shouted Sabrina, clapping her hands. 'So, let's get started, shall we?'

The girls jumped to their feet cheering.

'First I want you to do a few stretches, then take a lap around the pitch.'

The players stood and began stretching. Sabrina looked up at her visitor and smiled.

'Hey, Rosie.'

Rosie exhaled loudly. 'Wow, Sabrina, that was some peptalk. I was almost ready to sign up. So you're the coach of the Hurley Girlies?'

Sabrina nodded. 'Looks like it, yeah.'

Rosie gestured toward two of the players who were doing their stretches nearby. 'Gráinne and Eileen were talking to me in class this morning, saying they had no coach.'

'Yeah, well, Mr Forster rang me over the weekend. I talked to my super and he approved–said it would be good for community relations–so long as I can fit it into my schedule. And have my radio with me at all times,' she added, tapping the device secured to her belt.

'Are you a serious hurler?' asked Rosie.

'Well, I played for my college team, yeah. Not a star player, not by half–but I really love the game.'

'That's great. The only ones I know are those two,' said Rosie, nodding again toward Gráinne and Eileen. 'They're real sports, believe me. I watched 'em playin' footie a few weeks ago and they were brilliant. They ran circles around Del, Cary, and the other blokes.'

'Yeah, I was there, remember? They *were* brilliant.'

The occasion was a friendly football match on the Glenkerry GAA grounds in July. Two uni mates of Cary's were visiting and he had managed to enlist enough friends from around town for a match. Among them were several of the local gardaí including

Sabrina Selkirk and Delbert Samuels, an old schoolmate of Cary and Rosie's.

'So what're you doin' at *Coláiste*?'

Rosie told her about her new teaching post.

'That's grand, Rosie. Hey, maybe you can help us with recruiting. We need a few more players for the team. Can you talk up camogie in class?'

Rosie chuckled. 'With a peptalk like that you should have no trouble attracting players. But yeah, for sure, I'll talk it up.' Rosie paused, thinking. 'Oh, yeh know, there is this new girl, Molly Boyle. She doesn't seem to know anyone yet.'

'Well, camogie could be just the ticket for 'er. Maybe you could speak to 'er–tell 'er to come see me.'

Rosie nodded. 'I'll see what I can do.' Although the more she thought about it, the more she doubted whether the shy and retiring Molly Boyle would take to camogie.

By now the players were rounding the far end of the pitch.

'Well, I gotta get with my girls, so I'll see yeh. Say hi to Cary fer me.'

* * *

On her short bike trip home, Rosie stopped at the offices of the *Glenkerry Gazette* at the corner of the High Street and Upton Road.

'Cary?' she called as she entered. No reply.

'Cary?' she called again, standing at the foot of the stairs. She heard a grunt from above and started up.

'Rosie?' came a groggy reply as she appeared at his bedroom door. 'What time is it?'

She chuckled as she stepped into the room and smiled down at him. 'Almost four. Slow day at the *Glenkerry Gazette*, eh?'

Cary groaned, then sat up. She reached down and tousled his brown hair that, as usual, needed cutting. 'Time to get up and face the world, young man.'

Cary nodded.

'How was your early morning run?'

He looked up at her and smiled. Then he took her hand and tried to urge her down onto the bed next to him.

'I can't stay, Car. Gotta get home–chores to do. Buddy and Danielle are coming to supper tomorrow, so I have to do some tidying.'

Cary sat up and stretched. 'So how was your first day of school? Did those rugrats walk all over you?'

'Not really. A few smart arses, you know the type. But mostly good kids. And I was impressed with the artistic ability of some of them.' She sighed. 'But I been on my feet all day and I'm kinda exhausted, so I betta go.'

'Before you go, I have to tell you something, Rose.'

She sat down on the bed next to him. 'What's up? Somethin' wrong?'

Cary sighed. 'Yeah, kinda.'

He proceeded to tell her about the beach and his run. Then he told her about the body.

'Oh, my god, Car. How awful. Well, what did yeh do?'

He looked at her sheepishly. 'Well, first I boked, right into the water.'

'Oh, poor thing.' She took his hand. He had brown eyes that always looked a little sad, like a puppy's, but on this occasion his expression was particularly dour.

'It–he looked like a ghost or something, yeh know? Pasty, sort of spongy. But what really turned my stomach was a crab crawling over him–and a seaworm.' A bilious expression crept across his face. 'All I have to do is think of it and I start feeling sick again.'

'So, you called for help?'

'Oh, yeah, right away. But then I had to wait. And I looked at him again, and decided I should take a picture–with my mobile. I don't know why I thought of that. As soon as I did, I felt bad, like one a them paparazzi–yeh know?'

'So did you?'

Cary sighed and nodded. 'Yeah. But when I got home I deleted it. It just didn't seem right, yeh know?' He hesitated for a moment, as if still pondering the decision. 'Anyway, a few minutes later the gardaí came and I sat on the beach while this one garda asked me lots of questions.'

'What kind of questions?'

'Yeh know, when did I get there? What was I doin' on the beach that early? When did I first see the body? What did I do? That sort.'

'So who was it–the dead man? Someone from Wicklow?'

'No one I know. Taller than me, dark hair.'

'How old was he?'

'I really couldn't say. Mid-thirties, maybe.'

'And how did he die, Car? Did he drown?'

'I don't know. But he had a head injury of some sort. I suppose he might've fallen, yeh know, from the cliff, from the Black Castle. But I couldn't say for sure.'

'So what happens next?'

'The garda said they would issue a press release soon with more information, maybe an ID if they have it.'

'Gee, I'm sorry, Car. Sorry for the guy, and for you. That's gotta be upsetting.'

He stood reluctantly and followed Rosie down the steep stairway to the ground floor office.

'By the looks of things you been working,' she noted, pointing to his desk that was covered with stacks of papers and half a dozen empty coffee cups.

'Yeah, I was up most of the night. I wrote a bunch of stuff for next week's edition. But it's mostly filler, yeh know? Hen parties–club meetings–that sort. Nobody's gonna read the *Gazette* if that's the best I can do.' He sighed and looked dejected.

Rosie said, 'Don't let it get you down, Car. It takes time to build up a newspaper, like anything yeh know? You'll get there, I'm sure of it. Anyway, maybe now you got a story, eh?'

'Yeah, well, the gardaí don't want anything in the news yet. I suppose they have to contact the family first.'

'Yeah, of course. How awful.' They both paused contemplating that thought until Rosie spoke up.

'Oh, by the way, guess who's the new camogie coach at *Coláiste*? Sabrina Selkirk.'

'Really?'

'Yeah, I talked to her at practice after school. I guess her super approved the idea–he thinks it will be good for community relations.'

'Wow, that is great. She'll whip those girls into shape for sure.'

'Oh, Car,' she began, her eyes wide. 'I listened to her talkin' to the team for a few minutes. She was brilliant. She had those girls in the palm of her hand.'

'Really.'

'Maybe you should write a story about Sabrina, a profile, yeh know? Wasn't she born in Africa? Her family eventually came to the UK. Plus she's a marathoner. She won a race in Belfast a couple years ago. It'd make a great story.'

'Yeah, maybe so. Oh, about the camogie team, do you think you could take a team photo?'

'Oh, yeah, for sure. I'll ask Sabrina when would be best.'

Cary nodded. 'I think I'll have another little lie-in.'

'Okay, well, I'll see yeh later.'

* * *

As Rosie walked up the lane, she passed Cary's mother's house. Catherine was in her garden.

'Hi, Mrs M. How're you today?'

Catherine stood, wiping her hands on her overalls. 'I'm fine, Rosie, bless yeh. Have yeh seen that son a mine?'

'Yeah, I just called round at the *Gazette*. He told you, right, about the–the body?'

'Aye. He came by as soon as he got back to Glenkerry. Didn't want me to go hearin' about it on the radio or the telly–or the internet, he said. He was a bit out a sorts, understandably.'

Rosie nodded. 'Yeah, I think it's affected him a lot more than he's willin' to own. He was in bed, buried under the covers, when I got there.'

'Oh, dear. I wish I–well–I know he doesn't want his mother fussin' over 'im. But maybe I'll bring him an iced finger or two.' She put both hands on her hips. 'I have never known that boy to turn down iced fingers.' They both laughed. 'How sad for that man. Have they identified the body?'

'No. Not that Cary's heard, anyway. Well, I gotta get goin'.'

Rosie went on her way. Her house was just a short distance up Anglesey Lane. The O'Malleys and the McGurks had been neighbours for decades. After Patrick McGurk passed away, Rosie called on the McGurks almost daily, if only to say a quick hello. Now that she and Cary were a couple again, she felt especially close to Catherine, and the feeling was mutual. True, Catherine had once hoped that Cary and Siobhan Sullivan, a friend from uni, would bond, but Siobhan moved to London, and, after all, Cary and Siobhan were 'just mates,' as Cary insisted again and again. Plus Siobhan was an American, and she had too much drive, too much ambition, to dawdle about in tiny Glenkerry, or even in Dublin, for that matter–or so Catherine believed. But now that it was Cary and Rosie, Catherine couldn't be happier. Rosie was a Glenkerry girl, through and through, which she hoped meant that as long as the two were together, at least one of her sons would remain close by.

* * *

That evening Catherine walked the short distance down the lane to 1 Upton Road. The 'Closed' sign hung in the window, but the door was unlocked. Catherine let herself in.

'Cary? It's Mother. You up?' she called up the stairs.

She heard a groan. 'I brought you some sweets, love. Iced fingers.'

She heard bare feet hit the floor above her and in a few moments Cary descended the stairs in a t-shirt and pyjama bottoms. She wanted to tell him that he looked a mess and ought to get cleaned up. But she knew better.

'I'll just leave these here,' she said, placing a plate with several of the sweet pastries on the desk.

'Oh, thanks, Ma. Yeah, well, I could use a little pick-me-up.'

'Of course, you've had a traumatic experience. Anybody would need time to recover. So, there yeh go then, and I'll be on my way, so.' Before she left she added, 'Rosie called round earlier, while I was in the garden. Oh, my goodness, I forgot to ask her how her first day of school went.'

'Pretty good, I guess,' replied Cary, then added with a chuckle, 'Well, at least she survived, anyway.'

5 CONTACT US

Cary slept fitfully that night, unsettling images of bodies floating in and out of his dreams, glistening strands of seaweed writhing and undulating like sea snakes around bare arms and legs. When he finally woke shortly after dawn, he was tempted to pull the covers over his head and go back to sleep. But other worries soon began to resurface: the *Gazette* and his personal finances.

Finally he rose, slumped into his tiny kitchen, brewed some coffee, and sat eating one of the iced fingers his mother had brought him. Then, slowly and somewhat reluctantly, he made his way down the stairs and settled in at his desk.

The 'Contact Us' inbox on the *Gazette* dashboard was lit up with several new messages. 'Any information on the body found on the beach?' read one. 'Death in Wicklow town?' read another. Word was spreading, that was clear. No doubt onlookers in Wicklow had seen all the garda activity at Travelhawk Beach—perhaps some had watched the gurney being carried to the waiting ambulance.

Then he checked his mobile. There were two new texts, both from friends inquiring about the death. One was from an old classmate from *Coláiste* who heard he was the one who discovered the body. Another was from Gloria Hennessy, estate agent and a friend of his mother, asking how he was doing.

So much for keeping quiet about the dead man, thought Cary. Everyone knows already–or will soon. And they *should* know, after all. For one thing, someone somewhere might be missing a loved one. At least they'd like to be reassured that it was not the unfortunate fellow lying in the sand below the Black Castle. And what if that guy was a victim of foul play? That could mean there was a murderer on the loose, lurking in the quiet lanes or hiding in the deep, dark forests of County Wicklow. Shouldn't the public be warned?

They need to know, thought Cary. *They have a right to know.*

Just then a familiar face appeared at the door. He waved him in.

'Hey, mate,' said Del Samuels with a smile. Cary and Del were old friends, having attended *Coláiste* together and played on the school's football team. Del's family had emigrated to Ireland from Jamaica many years ago. Del was a member of *An Garda Síochána,* the Irish national police force, and had helped a great deal in the search for Rosie's mother.

'So, I hear you made some news yesterday, lad,' he said, wide-eyed.

Cary nodded and sighed. 'But journalists aren't supposed to *make* the news, yeh know–just *report* it. How'd you hear about it?'

'They sent around an internal memo to all gardaí, late morning. So what happened, you were runnin'?'

'Yeah, I got out real early and ran down the beach past the lighthouse, an hour or so. The sun was just comin' up. Thought it'd clear my head, which it did. But when I got back I could see around the headland below the Black Castle. And there he was, on the sand.'

'That musta been a jolt, eh?'

'Yeah, well, it wasn't a real nice way to finish my run.' He sighed. 'The guy was dead, no question–there was nothing to be done. So I called 9-9-9. Then I had to wait for donkey's years for them to come.' He was about to tell Del about taking the photo, then thought better of the idea.

'Who came?'

'Two guys, Sergeant Farrell and Garda Hughes. You must know 'em?'

'Oh, yeah, Mitch and Declan. Sabrina's worked with both of 'em at Wicklow. Mitch Farrell's a rugger. I played on a gardaí team with 'im for a while.'

'So what do you hear? Have they identified the dead man–I mean, the deceased?'

'Yeah, they have. He had some kinda ID card in his wallet. All in Arabic.'

'Arabic–really?'

'Yup. Luckily one of the Wicklow gardaí was able to translate it. The dead man's name is Kristoff Rahmannn. Syrian.'

'A refugee?' replied an astonished Cary.

'Well, they don't know anything more about him as yet. And that's not for public release, not yet anyway, right?'

'Oh, sure, right. But the sergeant told me there'd be a public announcement within a day.'

'Yeah, well, they still haven't located the guy's next of kin. And they don't normally release the identity of a victim until the family is notified. They usually need a family member to make a positive ID–but in a case like this, I don't know.'

'Syrian,' repeated Cary, shaking his head. 'So, what do they think, did he fall off the rocks?'

'Maybe–possibly. Forensics are still working on it. But he definitely suffered a severe blow to the head, possibly more than one–could be he fell and struck his head on the rocks several times before hitting the beach. There was no water in his lungs–that rules out drowning.'

'Do you think he was there long?' inquired Cary.

'I don't know, mate. I'm sure they'll know pretty soon–when the medical examiner makes her report. Why?'

Cary shrugged. 'I–I just felt bad for the bloke. I mean, the water was nearly up to him. If I hadn't come along, he might've been swept out to sea. And there were crabs and things.' He shuddered at the memory.

Del was watching his friend closely. He leaned down and spoke softly. 'Hey, mate, maybe yeh wanna talk to someone about it.'

'I did–the garda on the beach, Sergeant Farrell.'

'Yeah–no, I mean a counsellor–to help you process…'

Cary shook his head. 'I'm okay, Del–really. At the time I got sick, just for a minute, but I'm okay now.'

'No offence, Car, but you look like shite.'

'Thanks, Del–you're a true friend,' said Cary with a chuckle. 'Okay, so I didn't sleep too well. But I'm fine now.'

'And how's your lass doin' at *Coláiste*? They run her out yet?'

'No, nothing like that. She likes it, she says. And she came upon Sabrina out on the camogie pitch.'

Del and Sabrina Selkirk were a couple, although their relationship was strictly 'on the downlow,' as Del liked to say, for fear it might not meet with the approval of their supervisors should they find out about it.

'Yeah, she's coachin' those girls now–really crackin' the whip over 'em, I'll bet. Well, hey, I gotta get to the station now. Just wanted to be sure you're okay.'

'Listen, Del, if you hear any more about the victim, you'll let me know?'

'Will do, mate–will do. But remember, just between you, me, and these four walls–right?'

He looked down at the remainder of Cary's breakfast. 'Ooh, iced fingers. Need help finishin' them?'

'Yeah, sure,' replied Cary, holding the plate up for his friend.

Del grabbed one finger. 'Ta.' Then he shot his friend a doleful gaze.

Cary shrugged his shoulders and nodded. 'Go ahead.'

Del picked up a second finger and waved it at Cary. 'Later, mate.'

* * *

Cary sat at his desk thinking: a man from Syria–lying dead–on a beach in Wicklow. Even though the official public statement on the death had not yet been released, word was getting out, people were curious, perhaps even uneasy. And they would be looking to their local newspaper for the latest information.

No pressure, mate, thought Cary.

Today, Tuesday, 6:00 pm–that was his deadline–he had to send each week's issue of the *Gazette* to the printer by then if it was to be ready for distribution on Thursday morning. The deadline for advertising copy was noon, and Cary had already learned to be prepared for a flurry of last-minute submissions and revisions as the deadline approached.

Over the next few hours several dozen adverts arrived, most of them digital files sent to the *Gazette* inbox, but several in person: a home renovation business on the Arklow road, two local restaurants–the Fishmonger and the Grenadine–the Day Spa on Upton Road, and an automotive repair shop in Rathnew. Each drop-in client wanted to chat, and Cary did his best to be hospitable, even as he watched the in-box on his laptop swelling and the clock ticking.

The noon hour passed and Cary was still busy reworking the layout of several pages to accommodate new adverts. Plus he had three local news stories that he needed to fact-check: the church news section, the schools page, and of course sport, including the busy schedule of matches sponsored by the local Gaelic Athletic Association chapter, the GAA.

It was after one o'clock when he phoned in an order for a curried chicken wrap from Phinney's, then ran down the street to retrieve the sandwich and return to his office.

Meanwhile he kept checking his mobile, hoping to receive that promised public information statement from the gardaí regarding the death at Travelhawk Beach, but nothing appeared. It was without a doubt the biggest story in the county right now, and he had nothing to write–nothing, that is, that he was permitted to publish on the incident.

Finally, about ninety minutes before his deadline, the public statement appeared in his in-box:

The body of a middle-aged Caucasian male with black hair was found on a beach in Wicklow town on the morning of Monday 4

September. The identity of the deceased is being withheld pending notification of next of kin. An investigation into the circumstances of the death is ongoing and further details will be released when available. Any persons having information on the death are asked to contact the Wicklow garda station.

He quickly rearranged the front page, creating a box for the short item. He quoted the garda statement, then followed it with, 'For additional details on this breaking news story, please visit the *Gazette* website.'

Not much, thought Cary, *but at least it's something.*

6 ASSISTANT COACH

Rosie stopped by the camogie pitch the following afternoon as she left school to see how the Hurleys were doing. The girls were wearing their uniforms today, brilliant gold and green jerseys, gold skorts, green knee socks, and gold helmets with faceguards. True to her admonition of the previous day, Sabrina was focusing on the fundamentals of camogie.

'Okay, let's look first at your grip,' she said as the team stood in a semicircle around her. 'You have to grip the hurley properly. So watch me. My dominant hand grasps the top of the hurley, just like shaking hands, see? My thumb touches my index finger. My other hand, my weaker hand, is free to move up and down the handle, like this. Of course, if you're a leftie, it's the other way around. This we call the ready position, right? Okay, so show me your ready position.'

The girls quickly complied.

'Yep, that's it–good. Now, watch how my grip changes when I execute a swing. I simply slide my weaker hand up into the lock position with my dominant hand, like this. So now my hands are together and I'm ready to swing. See how I bend my elbows and knees while keeping my eye on the ball? Then I swing, mostly with my wrists, like this. Notice that my hurley makes a big letter C. See?'

She repeated herself several times as she demonstrated: 'Ready, lock, swing–ready, lock, swing.'

'One more thing. My weight shifts as I swing–from right to left, dominant side to weaker side.'

She then had the players arrange themselves in a single line. 'Okay–ready position–now lock position–now swing. Again. Ready-lock-swing. Again. Again. Okay–good–brilliant.'

'All right. Of course, you need to be able to execute a swing from your non-dominant side as well. Your hands remain in the same position, but now your weight shifts from your non-dominant side to your dominant, like this. Your non-dominant swing is bound to be a little weaker at first, that's only natural. But with practice you should be able to do both with nearly equal strength and accuracy.'

A few minutes later the players were practising swinging on the run, tracing a large circle around the pitch, just as Rosie approached Sabrina.

'They're lookin' good, Coach,' said Rosie.

Sabrina smiled. 'They have a lot of enthusiasm, I'll say that much for 'em. And energy. But as for technique, they need work. And all of them need to build strength and endurance.'

Just then Rosie noticed a familiar face among the players. 'Is that Molly I see over there? Molly Boyle?'

'Yeah, that's 'er. She showed up today with Eileen and Gráinne. A bit reluctant, I'd say.'

'Well, if enthusiasm counts for anything, those two will get to her, I've no doubt,' replied Rosie.

Sabrina turned her back to her players, then lowered her voice. 'Does that kid ever smile?'

Rosie nodded and sighed. 'Yeah, she was pretty grim-faced in Visual Arts today. Maybe it's just being new, yeh know? At that age, in a new school, new teachers, new classmates–I wouldn't blame 'er for feelin' a little intimidated.'

Sabrina turned and blew her whistle. The girls came in and gathered round her. Gráinne waved and Rosie waved back. 'Hey Molly,' said Rosie with a smile. Molly gave her a slight wave in reply and only the briefest eye contact.

'Well, I'm on,' said Sabrina to Rosie.

'Yeah, well, good luck. See yeh.'

'Hey, Rosie, can you wait a couple minutes? I wanna talk to you about something. Just let me get them started on this next drill first, okay?'

'Yeah, sure.'

Again Sabrina spoke to the team. 'Okay, then, good work. Now let's see how we execute a ground strike.' She demonstrated the important points of ground striking, hitting a ball on the ground with the hurley. Then she had the players line up in pairs for a drill.

'When you strike the sliotar on the ground it's important to line up your shoulders with your target–the goal, or maybe a teammate. Line yourself up and execute your swing, keeping your eye on the ball. Like this. Right? Again, I line up my shoulders, my eye is on the ball, then I swing. Like that.'

Rosie had been watching Sabrina carefully, admiring how she broke down the apparently simple skills of swinging and ground striking into a number of steps, how she talked to her players, how her self-assured style commanded their attention and respect.

As she watched she was aware of several other spectators along the sideline, one adult, perhaps a parent, and three boys who were alternately watching the camogie players and exchanging chuckles. One of them was Timothy Phinney, Gráinne's twin brother. He was slight of build with dark reddish-brown hair, like his sister's, but short and curly. Next to him was another boy, much taller, with black hair. He was heavy set, built like a rugby player, she thought. The third was one of her students, Brendan, taking occasional drags on a cigarette. When he saw his teacher looking their way, he furtively discarded the cigarette.

'Hey, Ms O.,' said Brendan cheerfully. Rosie wasn't fooled by that boy's bright demeanour. She suspected it had to do with a conversation they had after Visual Arts that morning. She had overheard him making comments about one of the girls. At the end of the lesson she asked him to stay behind.

'You understand the school's rules about harassment, Brendan, right?' He was looking sheepish. 'Making remarks about someone's appearance–their hair, for example. You know who I mean.'

'Yes miss. But I wasn't harassing her. I was complimenting her.'

'She didn't like it, Brendan. That makes it harassment.'

'Yes miss. I'm sorry, miss.'

Rosie smiled at the boy. She didn't trust him, neither his apology nor that angelic expression, not for one minute.

'I know your da, Brendan. I see 'im in the market now and then.' The boy's face paled. 'I don't think he'd be too happy if I had to speak to 'im about your behaviour, would he?'

'Please, Ms O. It won't happen again. I promise,' he replied.

Just then Sabrina returned to Rosie's side, her face glistening with sweat.

'Hey, I got a little problem I thought you might be able to help me with.'

'Yeah, sure, whatever I can do.'

'It's about Friday. I'm on the late shift at the station which means I can't be here. I was wondering if you could fill in fer me, three to half-four?'

Rosie laughed. 'Me, coach camogie? You gotta be kiddin'.'

'You don't need to do a lot of instruction with 'em. First they run two laps round the pitch followed by stretches. Then they do their drills–like this one. They already know them, we've been through them twice now. That'll take nearly half the time. Then let 'em play a match–yellow vests versus blue–they'll love that. All you have to do is stand and watch there's no kicking or tripping or that sort, yeh know? Please? Just this once? After this week I should be fine.'

'Well, I suppose.'

Sabrina beamed. 'Brilliant, Rosie, brilliant. I owe you big time– a coupla jars at Phinney's, maybe?' She blew her whistle again.

Rosie smiled but shook her head. 'Eh, two pints and you'll have to push me home in a barrow, Sabrina.' They both laughed. The team had gathered around once again.

'Okay, girls. Now, on Friday I gotta put on my garda hat, so I won't be at practice. But Ms O'Malley here–you all know her, right? She's gonna fill in fer me.'

Everyone cheered and Rosie blushed.

'And I expect you all to give her your full cooperation–no sass, no shemozzles–right?' her eye settling briefly on Isla MacDonald, the tallest member of the team.

Again the girls all cheered Rosie.

'See you Friday, then,' said Rosie to the team, then mounted her bicycle for the ride home. As she left she passed Tim and his tall dark-haired friend walking along the High Street together.

* * *

Near the town centre Rosie spotted Cary and Del Samuels just emerging from the Espresso Shop, coffee cups in hand. Cary waved and she pulled up at the kerb.

'Hey, takin' a break, eh?'

'Yeah. How was your day?'

'Not bad,' replied Rosie. 'Hey, Garda Samuels, just talked to yer girlfriend…' She clapped her hand over her mouth. 'Sorry. I meant yer *colleague* there, Garda Selkirk, on the camogie pitch.'

'Oh, yeah, she's the new coach,' replied Del. 'She was a big hurler in 'er college days.'

'I can tell,' said Rosie. 'And she's got a good bunch of girls this year, I'd say. Lots of *craic*. Maybe a little shy on the skill and experience, but full of enthusiasm, yeh know?'

'How's she find the time?' asked Cary.

'Her boss is all for it,' answered Del. 'He's lettin' her leave a bit early on Mondays and Wednesdays. Only problem is Fridays. She's gotta find someone to cover Fridays.'

Rosie nodded. 'Yeah, well, she found someone for this Friday— me.'

Cary was amazed. 'Whoa, Rosie O'Malley, camogie coach?'

'Just fer this week,' replied Rosie emphatically. 'I didn't want to disappoint her. And she's already got 'em into a routine and she says it'll be a breeze. We'll see. So whatta you two up to?'

'I been picking Del's brain for story ideas. Like I was saying yesterday, if I'm gonna sell papers the *Gazette* has to have more than adverts for bingo night and rusty old bangers.'

'So, any brainstorms?'

'We were talking about all the Ukrainian refugees living in Ireland. Maybe not in Glenkerry yet, but in Dublin, Cork, and even in Bray. I mean, everyone feels for those folks, right? And most Irish are proud to say that we're helping out. So I thought maybe I could interview a few Ukrainians and find out how they're doing, what kind a reception they've been receiving, that sorta thing.'

'Wow, that sounds like a great idea, Car. Any idea how to get in touch?'

'I suggested he talk with someone in Immigration Services, or the Red Cross in Dublin,' said Del.

'That reminds me,' said Rosie. 'One of Buddy's co-workers at the garage in Dalkey is Ukrainian. I think Buddy said he's been in Ireland a few years, maybe since before the Russian invasion, but I bet he would know some people. He's comin' to mine this evening, I'll ask him.'

* * *

Cary had a busy morning on Thursday. He interviewed Mr Forster, the principal of *Coláiste Gaeilge*, about the new school year, visited a care home in Ballinoch that had been hit hard by the Covid pandemic but was slowly recovering, then stopped to photograph a construction site on the Arklow road. But all the while he was pondering that dead man on the beach, what little he knew, and what more the gardaí might be learning. When he returned to the *Gazette* office, he texted Del: 'Got a few minutes?'

Del quickly replied. 'I'm in Dunbraugh. Back in an hour. I'll stop by.'

Cary tried to get some work done, but he was having difficulty concentrating on anything but the mysterious death. Finally his mobile vibrated. It was Del.

'Sorry. I got tied up with a family dispute–I hate those things. Hey, I'm right out front.' Cary looked up and saw a garda car parked in front of the office.

Cary and Del walked together along the footpath to the bridge, looking down at the swirling waters of the River Kerry.

'So, what do they know about the dead man?'

'Well, like I told you, his name is Kristoff Rahmann. He's Syrian–or at least he had a Syrian ID on him. I think he was forty-one, five foot eleven, black hair.'

'Have they reached his family yet?'

Del shook his head. 'Nah–it might not happen.'

'Why?'

'They've contacted the Syrian police in Damascus, reported the death, and asked for the family information. So far, no response.'

'God, that's awful. You'd think they'd feel some responsibility…'

'Yeah, you'd think. I guess the situation in Syria is that you have the Syrian police and you have the Syrian government. They're like this,' explained Del, crossing his fingers. 'They say that around Damascus the police are little more than government agents, thugs really, ready and willing to do Assad's dirty work. Not much law enforcement, just pickin' up enemies of the regime. The lucky ones get thrown in jail–many never get that far–if you get my meaning.'

'So, what does that mean for the investigation?'

'Well, it means the gardaí at Phoenix Park in Dublin take over, and they have to coordinate with Immigration Services and Iveagh House,' explained Del, referring to the headquarters of Ireland's Department of Foreign Affairs in Dublin.

'So I'm guessing that means things will move slowly, right?'

'Glacial, mate—glacial. There is an Irish consulate in Damascus, but whether they have any influence no one seems to know. You gotta realise that Assad rules that country with an iron fist. And he's very suspicious of westerners in general, including the Irish.'

'So was this Kristoff Rahmann in Ireland legally?'

Del shook his head. 'Immigration Services has no information on him.'

'And what about the forensic team? Do they think it was an accident? Or suicide? Or murder?'

'I don't know, Car. I'll ask, but I wouldn't be surprised if that report is slow to come down. Everybody's shorthanded these days, yeh know?' Del saw the expression on his friend's face. 'Don't take it to heart, lad. For all you know that Kristoff Rahmann could have been a Syrian agent, one of Assad's henchmen.'

'But what would he be doin' in Wicklow?'

'Good question, Car, good question.'

'Can you find out anything more?'

'Eh, I don't think so, mate.'

'What about Sabrina?'

Del cringed. 'I don't know…'

'Ask her, Del, please? She works with those guys every day at the Wicklow garda station. She's gotta have access to something more.'

'Yeah, maybe. I'll see what she says.'

By midday the *Gazette's* 'Contact Us' inbox was lit up with a number of new messages from readers, most having to do with the death at Travelhawk beach. Readers were concerned, several alarmed, pleading for more information. The pressure was on.

7 THE NEW NORMAL

That evening Sabrina called Rosie. 'I just emailed you the drills for tomorrow. They're pretty simple and the girls will know how to set them up. There are six in all, three girls to each station.'

'Yeah, I got it right here, thanks. It all looks good.'

'Couple other things, Rosie. First about mobiles. There's a new school policy, right?'

'Oh, yeah, we heard all about it. The older students are grumbling.'

'I know. And it applies to practice after school, too. I already had to speak to a couple of the girls about that. Probably just callin' home to ask mom or dad to pick them up afterwards. But still they have to wait until practice is over and they're off school grounds. If we start makin' exceptions next thing they'll be runnin' around with their hurley in one hand, their mobile in the other.'

Rosie laughed.

'And another thing, Rosie—jewellery.'

'Uh-huh.'

'No jewellery allowed in practice or in matches.'

'Oh, yeah, a course.'

'That includes bracelets, necklaces, rings, earrings, nose rings, and studs. Anything outside of their clothing that is.'

Rosie chuckled at that.

'When I told them outside their clothing, I said something about nipple rings. "It's your business" is what I told them. And of course they all giggled. Then I told them about this girl on my college team who took a jab to the breast from a hurley handle. They thought that was funny, too, until I told them that her ring tore right out. It bled a lot–the girl was in a lot of pain, and she had to have eight stitches.'

Rosie grimaced. 'I bet that made 'em stop and think.'

'Yeah, a little shock value,' replied Sabrina.

'So,' said Rosie in a sardonic tone, 'that makes three f-words: fundamentals, fun–and fear, eh?'

* * *

By the end of the day on Friday, her first week as a secondary school teacher, Rosie was exhausted–every bone in her body was aching and her head was pounding. But she was looking forward to filling in for Sabrina as she made her way to the camogie pitch. Most of the players were already warming up when she arrived including Gráinne, Eileen, and their new recruit, Molly. Rosie had a copy of that email message from Sabrina listing the warmups and drills the team should do first.

After a few stretches she sent them on a run, twice around the pitch. 'Not a sprint, now, an easy pace–but keep goin'–don't stop.'

'You not gonna run with us, Ms O.?' asked Gráinne.

Rosie smiled as she shook her head. 'I already got my exercise today, thanks.'

By the time the girls finished their run, Rosie had set up six drills, all of which Sabrina assured her they had done before:

dribbling, striking, blocking, hooking, hand-passing, and the like. Rosie watched with satisfaction as the players did the drills, rotating so that every girl had a chance to try each. She observed a wide range of ability among the team members and wished she could group them by skill level and concentrate on those that really needed instruction.

About forty-five minutes into the practice Rosie brought the players together, then divided them into two teams according to Sabrina's suggestion. Spirits soared as the practice match began.

For the next twenty minutes all went smoothly enough, the action moving steadily in both directions, neither team dominating. But Rosie could see that the biggest problem was the tendency of some players to swarm around the ball, producing a scrum. Again and again she had to stop play and urge the players to stick to their positions unless the ball was in their immediate area.

Eventually the older, more experienced players on both teams got the upper hand by controlling the ball, and the younger, weaker players could do little but watch as the ball whipped past them, sometimes between their legs. Rosie could tell that some of them were getting frustrated watching others carry most of the action. That included Molly Boyle.

Finally, several of the new girls on one team managed to get control of the ball, Molly among them. But just as she was lifting the ball and about to strike it, Isla blocked her, knocking the ball away toward a teammate. Molly lunged forward in an effort to recapture the ball but her hurley instead struck Isla hard on the knee.

Isla grimaced and fell to the ground gripping her knee.

'I'm sorry,' said Molly. 'I didn't mean to...'

'Yeah, right,' came Isla's sharp reply. 'Bitch.'

Molly's face turned bright red. 'I said I was sorry.'

Just then Rosie intervened. 'Hey, hey, she didn't mean it, Isla, okay?'

Play resumed but now Molly held back, far from the action.

A few minutes later Rosie blew her whistle. 'All right then, it's nearly half four. Good match, you lot, good match. Remember to do your running and drills at home like Coach Selkirk told yeh. Have a good weekend, yeah?'

Some of the girls headed toward the locker room and showers. Several others including Gráinne, Eileen, and Molly put their helmets and hurleys in their hold-alls, slung them over their shoulders, and walked through the gate to the street.

After the equipment was secured in the storage shed, Rosie pushed her bicycle through the gate. Molly was sitting alone on a bench.

'Good match, Molly,' she said cheerily.

Molly didn't respond.

'Don't pay Isla any mind.'

Molly shook her head and looked away down the street. Just then a car pulled up, a big black Range Rover with tinted windows. The driver opened her window and smiled at Molly who stood, lifted her hold-all, and walked toward the car.

'Hi,' said the woman to Rosie. 'I'm Anna, Anna Boyle, Molly's mother. You must be Ms Selkirk.'

'No, I'm Rosie O'Malley. I'm just fillin' in for Coach Selkirk today.'

'Oh, and you are her art teacher as well.'

Rosie nodded. 'Yes.' Molly was seated in the passenger seat but turned away from her mother and Rosie. 'She's done some beautiful drawings this week in class.'

'She loves to draw. Don't you, dear?'

Molly shrugged her shoulders.

'Well, it was nice meeting you, Ms O'Malley.'

'My pleasure. See yeh next week, Molly,' she added. But Molly offered no reply.

* * *

Rosie stopped briefly at the *Gazette* office. Cary was on his mobile talking to an advertiser but brightened when Rosie entered. He held up one finger, indicating he was almost finished with the conversation. Rosie sat down at her desk. She was supposed to do photography and layout for the paper, although she had yet to do much of either. And now with her teaching assignment it seemed unlikely that she would be able to put in too many hours for the newspaper. She slid open several drawers–they were empty except for a sketch she had drawn over a month ago for a new masthead.

His call finished, Cary opened his arms, gesturing for Rosie to come to him. She stepped up to him, leaned down, and kissed him.

'So, good day?' he asked.

'Yeah, pretty good. I had three classes in a row, then lunch, then a free block, then one more class.' She paused. 'And then the Hurleys.'

'Wow, that sounds exhausting.'

Rosie sighed, then slumped into Cary's lap. 'Yeah, but mostly good. Better now, yeh know, seein' you.'

He wrapped his hands around her waist and kissed her on the neck.

'I probably stink, Car.'

'You smell as sweet as an Irish breeze.'

'Now you sound like one a those adverts on the telly,' replied Rosie. They both chuckled.

'How about I treat you to supper at Phinney's a little later?' he asked.

'I thought you said you were skint. How 'bout *I* treat *you*? After all, I'm a workin' girl now.'

'Even better,' he replied. 'Seven or so?'

'Yeah, seven's good.'

'And you're invited to stay here tonight, if you like. Save you the long hike up the hill. Okay?'

'That'd be nice, Car.'

This was the new normal for Rosie and Cary–checking in daily, sometimes more than once–meals together at hers or his several times a week–sleepovers on most weekend nights.

They had been neighbours and friends since they were toddlers. In secondary school the relationship started to get more serious, even including a date for the Debs, the formal dance at the end of the school year. Both seemed happy with that, but truthfully, there had been something in Rosie's manner, a certain reserve, that told Cary, then just sixteen, that she was not ready to see their relationship advance. And when Rosie's father nixed the plan for the Debs, Cary had the feeling that it provided a convenient excuse for Rosie to back out. And that was the end of their brief–whatever it was. Cary was mystified and more than a little hurt. Through the rest of their *Coláiste* years the two remained friends, nothing more.

Then Cary left for university. But when he returned to Glenkerry for his father's funeral, there was Rosie, just as sweet and lovely as he remembered her, but distressed over the disappearance of her mother. Over some six weeks she and Cary worked together almost daily, trying to track down Mary O'Malley with the assistance of Del and Sabrina.

When at last they had located her, living in Galway with an old sweetheart, life got back to something like normal for Rosie. Cary by that time had agreed to remain in Glenkerry and restart his father's newspaper, and Rosie's encouragement of that plan was no small factor in his decision.

It was just a few weeks later, after a dinner date at the Grenadine, that Cary invited Rosie to spend the night at 1 Upton Road, a night of no turning back. For Rosie had a secret she had never shared with Cary. And even as they climbed the stairs to his flat on that July evening, she was fearful that her secret, once revealed, would end their new relationship before it had barely begun. But it had survived and by all appearances flourished in the few months since.

Rosie stood up and gave Cary one last hug. 'Oh, and that new masthead?' She held up the sketch. 'I'll get it done. I need some new pens. But as soon as I get 'em, I'll finish it–I promise.'

Cary watched her as she pushed her bicycle up Anglesey Lane. He sat thinking for several minutes, then drew out his mobile and placed a call to Del.

'Hey, Del. I'd really like to find out more of what the gardaí know about Kristoff Rahmann. Did you have a chance to ask Sabrina?'

'Yeah,' replied Del in a low voice. 'I asked her. She said she'd think about it. But I suspect she's afraid that her askin' around might raise some eyebrows, yeh know?'

'Ask her again, please?'

An hour later Del stopped at the *Gazette* office. 'I might have a few bits fer yeh, mate. But it's gotta be hush-hush. Sabrina could be in a lotta trouble if her super found out she was lookin' at files she wasn't authorised to see. As it was she had to pull in a favour from Mitch. I think he's gotta thing for her, yeh know?'

'Never mind that. She's into you, mate–everybody knows that. So, whatta you got?'

'Okay, well, first they had a response from the Syrian police. Or at least someone who seems to be in the police service. Anyway, he wouldn't confirm anything about Kristoff. All he wanted was more information.'

'Like what?'

'Where the body was found, the exact place and time, more description of the deceased, a pathologist's report, cause of death, and all. That's makin' the gardaí uneasy, yeh know?'

Cary looked mystified.

'Cause it seems like the Syrian police aren't interested in notifying the next of kin or anything, just in confirming the death.'

'What else, Del?'

'Well, immigration authorities in Lebanon have a record for a Kristoff Rahmann with a photo that matches the one on the ID. They say he was a native of Syria but moved to Beirut in 1998.'

Cary nodded. 'How about the forensic report?'

Del nodded. 'The evidence from the scene suggests the guy fell from the top of the cliff, from the Black Castle. Hit his head on the rocks–that's what killed him. The pathologist estimates the time of death at about midnight. The tide would have been low then but was coming in when you found him six hours later.'

'Do they think it was an accident?'

'There's no way of tellin' is what the report says. He could've been out there–who knows why in the middle of the night–and just lost his balance–there was some alcohol in his system.'

Del hesitated. 'But could he've been pushed? Yeah, I guess it's possible. They can't say for sure. There was no blood found above, and none on the rocks, but I'm not sure how closely they examined that rockface. It's nearly vertical, yeh know? It's even possible he was struck with a blunt object right on the beach, although there were no tracks in the sand, except for yours, no evidence anyone else was around. And no obvious weapon. Plus he had a lot of money on him, so that rules out theft as a motive.'

'And CCTV? Have they looked at any video of the area?'

'Yeah. The nearest camera is up on Castle Field, nearly 150 metres away. And there's no sign of anyone on or near the beach after 10 pm. But it's not a clear view. There's not much light around the castle and the images are pretty grainy. Plus the carnival was running that week–the Tilt-a-Whirl was parked square in front of the camera, unfortunately.'

'And what about Kristoff's ID? Is it genuine, do they think?'

'Well, it looks like a copy, not the original. And it's old, at least ten years old–it dates back to before there was any biometric information like eye scans or facial recognition. There's a photo of the guy, but the quality isn't great. And of course the ID and the other contents of his wallet were wet. So that didn't help.'

'Can you get me a copy, Del?'

'I'll try, mate, I'll try.'

Cary thanked Del, rang off, then sat at his desking thinking about the few new facts that Del had learned about the death of Kristoff Rahmann. It had occurred just a few hours before Cary discovered the body. It seemed the gardaí were leaning toward accident or suicide rather than foul play.

One thing was clear, though. Here was a story, an important story, one everyone in and around Glenkerry would want to read.

But those readers would be looking for details about the victim and his death in the next issue of the *Gazette*–not simply a repeat of the brief press statement by the gardaí. He would have to provide some additional information. His readers would be expecting that from their local newspaper. And after all, shouldn't that be the mission of all newspapers, of all journalists–to investigate, to inform their readers?

Of course, the *Gazette* was a weekly, so any news on the case would have to wait for the next issue. He couldn't hope to compete with the big city dailies, nor with the online news sources. But a weekly had one advantage, he reminded himself–seven days between issues, seven days to gather information, to digest that information, assemble it into a thoughtful and interesting story. And between issues he could post new developments on the paper's website.

But his only sources beyond that brief gardaí statement were two good friends, Del and Sabrina. Should anything he wrote implicate them, they would be called to account–their jobs might be in jeopardy. That would be very bad for them and for him. He needed more information, but he needed to obtain that information from some other source. But what other source could he turn to?

Then Cary did what every millennial would do first in such a situation, he turned to the internet. A quick search of 'Wicklow death' produced brief news items from several daily newspapers around Ireland that were little more than restatements of the garda public statement: *dead man found on beach in Wicklow town, more details pending contact of next of kin.*

On an impulse he did a search for 'Kristoff Rahmann.' Just one result: a character from a 1980s spy novel.

8 DATE NIGHT AT PHINNEY'S

Rosie arrived at Phinney's Pub a few minutes before seven. She sat at a table in the corner watching for Cary to come through the door. In a minute or two a smiling Gráinne stood at her table.

Gráinne's father, Liam, and her grandfather, John Phinney, owned the place, the most popular gathering spot in Glenkerry. Phinney's offered ale, stout, wine, and hard liquor, but they also served food, both for dining in and takeaway. And one night a week there was live entertainment on offer as well, featuring some of County Wicklow's undiscovered talent.

Gráinne and Tim began working at the pub when they were thirteen, at first washing dishes, but eventually waiting on tables, a practice permitted only for young family members of the proprietor of such an establishment. The experience had done wonders for Gráinne, enabling her to talk easily with everyone, young or old, male or female. She had once been quite shy but waiting tables at Phinney's had quickly cured her of that.

'Long time no see, yeah?' dimpled Gráinne.

Rosie chuckled. 'Hey, good match today, yeah? There's good energy on the team, I'd say.'

Gráinne smiled doubtfully. 'I get it–we try real hard but we're rubbish, right?'

'No, that's not what I mean. But I'm not an expert. I'm sure Sabrina–Coach Selkirk–can teach you guys a lot.'

'Yeah, she's good–really good.' Gráinne looked around. The pub was pretty quiet. 'Can I talk to yeh about somethin'?'

Rosie gestured toward the other chair and Gráinne sat. 'It's about Molly.'

Rosie nodded. 'Uh-huh. What about her?'

'She's all wound up, yeh know? All the time, like. That blow-up with Isla, that was just one thing. She got pissed off–I mean annoyed–at lunch the other day when one of the girls made an innocent remark about her. It's just, well, she doesn't make friends too easy. I been tryin', mainly cause we need her on the Hurleys. But she doesn't make it easy, yeh know?'

Rosie nodded. 'Yeah, I know what you mean–she's really hard to get with. Her family just moved 'ere from Cork, she told me. Maybe, yeh know–new town–new school.'

'If she could just like smile once in a while, just a bit, the others would take to her better.'

'You're right, Gran–you're absolutely right. But you and Eileen gettin' her to join the Hurleys, that's a huge step.' Gráinne shrugged her shoulders. 'No, really, I mean it. Give yourselves some credit. And keep workin' at 'er. Pretty soon I bet she'll start to fit in better.'

'Yeah, okay, I will. Eileen and me are runnin' tomorrow. I thought I'd invite Molly along, but she doesn't have a mobile. Can you believe it?'

'Well, maybe you can talk to her in school next week and plan something for the three of yeh–maybe a run, or just to hang out.'

Gráinne rolled her eyes. 'Somehow I can't see Molly "hangin' out".'

Rosie chuckled. 'Me either. I guess she's what you'd call a high maintenance friend.' Their eyes met in agreement. Just then Cary appeared. Gráinne stood and held the chair for him.

'Ooh, date night, eh?' she winked. 'I'll bring you guys menus.'

'So, you and Gráinne talking camogie, eh?' asked Cary.

'A coach's workday is never done,' she said with a melodramatic sigh. 'Anyway, look at you. Clean shirt, brushed hair. I gotta say, you clean up nice.'

'Yeah, well, I guess. But I still don't feel right, yeh know?'

Just then Gráinne returned with menus. He waited until she was out of earshot, then lowered his voice. 'That guy, I can't get the sight of him outta my head.'

'What are the gardaí sayin'? Have they found out anything more about him?'

'Not much, at least nothing they're willing to go public with. They issued a press release Tuesday but all it said was a middle-aged Caucasian male was found dead on the beach at Wicklow. Del says they've identified him. Kristoff Rahmann–he's a Syrian."

'Really?'

Cary pulled out his mobile, swiped it a few times, then showed Rosie an image.

'That's the guy's ID. Del sent it to me.'

Rosie stared at it.

'They've tried to contact the Syrian police about next of kin but so far they've heard nothing back.'

Rosie thought for a moment. 'Do yeh suppose he was a Syrian agent? Maybe the Syrian police don't wanna admit that.'

'Yeah, maybe. Del says Immigration Services has no record of this guy being in Ireland. So he must've entered illegally. If he has a family they're probably still in Syria.'

Rosie's brow was knit as she thought about it. 'But if it's true, I mean, if he was in Ireland illegally, isn't it kinda weird that he didn't have some kind of fake papers? Otherwise how could he, yeh know, drive, or rent a flat–or anything.'

'Yeah, you're right,' replied Cary. He hesitated, thinking. 'But for all we know he was here only for a short visit. Maybe some specific mission. Maybe he had a forged passport or visa but didn't happen to have it on him when he died.'

'Mission?' she asked, her eyes wide. 'Like a terrorist, or a spy?'

'Who knows? But you're right, to enter Ireland illegally and walk around with just a Syrian ID, that's gotta be risky. Even if he got stopped for something trivial like jaywalking, he could be detained, couldn't he, if he didn't have documents?'

'Yeah,' replied Rosie. 'But the gardaí must be lookin' at the case from all those angles, hopefully.'

'It sounds like they're leaning toward an accident–or suicide.'

'What about that story on refugees? Any news on that?' asked Rosie.

'Yeah, I talked to a woman from the Irish Red Cross today. She's gonna try to arrange for me to meet with some Ukrainians in Dublin or Wicklow–maybe next week sometime.'

'Wow, that ought to be interesting, Car.'

'Yeah, really. I'm hopin' to do a whole series on recent immigrants to Ireland. I think it will interest readers, don't you?'

'For sure,' answered Rosie. 'It will definitely sell papers.'

Cary sighed. 'So, how'd you do with the Hurley Girlies today?'

'Oh, Car, you shoulda been there to see them play a practice match. It was great fun.'

'So they're good, eh?'

'Well, they're enthusiastic, I'll say that much.' Just then Gráinne arrived with their pints.

'You guys ready to order?' she asked.

Rosie ordered a seafood salad, Cary opted for the steak and ale pie. After Gráinne walked away, Rosie continued. 'Gran and Eileen are two of the best on the team. They're good at manoeuvring the ball, lookin' around, settin' up plays. The others jus' go chargin' in.'

'Well that's great, Rosie. You think you might do some more with them?'

'Well, it's up to Sabrina. She's the coach. If she asks, I'll be glad to help out again once in a while.'

'Yeah, well, prepare yourself, Rose, cause from what I hear Sabrina's already talkin' like you're the assistant coach of the *Coláiste* camogie team. I just got a text from Del a little bit ago.'

* * *

A half hour later things were still quiet in the pub. The waitstaff were standing around, idly wiping clean tabletops and polishing clean glasses. Their meal and pints finished, Rosie and Cary were about to leave when Rosie spotted two teenagers at the front door. Both looked familiar. One was Molly Boyle.

Gráinne walked right up to them. 'Hey, Molly. I haven't seen you in here before. Do you live in Glenkerry?'

Molly nodded but looked sombre. 'Our ma called in an order.'

Then Gráinne looked at the boy and smiled. He was tall with black hair, the same boy Rosie had seen with Tim on the camogie pitch earlier in the week. 'Hi, I'm Gráinne.'

The boy blushed. 'I'm M-Michael–eh, Mike.'

'Yeah, I seen yeh in school, Mike. I didn't know yeh were Molly's brother. Nice to meet yeh. Hold on and I'll see if yer order is ready,' she said with a wink.

Just then Tim approached smiling. 'Bro,' he said to Mike, and the two bumped fists. 'Zup?'

'Gettin' takeout,' replied Mike. 'You work for the ole man, eh?'

'Yeah, Gran and me both. So, yeh callin' round tomorrow?'

Mike nodded. 'Husks are goin' down, mate,' he said with a grin. Again they bumped fists.

Gráinne returned with their order. 'Here you go. All paid fer. Enjoy.'

'Later,' said Tim to Mike.

'Yeah, l-later,' replied Mike.

Molly and Mike had just stepped out onto the street when Gráinne appeared at the door behind them.

'Hey, Molly, Eileen and me are runnin' tomorrow morning at the GAA grounds at half eight. You wanna join us?'

Molly shook her head. 'I got too much homework.'

Gráinne persisted. 'It'd be just a half hour.'

Mike looked at his sister. 'Why not, sis? You can s-spare a half hour.' He turned to Gráinne. 'Sh-she never goes anywhere.'

Gráinne persisted. 'Come on, it'll be fun. Good for Hurley team spirit, yeh know?'

Molly shrugged. 'Well, okay.'

'Great. And you can come, too, Mike. You look like a runner,' she added, even though he didn't.

He shook his head. 'Th-thanks, but that sounds like a g-girls-only event.'

'Well, okay–see you in school, then.' She turned to Molly. 'See yeh tomorrow, Molly. Remember–Hurleys Rule!'

9 THE SYRIAN CONNECTION

Cary woke around midnight and lay still, listening to Rosie breathing softly at his side. But his mind was back on the matter of the body on the beach, Kristoff Rahmann. The gardaí were not going to move very fast on the case, which seemed unfair to the man's family, whatever family he had. Wherever they were, surely they must be wondering about him. If he was a Syrian, what was he doing in Wicklow, Ireland? Was he a refugee? Or perhaps a Syrian agent up to no good? His thoughts drifted to Syria, that war-racked nation where justice was hard to come by. If only, he thought, he had a contact in the Middle East, someone who might know a little about what went on in Syria these days. Soon he fell back to sleep.

In the morning he made breakfast for the two of them. Finally Rosie prepared to leave. 'I got work to do at home gardening, animals. I'll see yeh later, okay? How about you come to mine and I'll make us a stir-fry for supper?'

'Yeah, grand.'

She hugged Cary, kissed him on the cheek, then departed.

Cary had cleaned up the kitchen and was about to shower when his mobile rang. It was Siobhan Sullivan, one of his best friends while he was at uni. She was in London, working for a software design company, living in a flat in Chelsea.

'Hey, Shiv, how are you?'

'I'm good, Car. Crazy busy, but good.' He could hear dishes rattling in the background. 'That's just Anders. He's doin' some housecleaning. It's a good thing *someone* cleans up around here,' she added with a chuckle. Anders was a Swede who worked with Siobhan. They shared a flat, the flat Cary was meant to share with Siobhan until his father died and all his plans turned to custard.

They proceeded to bring one another up to date on their jobs. Cary hinted that the *Gazette* was a work in progress. 'I don't know when it's ever gonna turn a profit. But I gotta just keep workin' at it, is all.'

Siobhan asked about Rosie. 'Oh, yeah, she's fine. She's got a teaching post at *Coláiste Gaeilge*, a maternity leave replacement for just a few months.'

'How's that going?'

'So far she likes it, yeah. Plus she's helpin' with the camogie team.'

'Wow–sounds like she's pretty busy.'

'Oh, yeah, I guess. We touch bases, yeh know, now and then.'

Cary and Siobhan met in their first year at university. Siobhan was American, from LA. They'd become good friends almost at once, mates, but just mates. At the time Cary was more than a little smitten with this American lass. But he felt certain she looked on him as just a friend and he was resigned to leaving it that way. Besides, he figured she must have a boyfriend–maybe at DCU, maybe back in LA. How could she not? And it had become an unspoken rule between Cary and Siobhan never to provide too many details about their love lives, partly because of the possibility that it might in some way be painful for the other.

Don't ask, don't tell, Cary was thinking to himself.

Then he told Siobhan about the body on the beach.

'Oh my god, Car, that must've been awful.'

'Yeah, well, it wasn't too pleasant.'

'So who was he? A local?'

'Nah. He was Syrian, imagine that? In County Wicklow? He had his Syrian ID on him. But the gardaí aren't having much luck finding out about him—or locating his family. He might have been a refugee. I'd like to try to find out about him. Plus I'm workin' on a story for the *Gazette* on refugees in Ireland and I have to learn more. But I have no idea how to go about it.'

'What about Sam, Car?'

'Sam?'

'Sameed Jones—from DCU.'

Sameed Jones grew up in Lebanon, Cary recalled. He came to Dublin for uni, also reading journalism. Sam's mother was Lebanese and a translator, his father was British and worked for an NGO in Beirut.

'Yeah, a course, why didn't I think of him? Where is he now, d'yeh know?'

'Yeah,' replied Siobhan, 'he's back in Beirut—workin' for his father's organisation—hopin' for a job in journalism. He calls now and then.'

'Gee, I should talk to him. He might be able to give me some background on Syria and Syrian refugees, maybe put me in touch with some people.'

'Yeah, Sam has lots of friends in Lebanon, Syria, and Turkey. Listen, why don't I text him with your number? Mobile reception is spotty where he lives, so it's easier letting him call when he's got service.'

'Yeah, that'd be great.'

'How's Catherine these days?' Siobhan had met Cary's mother on several occasions and was fond of her.

'Ma's okay, yeah. You know, mostly gardening, church, committees, that sort.'

'Tell her I said hi, yeah?'

Just then Rosie appeared at the door.

'Hey, I gotta go. Good talkin' with yeh–yep–right. See yeh.'

'Me again–I forgot my purse,' said Rosie, looking around the office. 'I guess maybe I left it upstairs. Who was that?'

'Siobhan, in London. She called just after yeh left.'

Rosie stiffened, her features visibly hardened. She'd met Siobhan. She knew about Siobhan and Cary at DCU. 'Just mates' was what Cary said of them over and over. Rosie wasn't convinced.

'Oh? How's she?' Rosie asked blandly.

'Yeah, she's good. She and Anders, both, yeah, real good. They sound happy, the two of them–you know, living together.'

Enough. You made your point, mate!

Cary went on. 'We had a friend at uni named Sam Jones. He's from Lebanon. Siobhan's gonna get me in touch with him. He knows people in Syria including some activists involved in the resistance movement there. I thought he might even be able to find out something about this guy, Kristoff Rahmann.'

* * *

At half eight Gráinne and Eileen arrived at the GAA pitch and began doing their stretches. As yet there was no sign of Molly.

'I hope she comes,' said Gráinne. 'I got the feeling after yesterday that she might quit the team. That's why I invited her today. Maybe show her we need her.'

'Right,' answered Eileen. 'Our first match is next Friday, yeh know. Six days. I hope we don't suck, yeah?'

Just then a black Range Rover turned into the car park and Molly climbed out. Then the car pulled slowly away.

'Hey, Molly,' said Eileen cheerfully. 'Ready for a run?'

'I guess,' replied Molly a bit doubtfully.

'No worries, just a few stretches, a few laps around the pitch, some more stretches, then maybe a caffeine fix at the Espresso Shop.'

Molly nodded. The trio did some hamstring, quad, and calf stretches together, then were off and running. They ran for nearly thirty minutes with a break after each lap. Molly straggled behind repeatedly, but Gráinne and Eileen slowed down each time to let her catch up.

When they had finished the trio walked the short distance to the Espresso Shop on the High Street. Gráinne and Eileen ordered caramel lattes for themselves and treated Molly to a mochaccino. They stepped out onto the footpath, then sat on a bench together.

'Molly,' said Gráinne softly. 'Don't let Isla get to yeh. She's big and likes to throw her weight around.' They all chuckled. 'If she slags you, just ignore her. She's a nightmare–but she's a really good full-forward. The Hurleys would be crap without her.'

Molly nodded, her eyes fixed on her drink.

'Where'd you live before you came to Glenkerry, Molly?' asked Eileen.

'In Cork.'

'Oh, I have an aunt and uncle in Cork,' exclaimed Eileen. 'I love that downtown shopping area, whatcha call it? Cornmarket? It's deadly.'

Molly nodded.

'I got some fabulous earrings at a little shop there. I wanna go back sometime.'

Again Molly nodded.

'Did you ever shop there, Molly?'

'Maybe, once with my ma and my brother, I think.'

'So how old is your brother?' asked Gráinne.

'He's two years older than me. He's in sixth year.'

'Does he, like, have a girlfriend?'

Molly grimaced, then shook her head.

'He's kinda cute,' offered Gráinne. Molly shrugged.

'So did you play camogie at your school in Cork?' asked Eileen.

'Yeah, for a while.'

'Cork is a big town for camogie and hurling, right? Doesn't Ashling Thompson come from Cork?'

Molly perked up. 'Yeah, she does. My mom took me and my brother to see her play once. She was amazing.'

'What about your dad? Didn't he go, too?'

She shook her head. 'He couldn't–it was a holy day for him.'

Just then Molly saw her mother's car pulling into the car park across the street.

'I gotta go.'

'Okay, Molly. See you Monday,' said Eileen.

'Yeah, Visual Arts–and practice,' added Gráinne.

Molly nodded and started to walk away. Then she turned. 'Ta,' she said, holding up her drink cup. And she smiled.

* * *

It was mid-morning the next day, Sunday, when Cary took a call on his mobile. It wasn't a normal mobile call, it was a VoIP, a voice over internet call, from Sameed Jones in Beirut. They spent several minutes talking about their mutual friends from DCU. Cary asked about Sam's sister whom he met once when she visited in Dublin.

'So, Siobhan says you're a newspaper publisher now, yeah?'

Cary chuckled. 'I'm tryin'. It's the *Glenkerry Gazette*.'

'Oh, yeah, your father's paper. Did he retire?'

Cary told him about his father's death just days before commencement.

'Gee, Car, I'm sorry for yeh.' There was a pause. 'So Shiv said you were working on a story on Syrian refugees in Ireland?'

'Well, it's more about Ukrainians right now. I'm hoping to meet a couple of recent arrivals sometime this week. It should be interesting. But something else has come up that I wondered if you could help me with, something to do with Syria.'

'Yeah, sure, like what?'

'A few days ago a man's body was found on the beach at Wicklow. The gardaí say they've identified him—he had a Syrian ID on him. It looks like he fell off a high ledge above the beach—hit his head.' Cary didn't want to explain that he was the one who found the body—it still made him queasy thinking about it. 'But the gardaí say they've been trying to get through to the Syrian police to contact the guy's family or next of kin. So far they've had no response.'

'Yeah, somehow that doesn't surprise me.'

'And I guess Immigration Services has no information on him, so they think he was in Ireland illegally. Anyway, that's where it stands. They don't know if he might have been an agent of the Syrian government tryin' to track down Syrian refugees in Ireland, or maybe he was a refugee himself.'

'So you said he fell. Was it an accident? Or was he pushed?'

'The coroner's report seems to be leaning to accident or suicide. But the investigation is going very slowly. I have a friend who's in the gardaí here in Glenkerry, and he says resources are stretched pretty thin these days, so it may take a while. But I'd like to run a story about it in the next issue of the *Gazette*, yeh know?'

'So, you want me to find out about him?'

'Yeah, if you could. His name is Kristoff Rahmann.' Cary spelled out the name. 'Caucasian, black hair, date of birth is 15 March 1982. I got a scan of his ID from a friend in the gardaí. I'll send it to you.'

'Kristoff Rahmann–hmm, the name doesn't sound familiar to me. But let me see what I can find out about him, okay? It might take a few days. Communication in and out of Syria is tricky. And there are bad guys everywhere. That's why I called on my VoIP account, yeh know what I mean? VoIP calls are encrypted and not easily traceable. So don't call me–I'll call you.'

'Okay, Sam, sure. Anything you can find out, I'd appreciate it, but don't take any chances, yeah?'

Cary rang off and sat thinking about the call. Syria was a big country, he knew–something like four times the population of Ireland. For over a decade it had been a quagmire of warring parties, the Free Syrian Army, Kurdish Rebel Fighters, the so-called Islamic State, Jabhat Fath al-Sham, Hezbollah, and the Syrian Democratic Forces. Assad's government forces were supported by

Russia and Iran, while Turkey, some Gulf states, and several European nations offered support to the anti-government forces. Meanwhile millions of Syrians had left the country, hundreds of thousands had died, families had been disrupted, hunger and economic devastation were everywhere.

* * *

That evening Cary walked up Anglesey Lane. He paid a brief visit to his mother who was about to leave for a meeting of *An Dílis*, a group dedicated to reforming the Roman Catholic Church in Ireland. She was also a member of Glenkerry Citizens for Justice that was involved in a number of charitable causes including providing housing for refugees in County Wicklow.

'I see the gardaí have released some information about the death of that young man,' said Catherine. 'But they've not identified him, so.'

'Yeah, well, everything is moving very slowly. They're still trying to contact the next of kin.'

'Those poor folks. I feel for them. I hope they're not from Glenkerry.'

'I doubt it, Ma,' He sighed. 'Well, I gotta go. Rosie's doin' a stir-fry.' He held up a bottle of wine he was bringing as his contribution.

'Ooh, lucky lass. Give 'er my love, Car.'

'Will do.'

When he stepped inside the front door of the O'Malley home, the enticing fragrance of garlic and oregano filled the air. In the kitchen he found Rosie labouring over a large skillet on the stove where a colourful mélange of aromatic ingredients simmered. He came up behind her and kissed her on the neck.

'Watch out, woman at work,' she said with a smile, her eye fixed on the pan as she stirred.

'Wow, what's in the stir-fry?'

'Let's see, snap peas, chard, celery, carrots, fennel, coriander, white wine vinegar, chanterelles–oh, and chicken.'

'You sure know the best way to a man's heart, Rosie.'

'Yes, I do,' she said. Suddenly she turned, glaring at him while pointing a long sharp kitchen knife at his throat. 'It's through the jugular vein, I'm told.'

They were still laughing as they carried their plates out to the table in the garden. Cary uncorked the wine and poured it. They sat sipping it in the hush of the evening, the wonderful mix of aromas wafting about them.

'You ready for another school week?' asked Cary.

Rosie smiled. 'I think so. I did a lot of planning today and I have to get into the art studio early tomorrow morning to make sure I have everything I need. We're painting this week, oils and acrylics.'

'Sounds like fun.'

'Yeah, well, it can be. But it can be very messy as well if you're not prepared. But I've done it before and I'll try to be prepared. Oh, Car, before I forget, can I ask you a favour?'

'Of course, anything.'

'So there's this form that the school nurse gave me to fill out. It's a health form.'

'Uh-huh.'

'They want me to list three emergency contacts, yeh know? People to call if there's some kind of emergency while I'm at school.'

'Oh, yeah, that makes sense.'

'Would it be okay with you if I put your name on the list?'

'Of course, yeah, why not?'

'Well, normally it would be family members, yeh know? But Buddy's in Shankill and Ma's in Galway. So I was thinking of them for second and third. Plus you–mebbe?'

'Yeh mean, first?'

Rosie nodded tentatively.

'Yeah, I guess so–of course.'

'Yeh're sure?' she asked.

'Yes, Rosie, I am sure. Okay?' He reached across the table and touched her hand. 'We're, well, a couple, aren't we?'

'Yeah, I think we are,' replied Rosie hesitantly. He brought her hand to his lips and kissed it gently. 'Yes,' she added with grin, 'I'd say we definitely are a couple.'

'Brilliant. And besides, what kind of emergency could there be? I mean, you're young–and healthy. Right?'

Rosie bit her lip. 'I talked to Margaret Healy on Friday, Car–she's the school nurse–about my...' She paused. 'About my health.'

Cary looked concerned.

'I told her about my ostomy. I thought I should. She should know, I figured. Wouldn't you agree?'

'Eh, I guess so. If you think.'

'Well, I didn't spell it out on the form. I just checked "Gastrointestinal disease" under Medical History.'

Cary wasn't sure what Rosie was saying. 'Uh-huh.'

'See, I don't know who has access to that form. Maybe the principal, or the human resources people, or members of the School Committee. See what I mean? I was hopin' that it could be just between her and me.'

'Yup, that makes sense. What did she say about that?'

'She's real nice. She grew up in Drogheda, got her nurse's training in Dublin. She even did a rotation in the ostomy clinic at Mercy, the same place where I had my surgery. So she's very casual about it. And she says nobody else needs to know. I mean, it's not ever likely to be an issue. I haven't had an ostomy-related problem in years, and when I do I can usually deal with it myself.'

'Well, that's great, Rose.'

'It's not that it's something I'm ashamed of. It's just, well, it's private.'

'For sure.'

'One other thing, though. I was thinkin', if I should ever have a problem, yeh know, at school, could you maybe come get me? Maybe borrow your ma's car? I couldn't exactly ride my bike home sick, yeh see.'

'Oh, yeah, no worries.'

Once they had finished their meal, they walked across the yard to the fence, then gazed across the pasture where the sheep were grazing placidly in the fading daylight.

'By the way, Sabrina called this afternoon. Like you said, she wants me to be her assistant coach–eh, *unofficial* assistant coach–of the Hurleys.'

'So, what did you say?'

'I'm in.'

10 HAWAIIAN SHIRTS AND COWBOY BOOTS

The next morning Cary paid a visit to Gloria Hennessy. Gloria was an estate agent–her office was just a few doors along the High Street from the *Gazette* office. She was in her fifties and an imposing figure, both in stature and in personality. Like many estate agents, she knew her town and its people. If anyone had their finger on the pulse of Glenkerry, it was Gloria.

'Ah, Ciaran McGurk,' she said with a twinkle in her eye as he stepped through her office door. 'Just the man I need to see.' She held up a sheet of paper. 'Here's this week's advert copy.'

Besides being a friend of Cary's mother, Gloria was also a major supporter of the *Gazette;* she purchased a full-page advertisement in every issue. And unlike certain other advertisers he could name, Gloria paid quickly, perhaps suspecting correctly that the newspaper's cash position was precarious.

'Oh, yeah, thanks, Gloria. I'll get right on that,' said Cary, quickly scanning the copy.

'We're featuring this new listing,' she said, her eyes shining as she handed him a glossy photograph. 'It's a new country estate house on Harmony Lane–five bedrooms, six baths, a three-car garage, pool, and spa.' She paused, watching with amusement as Cary's jaw dropped. 'On forty-five hectares–magnificent views of

Great Sugar Loaf,' she added, referring to the mountain that loomed to the north.

'Whoa, how much are they asking?'

'*One-and-a-half*,' she replied, speaking each word slowly and clearly.

Cary was gobsmacked. 'One and a half million euro? Who in Glenkerry–who in the *world* has that kind of money? Some Saudi prince? Or Russian oligarch?'

'Well, you know, Ireland is fast becoming the location of choice for holiday homes of the rich and famous–Americans, Brits, Germans, and others. Everyone it seems wants a little getaway in the Emerald Isle.'

'A little getaway?' replied Cary incredulously. He thumbed through a stack of photos of the house that Gloria had on her desk, shaking his head in disbelief. 'My entire flat could fit inside the dining room of this place with room to spare.'

Gloria guffawed.

'Actually that's just what I wanted to ask you about. You know what's going on in Glenkerry better than almost anyone. And I've been away at uni for three years, so I'm a little out of touch. Are there many recent immigrants living in Glenkerry these days? I mean, maybe expats from the States, or like you say, millionaires building their dream homes?'

Gloria leaned back in her chair, her hands behind her head. 'Well, there are some. Not a lot–but some. Brexit is one factor. Yeh know, Ireland's committed to the EU. After Brexit some Brits began looking on us with renewed interest, maybe on principle or maybe for business reasons. And of course there are Americans, especially in biotech, who have relocated to Ireland. I can think of maybe three couples from away who've bought homes in Glenkerry in the last few years plus one or two in the townlands.'

Cary nodded. 'It's funny, though, you don't see them on the High Street.'

Gloria grinned. 'Well, for one thing many are here only for short holidays–a few weeks in summer, or maybe over Christmas. And of course you might not notice an American oil tycoon if you saw him on the High Street–unless of course he was wearing a Hawaiian shirt and cowboy boots.'

They shared a laugh at the image.

Then she went on. 'Some folks have been here for decades–the Patels, yeh know–and the Samuels. Watch a football match down at the GAA grounds, you'll see more than a few young lads and lasses from Africa, the Caribbean, the Middle East, and of course Asia.'

'Yeah, I guess you're right, Gloria. What about refugees, or folks seeking asylum?'

'There are tens of thousands in Ireland, Cary–from Syria, Sudan, Somalia, Afghanistan, and now from Ukraine. Mostly in and around the cities where there are jobs and more affordable housing. But none in Glenkerry that I know of, not yet anyway.'

'Do you have any idea if there are people around here who are in Ireland illegally?'

She shook her head. 'No, I can't say as I do. But then, how would I know? They don't generally walk around with signs on 'em.' She paused. 'But I can tell you that some restaurants hire undocumented workers seasonally–they depend on them, truth be told. So yes, undocumented foreigners are around, but of course they keep a low profile.'

'Yeah, now that you mention it, I remember waitstaff in Dublin restaurants who didn't speak much English–they seemed to be mainly African or Southeast Asian.'

'Yep. And you'll find them in shops and restaurants around County Wicklow as well. And probably on farms, too, although farm workers are pretty much out of the public eye.'

'Could an employer get in trouble for hiring undocumented workers? I mean, could they get fined?'

'Well, I suppose, although you seldom hear of it. You should ask your friend Garda Samuels about that. My guess is the gardaí have more pressing matters to attend to–plus I hear they are terribly understaffed these days.' Gloria paused, then lowered her voice. 'But Ciaran, I'd be careful what I wrote about undocumented persons in Glenkerry or hereabouts. Some employers depend on illegal visitors as a major source of seasonal employment. If you draw attention to it in your paper, you might force the gardaí or Immigration Services to go after them.'

'Yeah, oh yeah. I'm not gonna write about them. I'm plannin' a story about refugees, folks who are here legally. Actually, I hope to meet and interview some Ukrainians around Dublin, maybe later this week.'

'Oh, well, that will be of interest to your readers, for sure. I think most Irish are proud to be taking in refugees. Just think of how many of our forebears were welcomed in America, Canada, Australia, New Zealand, during the famines–and since.'

'Yeah, that's what I'm thinking.'

'I recall your dad wrote some editorials in the old *Gazette* about Ireland's obligation to asylum seekers from war zones, places like Afghanistan and Iraq.'

'My ma was telling me about that. That's another reason I want to write something on the subject.'

'A fine idea, Cary. Say, you might want to discuss the matter with Kevin Leahy.' Kevin was a Glenkerry resident and a member of the County Council. He had proved very helpful in the fight against the 'Monster Mall' that Cary and Gloria worked on together. 'Kevin will have a broader perspective on the matter, yeh know–county-wide and beyond.'

'Yeah, Kevin Leahy, of course,' replied Car. 'I'll give him a call. Thanks, Gloria.' He stood up, about to leave.

'Cary, does this have anything to do with that body you found?'

'No, not really. I'm also working on a story about that for this week's *Gazette*, but so far there's very little to report.' He knew he needed to be discreet with Gloria. She was not one you could rely upon to keep a secret. 'Well, I guess they have identified him, or they think they have. But they haven't been able to contact the next of kin. That seems to be the holdup.'

'I hear he's a Syrian. Kristoff something,' said Gloria.

Cary was stunned but tried to act casual. 'Eh, where'd you hear that, Gloria?'

'One of the Dublin papers ran a story about it just this morning.'

'Really? I'll have to look into that.'

With that Cary took his leave. He stopped at the Espresso Shop where he sat at a table by the window sipping his latte while searching the web on his mobile.

'Body found on Wicklow beach identified,' read a headline on the Facebook page of a Dublin daily. The man's name was 'Kristof Raman,' the story reported–Syrian national, forty-one years of age.

'The gardaí continue their investigation into the circumstances of his death.'

Well, there it is, thought Cary, for all to see. While he had been privy to that information, he had been careful not to publish it. He wondered about that Dublin newspaper's source. Had the story been leaked by a member of the gardaí? Maybe someone hacked into the gardaí incident database. Or was it possible that the information had been disseminated in Syria, by the police or government authorities?

You have to write that story about the dead man, by tomorrow's deadline, he thought. But he was still nervous about how much he should feel free to report.

* * *

As soon as he got back to his office, Cary texted Professor Charles Jurgenson, his former journalism tutor and professor at DCU who had been very helpful to him during the battle over the 'Monster Mall' last summer. Cary had some questions, he explained, questions about journalistic ethics and standards. Would the professor have some time to speak with him?

Several hours later Cary's mobile buzzed–it was Professor Jurgenson. They spent a few minutes catching up, Cary telling his mentor about the *Gazette,* his hopes and challenges, then asking about the professor, his family, and the new semester at DCU. Finally Cary reviewed for the professor the few known facts about the death at Wicklow beach. He told him about his personal involvement which astonished the man. Then he got to the gist of his call.

'I've received some additional information from a personal friend in the gardaí about the identity of the victim. Off the record, yeh know? I promised not to make it public until the gardaí release the additional details.'

'What kind of details, Ciaran?'

'His name, age, that sort. And his country of origin.'

'So, I take it he was not Irish.'

'That's right. The man had an ID on his person. So they believe they know his name and his country of origin. He was from Syria.'

'Ah-hah. Perhaps a refugee who was granted asylum in Ireland?'

'But Immigration Services has no information on him.'

'Hmm. Syria is a tough country to deal with these days, that I know. Tightly controlled information.'

'Yeah. That's the problem, I guess. The Syrian police are not cooperating with the gardaí so far, for example in contacting the man's next of kin. But a few hours ago a friend in Glenkerry told me she saw the man's name in a Dublin newspaper. I found it on their Facebook page. They said the dead man's name was Kristoff Rahmann, from Syria. Which is what the gardaí found from his ID. How they obtained that information, I don't know.'

Cary paused.

'So I want to write something about the death for this week's *Gazette*, yeh know? I'd like to be able to include his name and the Syria connection without getting my garda friends in trouble. Is it permissible for me to use the information from this other newspaper? And do I need to attribute it to them?'

'Well,' began the professor, choosing his words carefully. 'This is a tricky area. There are some rules about such things in newspaper journalism. If that publication is the sole source, I mean, if they've obtained the information themselves, then yes, you would need to attribute it. After a certain amount of time it becomes public knowledge. But you probably don't want to wait; you want to get it into this week's issue, right?'

'Yes sir. And my deadline is late tomorrow.'

'Can you spell the name for me?'

Cary spelled out Kristoff Rahmann. He could hear a computer keyboard clicking over the mobile.

'I'm just checking something here, Ciaran. Hold on just a few seconds.' There was a short pause. 'Ah-hah, yep, here it is. *Al Jazeera* has a story about Kristoff Rahmann on their web page. It's dated about twenty-four hours ago. They're reporting his death in Wicklow, Ireland, on the fourth of September. And there's a paragraph about the man. He was a journalist in Syria until about 2012. They seem to suggest that he left Syria when he was implicated in a human trafficking operation.'

'Wow, really? That's amazing. *Al Jazeera*–are they credible?'

'Yeah, I'd say so. I mean, they have their critics, no question there. They've been accused of bias often enough. But as far as adhering to modern journalistic standards are concerned, they rate pretty high among the world's major news sources. When *Al Jazeera* publishes a story, they usually get the facts right. My sense is that they wouldn't run a story like this one unless they had a reliable source.'

Cary was perplexed. 'But I searched Google just a few hours ago. Why didn't I see the story there?'

'Remember our discussion in class about research methods? Your research can *start* with Google, Ciaran, but you mustn't *stop* there–ever. There are many reasons that you might not find a story on Google. Maybe your search terms aren't quite right. Or the story hasn't had time to propagate on the internet–that can sometimes take a few days. You're better off searching the news sources around the world directly. I think I gave your class a list a few years ago of some of the best sources for online news. And it includes *Al Jazeera.*'

'So I can use that story as a source?'

'Sure, although it's still good form to credit your source. But at least you don't have to worry about your friends in the gardaí, Ciaran–the whole world knows about Kristoff Rahmann now.'

Cary thanked the professor, then rang off. Immediately he went to his laptop and found the story to which Professor Jurgenson referred. How, he wondered, had *Al Jazeera* found out about Rahmann's death? And where did they come by the details of his work and his alleged involvement in human trafficking?

Cary knew he didn't have much time to ruminate on such questions. He began to write.

New information has come to light regarding the death at Travelhawk Beach in Wicklow on 4 September. According to a press release from the Wicklow gardaí, the victim was a middle-aged Caucasian male. The gardaí had identified the man but were withholding his name pending notification of next of kin.

In a story dated 10 September the Qatar-based international news service Al Jazeera is reporting that the victim has been identified as Kristoff Rahmann. A native of Syria, Rahmann worked as a journalist, first for a Damascus newspaper from 2004 to 2008, then as an independent journalist. Rahmann had dropped out of sight in 2012 after Syrian police sought to question him regarding his alleged role in a human trafficking scheme.

The gardaí continue their investigation of the circumstances of Rahmann's death and will release additional information as soon as it becomes available.

The Gazette is following the story closely. For updates visit our website.

It wasn't much, thought Cary. But it was all he had at the moment. And he would watch *Al Jazeera* and other news services carefully for the next twenty-four hours to see if there were any further developments in the case.

11 MOLLY DOES A BUNK

The Hurleys had just finished their warmup run followed by the usual stretches. Today's practice focused on dribbling, lifting, and striking the ball.

'Lifting–raising the ball off the ground–of course is very important in camogie, and it can be done in two ways–the roll lift and the jab lift,' began Sabrina as her team looked on intently. She first demonstrated the roll lift, rolling the ball toward herself with the hurley, then tapping it into her free hand.

After the players had practised the roll lift many times, she went on to demonstrate the jab lift. 'Now the jab lift is important because you can execute it on the run,' she observed, then demonstrated. 'That makes it very useful in a match when you are on the move. Jab, then lift the ball, then pass it or strike it to a teammate.'

She was watching the team do a drill on jab lifting when Rosie appeared along the sideline carrying her camera.

'Looks good, Sabrina.'

'Yeah, well, could be better,' replied the coach as she watched her players.

Just then Rosie saw Molly Boyle practising the drill with Aoife Byrne. Molly seemed to be comfortable with the routine and enjoying herself.

'She seems to be settlin' in, eh?' observed Rosie, nodding toward Molly.

'Yeah, still a bit standoffish, yeh know? But a little more relaxed. And smiling once in a while, too. Yeh know, she's a bit of a natural, I'd say. She's quick, agile–and her basic skills are solid. She told me she played on a team in Cork where she lived for a while.'

'That big girl, Isla, she's all over the place, eh?' noted Rosie as she watched.

'Yeah. Yeh know, she's sixteen–almost as tall as me–she probably outweighs me. But she's fast and aggressive–she's at the centre of nearly every play. And she's smart, too, game smart, that is. She's not much of a student, I hear–she barely qualified for the team this year because of her grades. But when she's on the pitch, she's amazing to watch. She studies her opponents, she plays to their weaknesses, she sees ahead–I don't know how she does it, but she seems to be thinking two or three plays ahead of everyone all the time.'

As they watched Isla barked at one of her teammates.

'But, as you can see, she's got a bit of a temper, too–I gotta work with her on her self-control.'

Rosie nodded. 'So, do you still want me to take the team photo for the *Gazette*?'

'Yeah, for sure. Let's give them five more minutes of this and then we'll take a break.'

Soon she called in the team. 'Ms O'Malley's gonna take a team photo today, okay? For the *Glenkerry Gazette*. So take a couple minutes to catch yer breath, maybe brush yer hair, then line up over here with the goal behind yeh, okay? Helmets off, a course.'

Just then Eileen approached Rosie. 'Ms O., got a sec?'

Rosie smiled and nodded.

'I was wonderin' if the *Gazette* would let me write like a little thing each week, I mean like, about the Hurleys, yeah?'

'That's somethin' you'd like to do?'

'Yeah, fer sure. I like to write. And they wouldn't have to pay me, I'd just, yeh know, do it fer the experience, like.'

'Wow, Eileen, that's a grand idea. Tell yeh what. Why don't you write something about the team, sort of an introduction for readers that don't know about you guys, or about camogie for that matter.'

Eileen quirked an eyebrow at that.

Rosie chuckled. 'Believe it or not, Eileen, there are some folks that don't know much about Gaelic sports. Write it up and give it to me. I'll pass it on to Mr McGurk—he's the editor. If he likes it, maybe he'll run it. Then see where it goes from there.'

'Thanks, Rosie, I mean Ms O.'

'No problem. Well, I gotta set up my shot.'

Rosie walked out to midfield facing one of the goals, noting the angle of the sun and the backdrop. Then the players started lining up. Rosie liked what she saw—the team's green and gold uniforms shone brightly in the late afternoon sun.

'Okay, squish in a bit, you guys. Isla, maybe you should move to the back row. Megan and Aoife to the front. There—that's better. Okay, ready?'

Just then Sabrina spoke up. 'Where's Molly?'

'She left,' said Gráinne softly.

'But she was here a minute ago.'

'Yeah,' said Gráinne, 'as soon as you told us Rosie was takin' pictures she scarpered.'

Sabrina sighed. 'Oh, darn.' Her eyes met Rosie's. 'Can you wait a sec?' Sabrina ran out through the gate to the street looking for

Molly. But she was nowhere to be found. She returned to the pitch shrugging her shoulders.

Rosie took several photos. 'Okay, thanks everyone. Now remember, next week's *Gazette*–be sure to buy a copy or two–or ten.'

Everyone laughed. Sabrina thanked Rosie, then gathered the team for another drill.

'Thanks, Rosie. Sorry about Molly.'

'Yeah, me too.'

* * *

On her way home Rosie stopped at the *Gazette* office. Cary was busy working on the Ukrainian refugee story but stopped, leaned back in his chair, and smiled as she entered.

'Hey, how was your day?'

'It was fine, Car, until the end.'

'Why? What happened?'

'Well, I got a photo of the Hurleys.' She showed him the image on her camera.

'Looks sharp, very colourful. So what's the problem?'

'It's Molly, Molly Boyle. She was there for practice and seemed to be doin' fine, but when I was ready to take the shot she was gone.'

She slumped into a chair.

'But it looks like an excellent photo, Rose, and she's just one kid, yeh know?'

'I know, but I was hopin' she was really startin' to fit in. I even caught her smilin' once during practice.'

'Don't take it personally.'

'By the way, Eileen Keough talked to me about writing a story on the Hurleys for the *Gazette*. It sounds like she might even like to do a regular column if you'd have 'er. Just for the experience.'

'Wow, well, can she write?'

Rosie chuckled. 'I don't know. I guess you'll find out pretty soon. I told her to write something and get it to me in school. Then I'll pass it to you.'

'Well, okay–I'll be glad to have a read.'

'Like I said, she just wants the experience. She doesn't expect to be paid.'

His expression brightened. 'It's sounding better every minute, Rose.'

Just then Rosie saw a familiar figure walking along the footpath across the High Street. It was Molly.

'There she is, Car–that's Molly. I'm gonna go after her and try to talk to her.' Rosie jumped out of the chair and started for the door. But at that moment her mobile rang. It was Sabrina.

'Hey, yeah. I'm with Cary at the *Gazette* office, just showin' him the photos.'

Rosie listened, sighing, nodding, her eyes meeting Cary's several times as she listened. Finally she replied.

'Okay, well, I'm sorry to hear that but, yeah, I understand. Don't feel bad, Sabrina–I mean, someone shoulda told you about that right from the start. Yeah, well, now we know, eh? Okay, see yeh.'

Rosie sank back into her chair. 'That was Sabrina. I guess there's this form all *Coláiste Gaeilge* parents fill out about photographing their kids. Parents can opt out. Molly's not supposed to be photographed, ever, in or outside of school.'

Cary had heard of this, but never in his school days had he known any classmate to be excluded from photos. 'I wonder why.'

'The clerk in the school office told Sabrina that it's pretty rare for a parent to choose this option. Usually it's to do with a family issue. She said a few years ago there was this couple that split up and it got messy. The mom took out a safety order against her ex for herself and her kids, that's how bad it was. They lived in Dublin but she brought the kids to Glenkerry every day and didn't want the father to find out where they were.'

Cary nodded. 'Do you suppose there's somethin' like that goin' on with the Boyles?'

'I don't know, maybe. I met the mom, Anna, and she seems nice enough.' She paused, her brow wrinkled. 'But I've never seen the dad, now that I think of it. And there's never been any mention of him.'

'Well, do you think maybe that has something to do with Molly's shyness?'

'Yeah, well, maybe so.'

Then her mobile buzzed, it was Sabrina, again. Rosie listened. When the call was over she looked up at Cary with a glum expression.

'Molly's quit the Hurleys.'

* * *

That evening Rosie sat alone in her kitchen having her supper, a bowl of soup—all veg from her own garden. She was turning over in her head what she knew about Molly Boyle. And she was feeling a little guilty, guilty that she'd urged Molly to join the Hurleys in the first place. Maybe she shouldn't have butted in. Maybe that girl needs to find her own way in her new school without some teacher, no matter how well-intentioned, trying to push her.

But the more she thought, the more Rosie wanted to try one more thing that might offer a ray of hope. It was Anna, Molly's mother, who called Sabrina. But Anna made it clear that it was Molly's decision to quit the team, not her own.

Rosie sent a text to Gráinne asking if she and Eileen could see her in school the next morning before the first lesson.

'It's about Molly. I need your help.'

As planned Gráinne and Eileen appeared in Rosie's classroom the following morning before the rest of the class began arriving. The three talked for several minutes. Then the two students went out into the hallway and waited for Molly.

A few minutes later Gráinne and Eileen walked into the classroom. Gráinne gave Rosie a thumbs-up signal. Then Molly entered, smiling.

Rosie breathed a sigh of relief. 'Just in time, guys. Today we start printmaking.'

* * *

At the end of the day, Rosie had a free hour, a chance to clean up her room and prepare for the next day. She was washing down the countertops when Gráinne appeared.

'Hey, Gran, look at how your print turned out.' She had made prints of leaves by dipping them in paint and pressing them onto heavy paper. Rosie had pinned one on the wall, a finely divided fern. 'That's brilliant, Gran.'

Gráinne blushed. 'Maybe, but I did a bunch that weren't so brilliant.'

'But yeh finally figured out just the right technique–just the right amount of paint, just the right amount of pressure–and with beautiful results. That's the way art is, yeh know? Trial 'n error–learn by your mistakes.'

'Ta,' said Gráinne. They both stood admiring the print.

'So, what did you and Eileen do to turn Molly around?' asked Rosie.

Gráinne chuckled. 'We begged her and pleaded with her, basically.' She sighed. 'Like you said, she's a high-maintenance friend.'

Then it was Rosie's turn to laugh. 'So what was Molly's problem?'

'Her ma doesn't want her in any school pictures. That embarrasses her and makes her feel like she doesn't belong, yeh know?'

'Yeah, I can see that.'

'So we just told her over and over how she does belong, how we want her on the team.'

'Well, fair play to you, Gran, to both a yeh.'

'But why is her ma so strict?' asked Gráinne.

'I don't know, Gran. Maybe it has something to do with their family situation.' Rosie paused. 'What about her dad? Is he around?'

'I'm not sure. She mentioned him once to Eileen and me. She was saying how her ma took her and Mike to see Ashling Thompson–yeh know, the All Star hurler–when they lived in Cork.'

'Oh?'

'When Eileen asked why her dad didn't go, she said it was a holy day in his religion.'

'Well, I suppose it's their business, not ours,' replied Rosie. 'But thanks fer helpin' out.'

'I don't know about Molly–she's just so nervous. It's almost like she's afraid of something, yeh know?'

Rosie wrinkled her brow. 'What about her brother? Do yeh know anything about 'im?'

'Yeah. Mike's cool.'

'Was that Mike with Timmy on the sideline the other day?'

'Yeah, they been hangin' out a lot–they mostly play video games.' Gráinne made an exaggerated grimace.

Rosie chuckled.

'Timmy wants me to go with 'im to the Boyles' on Saturday to play Fortnite with Mike and Molly.'

'Fun,' said Rosie with a smirk.

Gráinne huffed. 'I suppose.'

The Cliff Walk

12 ESCAPE FROM UKRAINE

It's Wednesday morning and Cary is riding his motorcycle to Bray. Over the previous few days he has had several telephone conversations with a representative of a national humanitarian organisation in Dublin who had contact with Ukrainian refugees in Dublin, Meath, and Wicklow. She has arranged for Cary to meet a couple in Bray who are willing to be interviewed. They both speak some English, he is assured.

Cary is anxious. He wants a good story, of course. But he also wants to respect the privacy of the couple, to allow them to tell only as much as they wish about the crisis in their homeland, their harrowing journey, and their new life in Ireland. In his university journalism courses he learned a lot about interviewing techniques, especially about how to draw subjects into saying more than they may have intended. That approach, he tells himself, might be acceptable for interviewing public figures like the *Taoiseach*, the Irish Prime Minister, or a member of the *Dáil*, the Irish legislature. But it is entirely inappropriate for this situation. Better no story at all, he thinks, than one that exploits the couple's misfortunes.

They are waiting for him in a small meeting room in the town hall with the representative of the Dublin organisation who arranged the meeting. They stand when Cary enters. The representative introduces them.

'Maryna, Ivan, may I introduce Ciaran McGurk? Ciaran is the editor and publisher of the *Glenkerry Gazette*.'

Cary smiles and shakes hands with each. 'Thank you so much for agreeing to see me, Mr and Mrs Goraya. It is a pleasure.'

Maryna smiles, then tips her head. 'You seem veery young, sir, to run a newspaper.'

Cary laughs. 'Yes, I suppose I am. I just graduated from university in May. The newspaper was my father's.'

'And your father ees now retired?'

Cary shakes his head. 'He passed away, just a few days before I graduated.'

Maryna shakes her head. Ivan speaks up. 'He would be very proud, your father–very proud.'

'Well, thank you, sir. I hope so.' That is something Cary has wondered about: would his father be pleased with what he was trying to do, restarting the *Gazette*? Or would he worry about him undertaking such a task, knowing what he did about the newspaper business? It's one of the many questions that prey on Cary's heart these days.

They sit. Cary opens his notepad. He might have brought a laptop, or a digital recorder, but he worried that such a device could make the Gorayas uncomfortable–and might be an obstacle to their conversation.

'Well, again, thank you for agreeing to meet with me. I imagine some of the details of your journey from Ukraine to Ireland may be painful for you to discuss. So, please, if I ask a question you would prefer not to answer, that's okay.'

* * *

Nearly ninety minutes later, Cary was exhausted both physically and emotionally. The Gorayas' story had touched him, it had moved him, it had humbled him.

'My life,' he told Rosie that evening, 'it seems so simple, so easy, compared to the Gorayas'. I can't even imagine what it would be like to watch my country invaded, to be forced to evacuate, to travel thousands of kilometres from my homeland, family, friends, and have to live in an unfamiliar place.'

'Well, you've got quite a story to tell your readers, yeah?'

Cary shook his head. 'I suppose. But what if I cock it up, Rosie? How do I write a story that is interesting for readers but not disrespectful, yeh know?'

'You'll do it, Car, I know you will.'

'Can I ask you to read a draught and tell me what you think?'

'Yeah, of course.'

The next day when Rosie checked her email she found the draught of Cary's story and read it.

UKRAINIAN COUPLE HAPPY TO BE LIVING IN
COUNTY WICKLOW BUT LONG TO RETURN TO
THEIR HOMELAND

Ciaran McGurk, Editor, Glenkerry Gazette

I spoke recently with Ivan and Maryna Goraya. We met just one day after the couple's fiftieth wedding anniversary.

Ivan and Maryna Goraya met in one of Ukraine's largest cities, Mariupol, where they both worked, Ivan for a steel manufacturer,

Maryna in a grocery store. After their marriage in 1973, the newlyweds rented a house in Anadol, a small town outside of Mariupol that was near enough to the city for Ivan to travel to work each day by bus. They raised three children in that house and eventually purchased it.

'Ukraine was a Soviet Socialist Republic back then,' recalled Ivan, shaking his head. 'It was a very sad time in the history of our country. Everyone lived in fear of the Russians. And the economy was in a very bad way–people could barely afford food for their families.'

'The day the Soviet Union collapsed,' recalled Maryna, 'it was like a dream. People were cheering and dancing in the streets–suddenly we had our beloved Ukraine back once again.' She smiled at the memory, but her smile quickly faded. 'We never believed the Russians would return,' she added ruefully.

Ivan and Maryna were still living in that same house in Anadol in February 2022 when Russia invaded Ukraine. Tears welled in Maryna's eyes as she remembered the days before the invasion.

'We heard rumours of an invasion, but we did not believe them. We thought we would be safe in Anadol. Our children told us we should be ready to leave, perhaps to Poland. Ivan's brother lives near Warsaw. But we would not even think of it.'

'On the second day of the invasion, we could hear gunfire and explosions in Mariupol,' recalled Ivan. 'Our sons, Oleg and Boris, they came to see us that morning. They told us we must leave. They already had a plan for us. They helped us pack–clothes, food, medicines, documents. They put our bags in their car. Their families all came to see us off, including our grandchildren. Then our sons drove us to the Polish border.'

'It was a very long journey,' explained Ivan, 'over 1000 kilometres. We could have travelled by train, but we heard that the trains were overcrowded with people leaving Ukraine. We drove day and night, mostly on small country roads. The main roads were filled with cars headed west to the Polish border. It was four days when we finally reached the border at a small town near Lviv.'

The Polish border patrol was well prepared for the arrival of refugees and within an hour the Gorayas were admitted. They said tearful goodbyes to their sons who then returned to Mariupol. Both planned to enlist in the Ukrainian army as soon as their families were safe.

Ivan and Maryna stayed with Ivan's brother and his wife in Warsaw for about a week. Then they read in the newspapers about a programme for Ukrainian refugees in Ireland. They visited the Irish embassy, spoke with a representative of the International Committee of the Red Cross, and less than a month later, in April 2022, departed by plane for Ireland. They were among the first Ukrainians to be admitted under the International Protection Act.

'As soon as we got off the plane in Dublin we were surrounded by many people, people we did not know—they greeted us like we were friends. They gave us flowers, and presents, and they took us by caravan to Bray,' recalled Ivan.

'We were very fortunate,' explains Maryna. 'They provided us a comfortable flat in the centre of Bray. We can walk to the grocer, to the pharmacy, even to the beach.'

'And the DART train is just a ten-minute walk,' added Ivan. 'We go into Dublin to church every Sunday.'

Maryna smiled. 'There is a grocery market in Dublin with Ukrainian food. We can get all our favourite Ukrainian delicacies there, borscht (soup made with beets), varenyky (dumplings filled with meat and vegetables), and banush (like polenta with meat).'

I asked how they had been treated since arriving in Ireland. 'Everyone has been so kind to us,' said Maryna. 'We are very thankful for the kindness of so many of the people of Ireland.'

Within a few weeks more refugees from Ukraine had arrived in Ireland and were settled in Bray, Enniskerry, and Dún Laoghaire. The Gorayas have attended many gatherings and gone on outings with their countrymen and women now living in Ireland.

I asked the Gorayas if anything about Ireland surprised them.

Maryna smiled. 'The countryside, it is so green and beautiful. We walked along the Cliff Walk in Bray one day; I could not believe all the beautiful flowers. Last week we visited Powerscourt in Enniskerry. What a magnificent place. It reminded us of the palace of Tsar Nicholas in Crimea.'

'You have so many different beers in Ireland compared to Ukraine,' observed Ivan with a smile, 'lagers and stouts and ales.'

I asked if they had heard any news from their children. Boris and Oleg are in the same unit in the Ukrainian army. Their wives, Maria and Anna, and their children moved together to Chernivtsi near the Romanian border.

'The children are attending school. Maria and Anna have jobs. They are all right, but they miss their husbands and they worry about them. We worry, too,' said Maryna.

Their daughter Alina, her husband Andre who is Estonian, and their one child are now living with Andre's family in Tallinn, the capital of Estonia.

'We miss them all very much. In Anadol we would see them often. But now we see them only on Skype,' said Ivan.

Editor's Note: In the coming weeks I will be reporting on a family from Syria who have settled in County Wicklow.

As soon as she finished reading the story Rosie texted Cary. 'Your article is lovely–beautifully written–very moving.'

13 GAME ON

'Okay, girls, today we focus on passing,' began Sabrina the next day as Rosie looked on. 'The key to passing is communication. You have to let your teammate who has the ball know you're open. So call her name, then be ready to receive her pass. Don't call unless you are open and ready.'

'Now, I asked you to memorise the names and numbers of your teammates, right? Numbers because in the heat of a match you may not always recognise a teammate by her hair or height or whatever. So you gotta know her number as well. Oh, and of course we have two Megans–Megan O'Kelly and Meghan O'Farrell. Megan O'Kelly here says you can call her Kelly, okay? So there's no confusion.'

Sabrina had Kelly stand a few feet away with the sliotar on the ground in front of her. 'Okay, I'm lookin' around and I'm free. So I call out "*Kelly*." My eye is on the ball, both hands on my hurley, my left hand ready to move as soon as Kelly passes to me.'

Sabrina nodded and Kelly lifted the ball with her hurley, then passed it. Sabrina received it, then struck it toward the goal.

'Simple, right? But not unless you communicate. Call your teammate's name, let her know you're there and open–your eyes are on the ball–you're ready to receive the pass. Okay? Watch.'

Now Sabrina started to dribble the ball. Kelly called her name: '*Coach*.' Sabrina lifted the ball deftly to her left hand, then tapped it to Kelly. 'Okay. "*Kelly*," ' said Sabrina. Kelly lifted the ball and passed it back to Sabrina. They demonstrated this over and over again, going one way down the pitch, then returning.

'All right. Find a partner and try it.'

With that the team broke up into pairs and began the drill. Sabrina stood watching closely for several minutes, making comments and corrections where needed.

Rosie was looking at the roster Sabrina had prepared for Saturday's match. 'You got Molly starting at left half-forward, eh?'

'Yeah. Like I said the other day, her skills are solid, better than most of the younger girls. I'm not sure how she'll perform in a match, but I thought I'd give her a try. I'll probably pull her out and substitute one of the younger girls at some point.'

'Oh, hey, let me show you something.' She took the clipboard from Rosie. 'On the back here I taped a list of the girls' emergency contact information if we should need it. Mrs Sweeney in the school office pulled all their files for me.'

Rosie scanned the list. 'Molly's mom is listed, but no father, eh?'

'Yeah. Molly's file was empty except for a sticky note with Mrs Boyle's number. She just registered a day or two before the start of the term. And I guess the records from Molly's old school haven't arrived yet.'

* * *

The first match of the season between *Coláiste Gaeilge* and St Michael's National School took place Saturday morning on the GAA pitch in Glenkerry. Sabrina was acting very relaxed, but Rosie sensed that she was nervous about the match. In a quiet moment she confided her worries to Rosie. Many of her players, especially the younger ones, were anxious. And she feared a poor showing today might doom them for the remainder of the season.

Just before the match was to begin, Sabrina gave her team a spirited peptalk, reminding them of the skills they had worked on in practice. She led them in a cheer. Then the referee's whistle blew. Rosie would be on the sideline, encouraging the players with her cheers, keeping the water tank full, wrapping ankles, and massaging cramped muscles when necessary.

The match began uneventfully, neither team scoring and the sliotar changing sides frequently. But after a few minutes the St Michael's squad seemed to find their pace and scored two quick goals in succession. This rattled the Hurleys and they appeared to forget all their practice on teamwork and playmaking. Even the veterans including Gráinne and Eileen played erratically. In the last minute of play Ava struck the ball through the uprights for one point. At half-time St Michael's was ahead, 6-1.

Sabrina gathered the team in a huddle.

'Now listen to me, Hurleys, okay? You can do this. You can. But you gotta focus on the fundamentals. Your eye on the ball–talk to your teammates–dribble–hand-pass–strike. Just like we practised, yeah? And go after the ball, hear me? Don't just wait for it to come to you, go after it. Hook–intercept–dispossess. Don't be thinkin' about winnin' or losin', about championships and trophies. Think about those fundamentals and the rest will take care of itself. Okay, are yeh with me, Hurleys?'

'Yeah,' came the cry, but weak.

'Really?'

'Yeah,' came the cry once again, but stronger.

'You can do this, mates,' shouted Sabrina. The team erupted in a loud 'Yeah.'

Just then Rosie noticed Cary standing along the sideline. She waved and held up crossed fingers. Cary smiled and gave her a thumbs up. Then the referee's whistle blew and the team lined up for the second period.

Sabrina's efforts to rally her girls seemed to be working. The team started to click, moving faster and passing the ball around much more skilfully than before. Lily dispossessed an opponent close to their goal, then passed the ball to Eileen who scored a goal. And minutes later Gráinne, Eileen, and Allegra took control of the ball and with a good deal of fancy stickwork managed to move it up the pitch and score a point through the uprights.

With only three minutes left in the match and behind by one point, the Hurleys seemed to have momentum on their side. They worked the ball surprisingly well, several times approaching the goal only to be dispossessed by their opponents. But with just a minute left in play, a scrum had formed midfield. Somehow out of that mob, Molly appeared, lifting the ball on her hurley, then passing it to Isla who scored the match-tying point just as the whistle blew.

Cheers went up for Isla and several of her teammates hugged her. But to Rosie's delight Isla pointed to Molly and gave her a thumbs up. A cheer then went up for Molly. Rosie watched with great pleasure as Isla and Molly stood together, clasped hands held high, both girls beaming.

The coaches and officials consulted. The pitch was needed for a hurling match scheduled to begin shortly. So there would be no extra time. The match was called.

Sabrina spoke to her team. 'You girls were brilliant, just brilliant. You didn't give up, you remembered your positions, you made your plays. So we didn't win, who cares? You played St Mike's to a tie–very respectable. And that last point, Isla and Molly, you guys rocked.'

Just then Molly's mother approached smiling. She opened her arms and her daughter ran to her and accepted a hug of congratulations. Mrs Boyle's eyes met Sabrina's, then Rosie's, as she mouthed, 'Thank you.'

Then it was off to Kelly's Cones, just across the street from the camogie pitch. The team sat on the grass licking their ice cream cones.

'Wow,' said Cary, the Hurleys looked good out there, at least the part of the match I saw.'

'Yeah, well, the first period was kind of a disaster. But I have to hand it to Sabrina, she really knows how to talk to those girls. Her voice, her face, she just–I don't know, Car, she has a way of building confidence. It's amazing to watch.'

'Is that Molly?' he asked, nodding to the trio of players near them.

Rosie nodded.

'Well, she must feel good about the match, yeh?' said Cary.

'Come,' said Rosie, and she drew Cary toward the trio and introduced them.

'You guys were brilliant out there–just awesome. Congrats,' said Cary.

With that Cary excused himself–he needed to be in the *Gazette* office at noon.

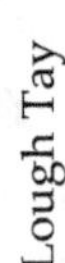

Lough Tay

14   THE WALLS HAVE EARS

It had been nearly a week since Cary's last conversation with Sam Jones. He had been busy, meeting with the Ukrainian families, doing research for his story, while at the same time trying to make contacts with advertisers and taking frequent calls, emails, and text messages about church events, lost sheep, and still more jumble sales. Finally, on Friday, he received a text from Sam. 'Have some information for you–will call tomorrow noon, your time.'

A few minutes after noon Cary was working on the refugee story when his mobile buzzed.

'Car, it's Sam. Yeah, sorry to take so long gettin' back to you. I'm not sure whether this is your man. But one of my contacts in Damascus thought he might have known a Kristoff Rahmann. He was active in the Syrian underground starting maybe 2005 or so. He did some writing against the Assad government for a resistance newspaper–got himself onto one of the government's hit lists. Then he disappeared–about 2012. My contact says he was never sure whether Rahmann left the country, was jailed, or killed.'

'Do you think it could be the same guy?'

'Well, the age seems about right, the general description, yeh know? He didn't know him personally, but he has a colleague who did know him, a newspaper editor. That guy is hard to reach–he's in Aleppo.'

Aleppo was a city that Cary had heard about, where resistance forces fought hard and the death and devastation had been some of the worst in all of Syria.

'But if he manages to get through to him, he'll see what else he can learn,' added Sam.

'Wow, well, thanks, Sam. I hope you aren't takin' any chances doin' this for me.'

Sam exhaled loudly into the phone. 'There's an old Arabic saying, *Aljudran laha adhan*–the walls have ears. In this part of the world nowadays, everything you do's a risk, mate, especially when it has to do with the Syrian underground. They are hunted constantly and when they are found they are eliminated–no questions asked–no explanations accepted.'

'Okay, well, thanks again.'

'Hey, Car, one more thought.'

'Yeah?'

'If that was the same Kristoff Rahmann you found on the beach, it's a little surprising that he would be walking around in Ireland with a Syrian ID, yeh know? Especially if he's in Ireland illegally.'

'Yeah, that's what we were thinking, Sam. You'd expect him to have some kind of fake papers, an acquired identity or whatever.'

'Exactly. And Car? If Rahmann was such a prominent member of the Syrian resistance, you gotta wonder if his death was an accident.'

'I guess I need to tell the gardaí, right?'

'Yeah, I suppose. Although they may know some of this already. But why don't you wait a few days, see if I can get any additional information.'

* * *

The weather was especially mild for late September and Cary and Rosie planned a trek around Lough Beag. Rosie packed them a lunch and some snacks and Cary stuffed a blanket into his pack. When he was arranging the rest of his kit a small foil packet fell out. Rosie picked it up and handed it to him, smiling.

'Sorry, mate, but I'm afraid we won't be able to make use of this today. I got my period.'

Cary nodded. 'Oh, yeah, sure. It was just a thought.'

Their eyes met. 'And a good one, Car. But not today, I'm afraid. Plus I'm not exactly a bare-naked in the great outdoors kinda girl, yeh know?'

Cary laughed. 'Yeah, no problem.'

They took a rough path from Rosie's house to the north. It crossed the summit of Anglesey Hill, named for the island off the coast of Wales that could be seen from the summit on a clear day. Then it descended into a dark, dense forest of spruce and pine. Rosie and Cary had walked this path a few times back in secondary school, being careful to meet out of sight of the O'Malley house where Rosie's father could see.

It was in this dense forest that Rosie once had spotted one of Ireland's most curious and enigmatic winged creatures, looking for all the world like a clump of lichens on a low-hanging branch.

'Remember that day, Car, when we saw the nightjar?' asked Rosie.

'Yeah, sure I do. But you saw it, Rosie–I would have walked right past the thing. It was weird, wasn't it?'

A short distance farther brought them to the shore of Lough Beag. Cary's recent memory of the lough was not a good one. It was the day the gardaí searched the waters while he watched and waited anxiously, fearing that Mary O'Malley had drowned here.

As it turned out, the lough was on her route the day she left, but she had continued on to Ballinoch, a tiny townland a few kilometres beyond, where she made good her escape by bus, first to Dublin and then to her new life in Galway.

They stood silently, listening to the warm breeze through the trees, watching a flock of ducks plying the shallow waters in search of a meal.

'I bet I never thanked you for comin' out here with the gardaí that day. I could never have done that, Car. I was so worried about my ma.'

'No worries. It all ended well, right? For your ma.'

'Yeah, it did.' She wrapped her arm around Cary's waist and sighed. 'That was only, what, two months, three months ago, but it seems like a million years.'

They followed the rough trail made by fishermen around the margin of the lough. At the far end a rocky promontory rose high above the water affording a view of the entire lough and beyond. Here they spread the blanket and enjoyed their meal.

'I had a long talk with Maura Ahearn last evening,' said Rosie. 'I've told you about Maura, right?'

'You mean your social worker at Mercy Hospital?'

'Yeah. She visited me almost every day the six weeks I was in hospital. I don't think I woulda made it without her. I was just twelve and I depended a lot on my parents, especially my ma. But even at age twelve there are things you don't wanna talk to your olds about, yeh know? And Maura always listened, never judged me or scolded me or acted like my opinions and feelings didn't matter. She was always accepting.'

'Yeah, well, I can imagine how you must've been glad to have her there.'

'And we been in touch ever since. For a while I went to these weekly group sessions she hosted for recovering ostomy patients. But even after I stopped going to those, she'd call and we'd talk. And she came to Glenkerry once and Ma made her a real nice supper.'

'That's great, Rosie, that you two have stayed in contact all these years.'

Rosie took a sip of fruit juice, then looked away toward the distant horizon.

'She asked me a favour, Car, last night. There's this girl at Mercy now, Sophie's her name. She's fourteen–she has colitis like I did–she's really sick. Maura asked if I'd be willing to meet her, to talk to her.'

'Wow, Rosie, that's–well...' He paused and looked into her eyes. 'She must really have faith in you to ask you to do that.'

Rosie looked at Cary then. He saw doubt, perhaps fear, in her eyes.

'What?'

'I don't know, Car. To be honest, it worries me. Like what do I say? What if I say the wrong thing? Or what if she doesn't feel like talkin' to a total stranger?'

Cary nodded. 'Yeah, I guess it's a lot of pressure on you.'

Rosie sighed. 'I couldn't sleep last night, thinkin' about it.'

Cary was looking carefully at Rosie's face, seeing the worry and the fear in her eyes. Then he turned and took in the view of Lough Beag below, surrounded by a forest of Sitka spruce and Scotch pine, its waters sparkling in the midday sun. Rosie had had so much to deal with–serious illness, fighting a battle she might not win, having to make a life-changing decision, all at age twelve. His childhood–well, it seemed so ordinary, so uncomplicated by comparison. He felt out of his depth trying to help Rosie grapple with that business.

'Hey.' He took her hand and she turned to him, her face tense. 'When you were in hospital like that girl, would you have wanted to talk to someone who'd been through it? I mean, someone other than a doctor, or a surgeon, or a social worker?'

Rosie hesitated, taking in the view. Cary was watching her face for some hint of a reaction. He saw tears welling up in her eyes. Then she nodded.

'I was so scared, and I felt so alone. If it was someone who listened–who understood–who cared–another girl or young woman who had what I had? Yeah, I think I would have.'

Cary slid over beside her and held her. He stroked her hair and kissed her cheek.

Just then a shadow passed over them and they both looked up startled. It was a merlin soaring low over their heads.

'We better get movin' or he'll think we're his elevenses,' said Rosie. They laughed together. Then they gathered up their kit, shouldered their rucksacks, and continued their circuit of Lough Beag.

For a time as they walked Rosie was silent. Then she stopped and turned to Cary.

'Yeh know, I think I'll tell Maura yes, I'll do it–I'll talk to Sophie.'

* * *

Eventually the footpath around Lough Beag brought them back to Anglesey Lane and they walked together down the narrow way, bordered on one side by pastures dotted with sheep, by a dense forest on the other. Far ahead of them a car approached, then turned and disappeared through a break in the stone wall on the forest side. It was a black Range Rover.

'That's the drive into the O'Donnell farm,' noted Cary. 'That place has been empty since Mrs O'Donnell passed. Maybe someone's bought it. I'm surprised Ma hasn't heard about that. Gloria Hennessy usually keeps her up to date on every estate sale in Glenkerry.' They both looked at the narrow lane as they passed. 'The drive into that house is long–and the house isn't visible from the road,' noted Cary. 'Someone must like their privacy.'

'Maybe so, Car, and I got a guess who. That black SUV? It looks just like the car Molly Boyle's mother drives. Maybe it's the Boyles who've bought the place.'

* * *

A few more days went by before Cary heard from Sam again. He was on his way back from an interview with another group of Ukrainian refugees, these in Ballyfermot, when his mobile sounded. He pulled his motorcycle off the road.

'Yeah, Sam, what's up?'

'Hey, I found out a little more about Kristoff Rahmann. I think you'll be interested.'

'Uh-huh.'

'That guy in Aleppo knew him. And like I said, Rahmann was active with the resistance at that time. And he left Syria in summer 2012. He wasn't sure where he went.'

'Do you think it's the same Kristoff Rahmann?'

'Well, the general description seems right, hair colour, height, and all.'

'Uh-huh.'

'But one more thing. This guy in Aleppo was a newspaper publisher–Rahmann worked for him. He looked up the man's employee record and found his birthdate. Car, it was the fifteenth of March 1982.'

'Which matches the ID,' replied Cary. 'Wow, I guess that clinches it then, huh? It's gotta be the same Kristoff Rahmann.'

'Yeah, so it seems, mate.'

'Hey, Sam, since we talked last week Rahmann's name came out. I saw it first in a Dublin newspaper, but then on the *Al Jazeera* website.'

'Is that right? *Al Jazeera*, huh?' replied Sam.

'Yeah. I'm curious about how they got the name.'

'Well, didn't you say the gardaí contacted the Syrian police?'

'Yeah, right away.'

'Well,' replied Sameed, 'I wouldn't be surprised if someone in the Syrian police passed the information on to *Al Jazeera*.'

'But why would they do that, I mean, before they'd contacted the next of kin?' asked Cary.

'The Syrian police are just an arm of Assad and his crowd. They're probably proud of the fact that a member of the resistance died all the way in Ireland. Even if they had nothing to do with it, they'd be only too happy to get credit–just another way they try to instill fear in the resistance. And as far as the family is concerned, I doubt the Syrian government gives a rat's ass for the family of a member of the resistance.'

'Yeah, well, I bet you're right, Sam. Hey, one other thing. *Al Jazeera* said Rahmann was accused of human trafficking back in 2012. They seemed to suggest that that was the reason he left Syria.'

Sam chuckled. 'Hah, that's ironic, Car–the Syrian authorities accusing a member of the resistance of trafficking? The Assad regime does that all the time. They falsely accuse their enemies of dirty deeds, then use that to justify assassination.'

'Yeah, I bet.'

'So, have you talked to the gardaí yet?' asked Sam.

'No, I haven't, Sam. But I think I should now, for sure.'

'Okay, but Car, if you do, you can't give them my name, yeh hear? If the gardaí tried to contact me, or if they gave the Lebanese police my name and asked them to talk to me, I can guarantee you I'd be on the top of Assad's hit list in a day. You know what I mean? Like I said, the walls have ears, mate. Really.'

'Yeah, Sam, I get it. Don't worry.'

With that Sam rang off. But Cary sat on his bike by the roadside staring at the mountainside ahead of him where a small herd of red deer were grazing. Finally he dialed Del but got his voice mail. 'Del, hey mate, it's me. Listen, I got some information– about Kristoff Rahmann. I think it's important. I'm on my way back from Ballyfermot–be home by half two. Could you call round? I need to talk to you.'

* * *

When Cary got back to his office he sat at his desk going over his notes. He was confused and worried. Confused about all this new information Sam had obtained. And worried that he could somehow be faulted by the gardaí for pursuing the case of Kristoff Rahmann rather than deferring to the authorities. That was why he needed so badly to talk to Garda Del Samuels. Just then Del appeared at his door.

'Hey, mate. I rushed here soon as I got your message. What's goin' on?'

'Let's go upstairs, okay?'

Cary made a pot of Bewley's and they sipped their tea in the small sitting room.

'I have this friend, he was at DCU with me. But he grew up in Lebanon and is living in Beirut now.'

'Uh-huh.'

'Last week I talked to him about this Kristoff Rahmann.'

'What, did he know the guy?'

'Well no, not exactly. But he has a friend in Damascus, and another in Aleppo, up north. They knew a guy by that name who was active in the Syrian underground at the time war broke out in 2011.'

Del raised an eyebrow at that. 'Wow. Are they sure it's the same guy?'

'Well, the description on that Syrian ID sounds right. But get this, Del. The guy in Aleppo knew Rahmann. Rahmann worked for him. He found his personnel file. It showed Rahmann's birthday was the fifteenth of March 1982. And that's the date of birth on the ID.'

'Wow, well, that must be the guy, then, huh? Did they know he was in Ireland?'

'No. All that close friend knew was that Kristoff Rahmann disappeared in 2012. Without a word.'

'Well, did he have family there? Maybe still there?'

'That I don't know. It's hard to get hold of this fellow. I guess it's dangerous still around Aleppo, everybody feels like they're being watched, yeh know?'

'Yeah, I get it. But Car, you need to talk to my super, and soon.'

Cary exhaled, then nodded. 'I know.'

'How about if I talk to him first?' offered Del.

'Yeah, okay Del.'

* * *

With his deadline approaching Cary spent most of the afternoon editing and laying out adverts, then revising and fact-checking his news stories including another update on the Kristoff Rahmann investigation. And he put the finishing touches on his story about the Gorayas.

At about half four Rosie appeared. Cary smiled. 'Hey, how was your day?'

'All right,' she replied. 'Yeah. Pretty smooth all in all.' She drew a sheet of paper from her backpack. Eileen just gave me this, Car. About the Hurleys, remember?'

'Oh, yeah. Let's see what she's got.' He sat reading, wrinkled his brow once or twice, then chuckled.

'So, whatta yeh think? Can you use it?'

'Well, her grammar's a little fractured,' said Cary with a grin. 'But other than that, I'd say I can use it.' He looked at the clock anxiously. 'I'll see if I can get it in this edition. My deadline is in about an hour.'

'Anything I can do?'

'Nah, thanks. I'll be fine. Go along. I'll call round this evening, okay?'

Travelhawk Beach

15   SUPERINTENDENT LEWIS

The next morning Del appeared at the *Gazette* office followed by his boss. Superintendent Donald Lewis was a tall man, nearly bald but for a fringe of grey hair on his temples and a bushy grey mustache. He looked sternly at Cary.

'Apparently we need to talk, Mr McGurk.'

'Yes sir,' replied Cary. He showed them into the back room where they sat around a small table.

'Garda Samuels tells me you have some information that may be important in the matter of the death of Kristoff Rahmann in Wicklow town. Is that right?'

'Yes sir, that is correct, sir.'

'How exactly did you come across this information, Mr McGurk?'

'Well, I saw that story in *Al Jazeera* about ten days ago. They identified the dead man as Kristoff Rahmann.'

Superintendent Lewis nodded. 'Yes, I heard about that.'

'Then I remembered I had a friend from university who grew up in Lebanon. And I knew he had friends and contacts in Syria. He's living in Beirut now. So I called him and asked him if he could find out anything about this Kristoff Rahmann.'

'Okay, so this friend of yours made some calls, and he found someone who knew Kristoff Rahmann, or at least someone of that name. Right?'

'Yes sir. This guy still lives in Damascus. He recognised the name, thought he might have been involved in the Syrian resistance movement.'

'Uh-huh. Which is what, an underground group working to overthrow the government?'

'Yes sir. There are actually quite a few different groups.'

'And you feel certain this is the same man?'

'Well, sir, the fellow in Damascus talked to a colleague in Aleppo, a city north of Damascus–close to the Turkish border. At one time this man published a newspaper in Aleppo. It turns out he actually hired Kristoff Rahmann to work for his paper back before war broke out in Syria. He still has an employee file for Rahmann. The date of birth is the same as on that ID, 15 March 1982.'

'And how did you happen to know that was the date on Rahmann's ID?'

Del spoke up. 'I told him, sir. So he could make sure it was the same man.'

'Okay, so it sounds like that's the man all right.' The superintendent paused. 'Anything else?'

'Well, sir, Garda Samuels tells me the death is being treated as an accident or suicide. Knowing what we do now about the victim, doesn't it seem likely that he was murdered? Assassinated? By agents of the Assad government?'

'Whoa, now, just a minute–aren't you getting ahead of yourself, young man? As I recall, solid evidence of foul play is really not there–no weapon, no witnesses, nothing on CCTV–and no tracks in the sand–except yours, of course. And the forensic report is inconclusive. So this guy gets on some blacklist for writing or publishing against the Syrian government, and now, ten plus years later, he turns up dead in Ireland. And you're saying he must have been murdered, or assassinated? What you have is entirely circumstantial evidence, isn't it?'

Cary sighed. 'I guess. But doesn't it make sense? I've heard there are Syrian agents all over Europe and the Middle East trying to track down members of the resistance and eliminate them.'

'Uh-huh.'

'And another thing, how did *Al Jazeera* find out about the death? My friend in Lebanon thinks the Syrian police or the government must have tipped off *Al Jazeera* about the death of Mr Rahmann hoping it would send a message to his enemies, in Syria and elsewhere. They're even hinting that Rahmann was involved in illegal human trafficking.'

Superintendent Lewis cast Cary a dubious look. 'Maybe so, maybe so. But that still doesn't prove that Kristoff Rahmann was murdered, just because the Syrian government had it in for him. And even if they did want him eliminated–tracking him all the way to Ireland? That seems a bit of a stretch, doesn't it?' He sighed as he stood up. 'Look, son, I'll pass this information along to Chief Superintendent Morris in Wicklow–he's in charge of this case. But unless there is more physical evidence from the crime scene, I doubt it will change their thinking.'

'My super has a point, Car,' began Del after Superintendent Lewis had departed. 'The connection of the death of this man to the Syrian government is a long shot. And if the guy fell by accident, or took his own life, his distant past is probably irrelevant. The only thing that will change their minds is solid evidence of foul play. So unless you have some additional information, I don't think they're about to shift gears, yeah?'

Cary looked discouraged. 'I suppose you're right. I mean, it makes sense, but...' He hesitated for a moment, then cast his friend a sheepish look. 'Listen, Del, there is one other thing. I probably should have mentioned it sooner, I know, but that day, on the beach, before the gardaí arrived? I took a photo of the body with my mobile.'

'Oh?' replied Del.

'The minute I took it I felt weird, yeh know?'

'So you didn't tell Mitch?'

Cary shook his head. 'Honestly, I forgot all about it until that night. Then I deleted it from my mobile. Like I said, it just didn't feel right, yeh know? But ever since I've been thinking there was some little detail on the body that I was forgetting.'

Del looked Cary in the eye. Then he held out one hand, palm up, wiggling his fingers. Cary reached into his pocket, drew out his mobile and placed it in Del's outstretched hand.

'You think you can retrieve the photo?'

Del shrugged. 'Maybe–don't know. But it's worth tryin'. I'll see what I can do. What's your passcode?'

Then Del flashed a crooked smile. 'Please tell me I'm not gonna have to look at any sexts–or revealing selfies, mate.'

'Not to worry,' responded Cary with a chuckle. 'Those are all on my other mobile.'

* * *

Several hours later Del returned with Cary's mobile. On it was the photo he had taken at Travelhawk Beach, the photo of the dead man. He held it out for Cary to see.

'Your wish, mate.'

'Wow, thanks, Del. How'd you do that?'

'Sergeant Walsh–Brian–he's a whiz with these things.'

Del sat. 'Here's the thing, lad. When you delete something from your mobile, laptop, any device–an image or any document, for that matter–it doesn't really get deleted, it gets marked for deletion, yeh know? Meaning only when that space is needed is it overwritten. The trick is to relocate a deleted file before it gets overwritten. But Bri has an app that does it.'

Cary was only half listening–mostly he was staring at that image. Then he sent it to his laptop to get a better look. He and Del both leaned over the screen peering at the enlarged image.

'He had a ring. See?' observed Cary.

'Yeah, Car, and tattoos.'

'Wow, yeah. You know, I don't think I noticed them with all that seaweed covering him. On both forearms. Do you think I should tell Superintendent Lewis about this?'

'Yeah, definitely. The forensic team took plenty of photos themselves, of course. So this may not tell them anything they don't already know. But still, I think you should tell him.'

* * *

After Del left Cary sat looking at the image. The ring and those tattoos. Just details, he was thinking, details of little importance. Besides, the gardaí surely saw them as well, and no doubt photographed them.

Later in the day he received another call from Sam.

'A couple more things from that guy in Aleppo. He said Rahmann was Muslim, like most Syrians. He attended the American University of Beirut for a time. And he was married in

Damascus around 2004 while he was working for that newspaper. To an Irish woman.'

'Hmm, really?' replied Cary. 'Well, that might explain why he ended up in Ireland. Do you know her name? Her birth name, I mean?'

'No, Car, sorry. And one other thing, he doubts that business about Rahmann being involved in trafficking. He thinks it's just part of Assad's effort to discredit opponents of the regime.'

'Okay, Sam. Well, that's helpful, mate.'

Cary was about to ring off when he had another thought. 'Hey, Sam. Another thing. The dead man had tattoos–brightly-coloured designs, like grids–on both arms.'

'Hmm, that's curious.'

'Whatta you mean?'

'Well, that fellow in Aleppo, the newspaper publisher, he said Rahmann was Muslim.'

'Yeah?'

'Most Muslims don't get tattooed–most devout Muslims, anyway. It's not halal, Car.'

'Really. That's surprising then, huh?' He paused. 'Well, thanks again, Sam.'

'Sure thing, Car. Let me know how the investigation develops.'

Cary walked the three minutes along the High Street to the Glenkerry garda station. Del was seated at his desk and Cary reported on his conversation with Sam.

'Listen, we gotta tell my super, Car. And soon. He needs to know this stuff, mate.'

Cary nodded. 'If you say so, Del.'

Superintendent Lewis was in a meeting and Cary sat waiting in an uncomfortable chair outside his office, staring at his mobile all the while. When Lewis finally appeared Cary stood as Del spoke up.

'Sir, Mr McGurk has some additional information I think you should see.'

'Come through,' grumbled Superintendent Lewis with a hint of irritation in his voice.

'Sir, Mr McGurk just had another call from his friend in Beirut.' He nodded to Cary.

'Yes sir,' began Cary. 'Three things, sir. One, he learned that Rahmann married an Irish woman, probably around 2004, sir.'

'Is that so? Does he know her name?'

'No, sir. And sir, this man in Aleppo, the one that published a newspaper? Like I said this morning, Rahmann worked for him so he knew him pretty well. And he is very sceptical of that claim that Rahmann was involved in trafficking. He told my friend that that was a common tactic of the Syrian government to justify eliminating any opposition.'

Del spoke again. 'One other thing, sir. Mr McGurk confided in me that he took a photo of the dead man with his mobile, on the beach that day, before the gardaí arrived. He deleted it but I recovered it for him. Or rather Sergeant Walsh did.'

Lewis perked up a bit. Del nodded to Cary who handed him his mobile with the image on the screen.

'Uh-huh. Okay. What of it?'

'It's those tattoos, sir,' began Cary. He went on to explain what Sam had told him about Kristoff's Islamic faith and tattoos.

'So, what are you saying, Mr McGurk? Are you suggesting that the deceased is *not* Kristoff Rahmann, that Rahmann would not have had tattoos?'

'Possibly, sir, possibly.'

Lewis paused, turning a pen in his fingers. Then he directed his gaze to Cary with a slight smile.

'Who was it once said that the simplest explanation of something is usually the correct explanation?' asked Lewis.

Cary flashed an embarrassed smile. 'Uh, Sherlock Holmes? Or maybe Hercule Poirot?'

'Or maybe Lieutenant Columbo,' replied Lewis with a grin. 'What I'm saying is there's probably a simple explanation. Like maybe Rahmann was not a particularly devout Muslim.'

Cary nodded.

'Or maybe he got those tattoos after he left Syria, maybe after he came to Ireland. Isn't that possible?'

Cary thought for a moment. Then he nodded slowly. 'Yes sir, I suppose it is.'

'Listen, Mr McGurk. These are interesting theories you have. And like I said, I will pass them all along to Chief Superintendent Morris in Wicklow, okay?' Lewis stood. The meeting, it was clear, was over. Cary and Del stood.

'Garda Samuels, have Mr McGurk make a written statement.'

'Yes sir.'

Then Lewis turned to Cary. 'We will of course need the name and contact information for this friend of yours who knows so much about Mr Rahmann.' Just then the Superintendent's mobile buzzed. 'You'll have to excuse me.'

Del and Cary left the office before Cary could respond. At his desk Del pulled out a form and handed it to Cary.

'Del,' he whispered, 'I can't give them my friend's name–I can't.'

'Just fill out the form, Car. And where it asks for your sources, just leave it blank–for now.'

16 BANK OF SIX

Ever since the St Michael's match, Sabrina had been drilling her team on the basics, again and again repeating her mantra–'Think fundamentals'–'Focus on the fundamentals.'

'Okay, today I want to talk a bit about defence,' began Sabrina at Wednesday's practice. 'It doesn't matter how strong our offence is, if we can't defend our goal, we're in trouble. Yeah? Now we need you defensive players to be solid–like a brick wall. Make the other team work to get through, make 'em work hard. Show them that you are ready and waiting to break up their plays. Nothin' a defender loves more than a good hook, a block, a tackle, a dispossession. Okay?'

She pointed to a whiteboard set on an easel showing the pitch and the positions of all the players, offence and defence. 'Now in the back we have our defensive block. That's the three half-backs, two corner-backs, and full-back, right? What we call the "bank of six." '

'Each of you has your assigned position. Your job is to hold that position, right? Hold it–own it–*be* your position–understand?'

'Now your opponent will try to draw you out of your position.' Sabrina's eyes flashed as she shook her head. *'Don't let her.* Hold fast–be strong–got it?'

'Fer example, if their centre half-forward tries to pull our centre half-back, Lily, out of her position, like this…'. She drew an arrow on the white board. 'If she succeeds, if Lily leaves her position, then a huge gap opens up in our defence–dead centre in front of the goal.' With a flourish she drew a big red X representing the gap. 'Don't let her do that to you, Lily, right?'

Lily nodded.

'Or say their midfielder tries to draw our left half-back, Ella, like this.' She drew another arrow. 'If you let her draw you away, you'll leave a big opening on that side. Right?' Ella nodded.

'The 65-metre line should be your guide, defence. Do you hear me? 65 metres. Don't cross it–full stop. Okay?'

She looked around, making eye contact with each of the defensive players.

'Moral of the story? Hold your position. If the ball comes your way, of course, you're gonna take control of it, lift it, then hand-pass it or strike it to a teammate. That way you've held your position and improved your team's chance of moving the sliotar up the pitch.'

'Offence, it's your responsibility to get that ball from your defence, then move it toward the goal. That's your job, right Allegra? Molly? Robyn? Let the bank of six stay where they belong, see?' She drew a red box around those six positions. 'Don't expect them to do your job for you.'

Sabrina then broke the team into two groups to do a drill that required the defensive players to hold their ground.

Rosie was watching Sabrina's performance with a mixture of amazement and admiration. She had a way, thought Rosie, a way of focusing her audience on her message, of lifting and inspiring them to action.

* * *

Cary rushed off early the next morning for a dentist appointment. When he returned he found a number of voice mail messages and texts awaiting him. The new issue of the *Gazette* including his article on the Ukrainian refugees had just come out, and many of the messages pertained to it, praising his reporting and encouraging him to write more of the same. There were personal messages from Gloria Hennessy and County Councillor Kevin Leahy.

Catherine appeared at his door in midafternoon, beaming her appreciation for the story.

'Your father'd be so proud,' she said as she hugged her son.

The Contact Us feedback was generally laudatory as well, although several readers expressed concerns about Ireland's refugee policy, especially in light of the lack of housing across the country, a problem that was already on Cary's mind for a future story. And one reader made derogatory comments about the refugee settlement programme and refugees in general, calling them parasites.

But Cary was also surprised at the enthusiastic response to Eileen's story on the Hurleys accompanied by Rosie's team photo. He sent a text to Eileen: 'Great story on the Hurleys–come by and we can talk about more story ideas.'

Great Sugar Loaf

17 THE GREY SKODA

It's after midnight and Cary is suddenly awakened by a noise, a faint rattle. He lies in bed listening, wondering if what he heard was merely part of a dream. Then he hears another noise, this time a more distinct rasping sound. He rises, steps into the hallway and stands at the top of the stairs listening. After a pause, the noise resumes.

He switches on the light, then climbs down the stairs cautiously. On the ground floor he waits and listens. Hearing nothing, he walks to the front door and looks out onto the street. All is quiet. He checks the back door. It is closed and locked. He opens it and steps out onto the patio but sees nothing. Then, as he turns back to the building, he notices scratches around the door latch and strike plate. Maybe they had been there before, he thinks, and he had never noticed them. He climbs the stairs and crawls back into bed but lies anxiously, listening. At last he falls asleep.

The next morning while waiting for his tea to steep, he steps out onto the patio again and stands looking at the distant view, thinking about what he needs to do this day. But when he turns to go back inside, he sees something he had not previously noticed, a slight indentation in the door frame opposite the latch, as if someone had been trying to pry the door open.

* * *

'Well, Ciaran McGurk,' began Gloria Hennessy as he entered her office on the High Street, just a few doors down from the *Gazette* office, 'aren't you a sight for sore eyes–literally?' She was seated at her desk wearing dark sunglasses.

'What the heck, Gloria–what's up with the shades? You trying to hide from the Tax Department?'

Gloria laughed. 'No, lad–nothin' like that. Didn't your ma tell yeh? I had cataract surgery a few days ago. That's all. How do they look, Car? I hate to think of some handsome young man passing me by because of them. Maybe he'll think I'm a movie star or something.'

'They look brilliant, really.'

'They damn well better,' she said with a chuckle. 'They set me back a few quid, I'll tell you.'

'How long do you have to wear them?'

'Just a week is all. So, how're you doin' these days?'

'Okay, thanks. But last night, gone twelve, I heard a noise, from downstairs. Like tapping, metal on metal, you know? I went down and looked around but didn't see anything–started to think it was all my imagination. Then this morning I noticed the latch on the rear door, it looked like maybe someone had tried to jimmy it.'

Gloria nodded. 'Oh, dear, that's not good. Well, Mr Hogan next door, at the fish shop? He had some things nicked from that shed out behind his shop. Nothin' of great value, just a few tools is all.'

'When was that?'

'Oh, I'd say a month back, maybe two. After that I had Bill Finneran, the carpenter, come in and repair my doors, front and back, make them more secure. Maybe you should do the same, eh?'

Cary grimaced. All he needed right now was more expenses.

'You have some valuable equipment, right? A copier, a computer.'

Cary nodded. 'Yeah.'

'Maybe you ought to install one of those electronic alarm systems folks are getting nowadays for their homes.'

'Yeah, maybe so.'

'So, a fine story on the Ukrainians, Ciaran. I enjoyed it. What those folks have had to endure, eh?'

'Yeah, it's hard to imagine, I mean, having your life, your whole world turned upside down.'

'Well, and it's wonderful to hear that we Irish are doing our part. We dropped the ball with the Afghans and the Syrians, yeh know? Shameful.'

'Yeah. Well, I'm meeting with a Syrian couple in Rathnew this afternoon.'

'I look forward to reading about them. So, what's the news on that dead body you stumbled on, that Kristoff fellow?'

'Yeah, well, not much. I've got a couple of possible sources for more information, but nothin' solid yet.' He paused. 'Well, I betta get goin'.' He turned toward the door, then back to Gloria. 'Say, is that a new car you got out front, that grey Skoda?'

'No, that's not mine. I'm not drivin' for a few days because of my eyes. A gentleman friend drove me to the office and he's pickin' me up later. I don't know who belongs to that thing–it's been parked there all morning.'

* * *

Several hours later Cary was making tea for himself. As he waited for the water to boil, he gazed out his kitchen window that afforded a good view along the High Street. There was that grey Skoda, still parked in front of Gloria's office where he had seen it earlier in the day. But as he watched a man emerged from Phinney's and stood by the car for several minutes. He was dark-haired and wore dark glasses. As Cary watched, the man climbed into the car and drove away.

After he had finished his tea, Cary walked the short distance to Phinney's and entered.

'Hey, Liam,' he began. 'Say, was there a guy here earlier–dark hair, sunglasses? Stayed a long time.'

'Yeah, I know who yeh mean. He sat by the window. Didn't talk to a soul–mostly reading and looking out the window. Kept orderin' double shot espressos–musta had four or five before he was finished. If I had that much caffeine I wouldn't sleep for a week, yeh know?'

Cary chuckled. 'So, no one you know?'

'Nope–never seen him before in my life. Why?'

'No reason. Just curious.'

Then Cary told Liam about the break-in, or attempted break-in, or whatever.

'Yeah, well, we lock up everything pretty tight here every night. Most pubs do these days, yeh know?'

Cary nodded. 'Well, thanks, Liam.'

'Oh, one thing I noticed should please you, son. That guy? He was reading the *Gazette* the whole time.'

* * *

That afternoon Cary rode his motorcycle to Rathnew to interview a Syrian couple he'd been introduced to. A kilometre or so out of

Glenkerry he noticed a small grey car behind him. When he turned into the town centre he caught a better glimpse of the car in his mirror–it was that Skoda again. Cary tensed, watching the car in his mirrors. He pulled over and parked his bike. The Skoda pulled over as well some distance behind him.

Cary sat on his bike for several minutes, trying to decide what to do. He pulled out his mobile and considered calling 9-9-9 but decided against it. It would take some time for a garda car to arrive, of that he was certain. And probably the suspicious tailer would be long gone by then.

Nervously he dismounted. He walked along the footpath in the direction of the Skoda, trying to look casual. Now he could just make out the driver, a man with sunglasses. As he approached the car suddenly lurched forward and sped past him down the street. Cary pulled out his mobile but by the time he snapped a photo the car was nearly out of sight. He returned to his bike and rode the short distance to the community centre where he had arranged to meet Hamid and Mira Osman.

Cary listened as the Osmans told their story. They were living in Homs, one of Syria's largest cities, when war broke out in 2011. Parts of that city were under the control of the Free Syrian Army, one of the many groups fighting against the Syrian government, and for a time the Osmans felt safe there. But early in 2013 their neighbourhood came under heavy fire from government forces and the Osmans decided to leave. Like hundreds of thousands of other Syrians, the Osmans spent many months in a refugee camp in northern Syria.

'It was cold, there was no electricity, and not enough food. We were very frightened all the time in that place,' said Mira.

Finally in April, 2014, the family embarked on the difficult journey to Turkey, making their way eventually to Istanbul where they were taken in by friends.

'We applied to many countries for asylum and we waited and waited for some good news,' recalled Hamid.

Finally in January 2015 the Osmans received the news they had been hoping for: they had been granted refugee status in Ireland. A charitable organisation arranged for their flight from Istanbul to Dublin. When they arrived in Dublin they were immediately transported to a reception centre outside Dublin.

'We were told that it was only a temporary situation,' explained Mira. 'It was an old warehouse that had been converted into small flats.'

'It would have been fine for a few days,' continued Hamid. 'But we were there nearly two years.'

Eventually Hamid managed to get a job in a nearby factory, but it only lasted a few months.

The Osmans have three children, Amin, Fatima, and Lila, who were seven, four, and two years of age at the time. A school of sorts was provided at the reception centre but it was overcrowded and disorganised.

'The children were not happy there,' said Mira.

Finally a church-supported organisation found the Osmans a flat in Rathnew.

'It is very nice,' noted Mira, 'and the kids even have a little yard to play in. And they all attended the national school just a short distance away.'

Hamid now works for a cleaning service in Wicklow town.

Cary asked if the Osmans hoped to return to Syria one day.

'I don't know, I just don't know,' replied Mira. She smiled but her eyes teared up. 'We've been away almost ten years. Honestly, the kids have little memory of our life in Syria. Ireland feels like home to them now.'

Amin now lives and works in Dublin. Fatima and Lila are still in secondary school.

Their experience in the Dublin reception centre soured the Osmans on Ireland for a time. But they feel content today in their Rathnew home.

When the interview was over, Hamid and Mira took Cary outside to the playground where they watched Fatima and Lila kicking a football around with several schoolmates.

* * *

After the interview Cary departed on his bike, his eyes anxiously watching his mirrors all the way home. Back in Glenkerry, he went directly to the garda station and found Del Samuels at his desk.

'Hey, mate. You okay? You look stressed,' observed Del.

Cary slumped into a chair, then recounted his story, starting with midnight of the previous night. He showed Del the photo of the car barely visible as it sped away.

'I'm bettin' that guy was the same one who tried to break in last night–and was watchin' my place this morning.' He looked at his friend with desperation in his eyes. 'I don't get it, Del. Who is this guy and what does he want from me?'

'I don't know, mate–I don't know. Listen–relax, eh? How about some tea? Then I'll write this up.'

He made his friend a cup of tea. Del had a way with people that made him an ideal garda. He was calm with a reassuring air of confidence about him that worked well with all he encountered. And he had a pleasing smile and a sense of humour that could put many a distraught client at ease. But it wasn't working on this client.

'Okay, then. Start from the beginning.' Step by step he walked Cary through the sequence of events that began with the attempted break-in, all the while making notes on a lined notepad.

'Now, how about a description? Tell me everything you remember about this guy.'

Cary sighed. 'Well, he's maybe a bit taller than me, say just under six feet. Dark hair. Wearing dark trousers, a brown t-shirt, and a cap with a visor.'

'Age?'

Cary exhaled. 'I'd say late twenties, maybe thirty. Liam noticed he was reading the *Gazette*.'

'And this all started around midnight last night, right?'

Cary nodded but was deep in his own thoughts. 'If he was trying to rob the *Gazette* office, and I scared him off, the last thing you'd expect him to do would be to hang around the next day, and follow me to Rathnew, right?'

'Yeah, you're right, Car. Well, maybe he was lookin' for something in your office, your notes or something. He probably didn't realise anyone was living upstairs.'

'Do you think maybe while this guy's followin' me around, he has a partner who'll try to break in again?'

'Possibly, possibly. But in my experience these sorts usually work alone.'

'But what could anyone want from the *Gazette* office? All I have is a laptop and a small printer. I usually take the laptop with me. So there's not much to interest a thief.'

Del was only half-listening. 'Wait, Car. Your story on the Ukrainian refugees, when did that come out? When did that issue reach the shops?'

'Well, uh, yesterday, Thursday, in the morning.'

'Uh-huh. And all this started last night, maybe twelve hours later, right?'

'Yeah, so?'

'Is it possible there's a connection? Suppose someone saw your story in the *Gazette* yesterday morning and suddenly took an interest in the paper–or in you.'

'You think?'

'What was the reaction to the refugee story, Cary? Have you heard from many readers yet?'

'Yeah, a few. Mostly really positive. But there were a few responses in our feedback that were not so positive. Two were people concerned about the lack of housing in Ireland and asking why we were providing homes for refugees when we can't even house our own people.'

'Well, good point, eh?'

'Yeah. And I'm working on a story about the housing situation in County Wicklow. But there was one nasty comment from someone that included a lot of anti-immigrant and anti-foreigner language.'

'Why don't you forward that to me, Car, yeah? I'll see if I can track down the writer. Just out of curiosity. I'm not sayin' he's your stalker, but...'

'Am I in danger, Del? Do you think?'

'I really doubt it, mate. But it's probably a good idea to keep your eyes open for a while, watch for anyone tailing you, and call the gardaí anytime you see the guy or anything suspicious, yeah?'

Cary nodded reluctantly.

'Oh, and one other thing,' Del continued. 'An interesting development in the Kristoff Rahmann case. A family member has come forward.'

'You mean in Ireland?'

'Nope, in Lebanon. An uncle, I think they said. He saw the *Al Jazeera* story. He went to the Beirut police. They showed him a photo of the dead man provided by the gardaí. He confirmed that it was Kristoff Rahmann.'

'Is that right?'

'And he told them he believed Rahmann was assassinated by Syrian agents.'

* * *

Spirits had been high all week as the Hurleys prepared for their next match against a team from Arklow. But the night before the match Sabrina received a call from Isla's mother. Isla had a fever, possibly the flu. She would not be playing on Friday.

When word of Isla's absence spread in school the next morning, the team's spirits plummeted. Isla might not have been everyone's personal favourite, but she was pivotal to the team. She was surprisingly agile and tireless for her size–she somehow managed to be at the centre of nearly every play. Sabrina moved Robyn Furlong to full-forward and assigned Sofia Walsh to centre half-forward.

From the minute the opening whistle blew, Rosie could see that the Hurleys were in trouble. They seemed to come unravelled, missing one opportunity after another to take the initiative, to move the ball in their direction, to score points. The defence appeared to have forgotten all Sabrina had told them about holding their ground and breaking up their opponents' play. At half-time the Hurleys trailed four points to nil.

Rosie watched as Sabrina tried to rally her team.

'Listen, you lot. You can do this, you hear me? You can turn the tide next period. I know you can. First, defence, yeah? You gotta hold your positions, like we've talked about and drilled on, remember? Make them work for every inch of turf, right? Corner-backs, stay in tight, move the sliotar away from the goal. Full-back, the same. Look around you, girls. Always know who your nearest teammates are and be ready to feed them that ball if you get it. Offence, push harder. And sing out when you're free, remember? Let your teammate know where you are, then be ready for a pass. Okay? Katie, Ava, Robyn, if you get the ball anywhere near the goal, take a shot, don't be shy.'

The whistle blew. Sabrina looked around at her team. 'You can do this,' she repeated. 'I know you can. Okay? Let's go.'

They all cheered as they broke from the huddle.

The second period started more hopefully. The Hurleys seemed to show a little more confidence. But just when things seemed to be going their way, the Arklow team scored a goal. That put an end to the brief spurt of optimism and energy. From then on it was Arklow's match. The final score: Arklow 7, Hurleys 1.

After the match Sabrina tried bravely to find something to praise her players for. But it wasn't easy. They had completely fallen apart without Isla. And now the Hurleys were utterly demoralised.

* * *

Rosie appeared at Cary's door around five o'clock. She found him sitting at his desk clicking away on his laptop. He leaned back, stretched, and smiled.

'Sorry I couldn't be at that match today. How did the Hurleys do?'

Rosie exhaled loudly, then slumped into a chair. 'It was a disaster, Car. They fell apart–really. Sabrina tried her best to turn them around at half-time, but it was no use.'

'Gee, I'm sorry Rose.'

'I guess it's true, Isla is the key to that team. Without her, they're rubbish.'

'What about school? How did that go?'

'Exhausting. After five days of painting the art studio was a bloody kip. I spent over two hours cleaning brushes and reorganising the paints. I'm knackered.'

He took her hand. 'Sorry. But I'm sure your students enjoyed it.'

'Yeah, most of them. But some of those kids, you can't turn your back on 'em for a second.' Rosie tousled his hair. 'Boys, eh?'

Cary chuckled. 'You're probably smiling too much, Rosie. Remember my advice?'

Rosie put on the best scowl she could manage.

'There yeh go.' They both laughed.

'So, everything okay at the *Gazette*? Did you get any more feedback on the Ukrainian refugee story?'

'Yeah, a few texts and emails. Reverend O'Ryan came by and was very complimentary,' referring to the pastor of St Mark's, the Church of Ireland parish in Glenkerry. Cary was about to tell Rosie of the attempted break-in and the guy in the grey Skoda when she sighed.

'Well, I gotta get home and rest up. Whatta ya say we go to that new shop, A Pizza Paradise? My treat?'

Cary stood and smiled. 'I'd love that, Rosie. I really would. But somehow I don't feel like goin' out tonight. What about if I get us some takeaway and bring it up to yours, half six or so?'

Rosie smiled. 'Sure, if you like. Bring your toothbrush, mate. No sharing allowed.'

* * *

That evening Rosie and Cary sat in the O'Malley yard savouring their fish and chips along with a salad assembled from Rosie's garden. Rosie was enjoying the sounds of a September evening, the musical chirps of the crickets accompanied by the raspy thrum of the katydids. Overhead swallows soared and swooped in search of a winged meal. But Cary seemed glum.

'You're kinda quiet tonight, Car. Everything okay?'

He exhaled. 'I guess.' Then he shrugged. 'I don't know, to be honest, I'm a little worried.'

'Worried? You mean about the *Gazette*? Finances, subscriptions, all that?'

He shook his head. 'Well, there's that. But, well, I didn't want to upset you, but someone tried to break into the *Gazette* office last night. They jimmied the back door.'

Rosie was wide-eyed at this news and she listened carefully as Cary recounted the events of the day.

'Del was wondering if it could somehow be connected to the Ukrainian refugee story. Most of the readers I heard from have been very positive, but not all.'

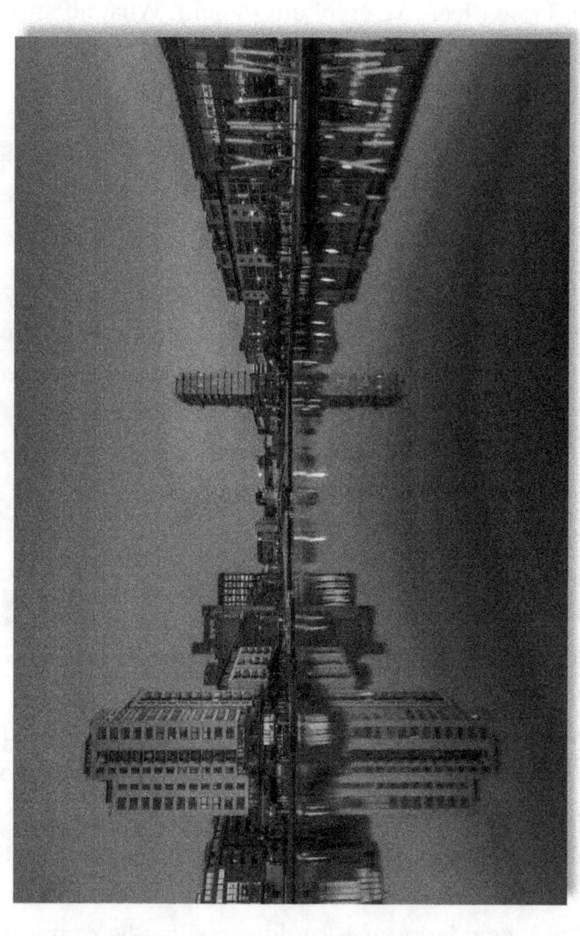

Dublin

18 SOPHIE'S CHOICE

The next morning Cary drove Rosie to Dublin in his mother's car. He dropped her off at the entrance to Mercy Hospital, then parked in a car park down the street.

Rosie walked up the wide granite stairway to the main entrance. The mere sight of this place made her shudder. This had been her home for nearly two months some ten years ago and the memory of that time hung like a heavy weight upon her spirit even now.

At the reception desk she asked for Maura Ahearn, the social worker who had been Rosie's rock, her guardian angel during that difficult time. Maura had continued to see her for several years after her surgery. But it had been nearly four years since they last met.

Rosie sat nervously in the waiting room until Maura appeared smiling. They shook hands, then hugged. Maura led Rosie to her office several floors up. She asked about Rosie's family and her work. Rosie asked about Maura's family–she remembered that she had a husband and several children. Finally Maura explained the reason she had asked for Rosie's help.

'Her name is Sophie. She's fourteen. Her parents–Roger and Fiona–live in County Meath. Roger is a building contractor, Fiona's a physio. Sophie is their only child. She's had colitis for almost two years. For a while medications were helping her, but about six months ago her condition suddenly worsened. She had abdominal pain, bleeding, chronic diarrhea. She was admitted to Mercy twice before, but each time she was discharged after a few days when her condition seemed to be improving. But about a month ago it got worse once again and she was readmitted. It looks like it might be Crohn's, although that diagnosis, as you know, is often hard to make with certainty.'

This sounded so familiar to Rosie, like a flashback of her own life and her own battle with gastrointestinal disease.

'Last week they talked to her about ostomy surgery. She has been very resistant.'

Rosie nodded. 'Yeah, I get that.'

'She's frightened, of course, although she puts up a brave front. And she's angry–angry with the hospital staff–angry with her parents–angry with the world.'

Again Rosie nodded. 'Yeah, I remember that feeling, that nobody really understands what you're goin' through, that it's you against them–against the world.'

'That's exactly why I thought of you. She reminds me so much of you back then, Rosie. I thought perhaps you could get through to her. Or I should say, maybe she'll let you into her world. And maybe, just maybe, she'll listen to you.'

'But I'm not sure what I should say.'

Maura smiled and shook her head. 'Just tell her your story, that's all. Don't worry about the details of her case, of her disease. Just talk to her, yeh know? Woman to woman.'

'Okay, I'll do what I can.'

Maura smiled. 'That's all we ask, Rosie.'

She led Rosie down a long corridor, up an elevator, then down another long corridor. Finally they arrived at a patient room and

Maura tapped on the door. A woman opened it, smiling weakly, anxiously, and stepped into the corridor.

'Fiona, this is Rosie O'Malley.' They shook hands. Just then a man appeared from the room.

'And this is Roger. Fiona and Roger are Sophie's parents.'

'Maura tells us you're a teacher.'

'Yes, well, I'm teaching art at *Coláiste Gaeilge* in Glenkerry. It's just a temporary position.'

'And you're an artist, a gardener, and accomplished in camogie and Taekwondo.'

'Accomplished?' answered Rosie with a dubious smile. 'I don't know about that.'

'Well, Maura has told us so much about you, and we would be very grateful if you could talk to Sophie.' Tears welled up in Fiona's eyes as she spoke. 'She's a very unhappy girl...' She exhaled loudly. 'A very angry girl...' Again she breathed loudly, struggling to maintain her composure. 'And a very sick girl.'

'Well, I would be happy to speak with her.'

'We're at our wits' end, Rosie.'

No pressure, thought Rosie. She felt as though she was being drawn into a vortex of gloom, a deadly downward spiral, along with Sophie and her family.

Rosie nodded and reached out for Fiona's hand. 'I'll try my best, I promise.' She turned to Roger, and then to Maura, smiling gamely.

'Well, come on in and let's introduce you to Sophie.'

With that the four entered the room. There was Sophie, lying in a bed with IVs in her arms, her face thin and drawn, her skin pallid, her eyes dull and sunken. It was difficult for Rosie to realise that this was a fourteen-year-old girl she was seeing, not an elderly care home patient waiting for the end to come.

'Sophie,' began Maura softly. She reached out and stroked the girl's hand gently. 'Honey, I want you to meet someone.'

Rosie stepped forward. 'Hello, Sophie, I'm Rosie–Rosie O'Malley.'

Maura pulled a chair up to the bed and Rosie sat looking into those blank eyes.

'Rosie's an old friend of mine.'

'That's right,' began Rosie. 'I first met Maura almost ten years ago right here at Mercy. And we became friends when I spent six weeks here. In fact, I think my room was on this very floor.'

Sophie's face was expressionless.

'We'll wait outside,' said Maura. And she, Fiona, and Roger left Rosie and Sophie alone.

Rosie was unsure how to begin. She looked up at a bulletin board next to Sophie's bed. There were two photos of Sophie, one with her family and one with a group of smiling girls in camogie kit.

'Do you play camogie, Sophie?'

She nodded slightly.

'I love camogie. I played in secondary school, not for the school team but a community team. And now I'm coachin' our *Coláiste* team.' Then she added with a smile, 'They call themselves the Hurley Girlies.' Sophie didn't respond but looked away toward the window.

Rosie decided to come straight to the point. 'Sophie, I had colitis.' The girl turned and looked at Rosie, a glimmer of acknowledgement in her eyes.

Rosie smiled. 'I was scared, yeh know? Scared and angry.'

At that Sophie nodded slightly.

'I couldn't understand why this was happening to me. And I felt like no one had any idea what I was goin' through, how I was feelin'. It was so frustrating–so humiliating.'

Rosie paused, feeling a sudden surge of anger. 'One of my doctors, he was so cold. And he didn't talk to me, yeh know? He talked to my parents about me right in front of me like I wasn't even there. I was only eleven or twelve, but I wanted to be part of the conversation. But that wasn't how he worked.' Rosie sighed. 'I really hated him–just the sight of him made my stomach hurt even more.' Then Rosie laughed a nervous laugh.

Sophie nodded. Then she spoke softly, her words barely audible. 'But you got better?'

'Yeah, I did. This surgeon came in to see me one day. And he was different. You sometimes hear how surgeons are so distant, like they forget there's a human being they're talking to–or operating on.'

Again Sophie nodded and Rosie wondered what kinds of experiences this girl had had with doctors and surgeons.

'He sat down beside my bed and talked to me. And he asked me how I was feelin'. And I told him something I never told anyone, not even my parents.' Rosie paused, biting her lip. 'I told him I didn't want to go on fighting this colitis, or Crohn's, or whatever it was–that I wanted to die.'

Again she paused, trying to keep her composure. 'I figured he'd try to change my mind. But he listened and nodded. And he seemed to be saying that he understood how I was feelin'. He told me he had a daughter who died of cancer a few years earlier, and he knew what I was sayin'.'

'But then he told me about this surgery–ostomy. I mean, I had never even heard of such a thing. It sounded like something out of science fiction, yeh know? The idea that they could remove your intestines, or part of your intestines–it was unbelievable. And he made it sound like a simple operation–I'm sure it's not that simple–but he told me he had done hundreds of ostomies in his career–he had been a surgeon here for at least twenty years–and he assured me that it was safe and not too complicated.'

Now Sophie was watching Rosie and listening intently. 'So you had the surgery?'

Rosie nodded. 'I remember that very day thinking to myself, "I like this man–and I believe him–I'm gonna stop worryin' and just put my trust in him." And right away I felt such relief, even before I had the surgery.'

'What about your parents?'

'Yeah, he talked to them and they agreed. I know my ma was worried, but I told her I wanted to do it. And the sooner the better. I mean, she knew how miserable I was and that I couldn't go on the way things had been. It was like *I* had to convince *her*. But she finally agreed. And she convinced my da.'

'So was it like the surgeon said it would be?'

'Yeah, pretty much. I mean, you don't recover from abdominal surgery overnight, he told me that. And it was a few weeks before I felt like I could stand up and walk without worryin' that my incisions were gonna split open and my insides tumble out.' Rosie chuckled. 'But the constant tummy pains were gone, Sophie…' She snapped her fingers. 'Just like that.'

'And I remember the day they brought me home from the hospital, and what it felt like to be back home, walkin' in my garden, breathin' fresh air, and eatin' something other than hospital food.' Rosie chuckled and saw a slight smile on Sophie's lips. 'And sleepin' in my own bed.'

'And here I am almost ten years later and I feel fine, I'm teaching art at the same school in my town, and, like I said, I'm the assistant coach of the school's camogie team—the *unofficial* assistant coach.'

At the word 'camogie' Sophie brightened.

'The coach, she's a good friend of mine. She played on her college camogie team. She has this jersey. It says, "A day without camogie is like–just kidding–I have no idea." ' Sophie smiled.

Rosie touched her hand. 'You miss it, yeah? Well, I bet you will play again, Sophie, if you have the surgery. I'm not sayin' you'll be in the Championship League, but you'll be playin' with your friends. It might take a while, but it's possible.'

Sophie nodded again.

'I'd pretty much given up hope of ever doin' anything again, of ever gettin' outta this place.' Rosie's eyes scanned the room. 'But I did.' She paused. 'So, will you consider havin' the surgery, Sophie?'

'Maybe,' was all she could muster. 'I'll think about it.'

Rosie was suddenly feeling a rush of encouragement.

'Maybe,' she thought, *'I'll take that.'*

'Well, I better get goin'.'

But Sophie wasn't quite ready for her to leave. 'So Maura told me you have a boyfriend.'

Rosie nodded and smiled. 'His name is Cary. He drove me here today.'

'Does he know?'

Rosie smiled and nodded. 'We've been friends since primary school. When I was sick, he sent me cards he made himself. And we talked on the phone now and then. He came to see me at home once when I was really sick. I felt bad he had to see me that way–I know it scared him, the way I looked. Then I was in hospital and didn't see him for months.'

'After my surgery and I was back home, I started feeling better and wanted to go out and play, but my parents wouldn't allow it.' Rosie chuckled at the memory. 'One day when my da was at work and my ma was at a church meeting, I called Cary and asked him if he would come over for a little kickabout.' Rosie smiled. 'I'd gained nearly two stone. I even thought of putting on some blush, but then I looked in the mirror and decided I didn't need it, my colour was back. You shoulda seen his face when he saw me.'

'We dated for a while in secondary school. But, well, you're fourteen, right? So you understand what I mean when I say that things change for a boy and a girl around that time. And I knew that change was comin', that he'd be expecting something more. And I panicked. I couldn't face it, tellin' him. So I backed off. I felt awful about it, that I couldn't tell him, or didn't trust him. Or maybe I just didn't know how to tell him, yeh know? I was just afraid that when I did, he'd freak out. And I was afraid that that was the way it was for someone like me. That I'd never, well, be able to go to the "next level".' She put air quotes around the two words with her fingers and they both laughed.

'He went off to uni and we barely spoke for three years. But when he came back to Glenkerry, we, well, we picked up where we left off.'

Their eyes met. 'You told him?'

'Yes, Sophie–I told him everything. And he was okay with it, and he said over and over how amazed and impressed he was with what I've been through and how I'd gotten on with my life.'

'So you're together?'

'Yes, we been together for, uh, almost three months I guess it is now. And it's wonderful. And Sophie, when I say we're "together," you know what I mean, right?'

Sophie nodded and smiled. There was even a slight blush to her pallor.

'Listen, Sophie.' She paused, looking squarely into the girl's eyes. 'You've got lots to look forward to if you have the surgery— lots. And people like Maura, and me, we'll be here for you. And of course your parents, too. Plus a whole community of people like me who have had ostomies.'

Sophie was looking at Rosie, her face showing a little less strain than a while ago.

'Well, I better get going then.' Rosie stood.

Sophie's hand reached out for hers. 'Thank you,' said Sophie in a whisper.

* * *

Cary had been waiting in the hospital lobby. He was looking idly at his mobile when Rosie appeared. He stood up and smiled.

'So, how'd it go?'

With that Rosie's face turned bright red and she leaned against him, sobbing. He stroked her hair, then gestured for her to sit. She wiped her eyes, then sat quietly for a moment, trying to compose herself.

Cary held her hand. 'Rosie?'

She looked up at him with pain written in her eyes. 'It was like lookin' in a mirror, Car. Seein' myself ten years ago.'

'Did you talk to her?'

Rosie nodded.

'Do you think she listened?'

'Yeah, I do.'

'Is she gonna have the surgery?'

'I don't know, Car. She's just a scared little girl is what she is. But she loves camogie.'

'Camogie?'

'Yeah. And I promised her if she had the surgery, she'd play again.'

Cary bit his lip. 'What did she say, about the surgery I mean?'

'She said she'd think about it.'

'Well, Rose, you did yer best, right?'

Rosie grimaced. 'I'm not sure it's enough. I just don't know.'

'Hey, let's go home, yeah?'

* * *

Sunday evening Rosie was deadheading in her garden while Cary sat at the picnic table with his laptop working on the Syrian refugee story. Rosie's mobile buzzed. She wiped her hands on her apron, then drew out her mobile and took the call while standing in the middle of her garden.

After several minutes, the call ended, Rosie walked toward Cary smiling. 'That was Maura.'

'Oh?'

'Sophie's agreed to have the surgery.' She beamed for a moment, then dissolved in tears.

Cary stood and embraced her. 'Thanks to you, eh?'

Rosie shrugged. 'I don't know about that. Maybe a bit.'

He hugged her again, then stroked her hair. Then he lifted her chin until their eyes met.

'Rosie O'Malley?' he began, looking deep into her eyes.

Rosie's eyes were riveted on his.

'Yeah?'

Cary seemed to be struggling for words.

'What?'

'Just that–you are amazing.'

Lugnaquilla

19 THE INTERROGATION

The next morning found Cary sitting nervously in a windowless room in the Wicklow garda station. He had received a call from Sergeant Farrell, the same man who interviewed him on the beach three weeks earlier. He was requested to provide further assistance to the gardaí in the matter of the death of Kristoff Rahmann on Travelhawk Beach.

'Mr McGurk, sir, would you like a cup of tea–or coffee?' asked the sergeant.

Cary shook his head. 'No, thank you, Sergeant.'

'Chief Superintendent Morris and Superintendent Lewis will be in shortly.'

There was another long wait. Cary grew increasingly anxious. Finally Chief Superintendent James Morris appeared, a tall, unsmiling man with greying hair. He was followed by Superintendent Lewis, Sergeant Farrell, and a woman Cary didn't recognise. The four sat at the table facing him.

'Mr McGurk, I'm Chief Superintendent Morris. You know Superintendent Lewis and Sergeant Farrell, right?' Cary nodded. 'And this is Ms McClintock. She's from Iveagh House in Dublin– Immigration Services.'

Cary nodded as he made eye contact with each of his interrogators.

'Okay,' began Chief Superintendent Morris. 'Well, we understand that you have been doing some, eh, investigating, shall we say, into Kristoff Rahmann?'

Cary tensed. 'I just thought since I had this friend from university who lives in Beirut, Lebanon, that I'd ask him to see what he could find out about the guy.'

The two superintendents exchanged stern expressions.

'So, Superintendent Lewis interviewed you. And you reported that your friend in Lebanon was able to contact someone in Syria who knew Kristoff Rahmann, or a man by that name.'

'Yes sir, that's right. Two Syrian contacts, actually, one in Damascus and one in Aleppo.'

Morris sighed. 'Two contacts, okay. So if I get this right, you were told that this Kristoff Rahmann lived in Syria, was active in the Syrian underground back in 2012 or so, then disappeared. Is that correct?'

'Yes sir, that is what I was told.'

'And what made you think that man was the same Kristoff Rahmann as the deceased man on the beach?'

'Well, the general description fit—height, weight, hair colour, skin colour, age.'

'Uh-huh.'

'But also the date of birth checked out. The guy in Aleppo published a newspaper. Kristoff Rahmann worked for him, so he had an employee file for the man. The date of birth was the same, the 15th of March, 1982.'

'All right. So there's good reason to suspect that the Kristoff Rahmann of the ID is the same Kristoff Rahmann described by your friend from Syria.' He exchanged glances with his colleagues.

'According to Superintendent Lewis you voiced the opinion that Mr Rahmann might have been murdered or assassinated—because of his past history. Is that correct?'

'Yes sir. It's just that, well, in his writing Rahmann was outspoken about his opposition to the Assad regime.'

'Uh-huh.'

'And my contact in Beirut told me that Assad's people are known for going after journalists and others who criticise the government. So it seems to me very possible that that's what happened to Mr Rahmann.'

'Even some ten years after you say he left Syria? Really?'

'Well, it was just a thought.'

Morris exchanged glances with Superintendent Lewis and Ms McClintock, then took a deep breath.

'Now we need to go over with you once again the details surrounding your discovery of the body. I know you've already told this story more than once, but we'd like to hear it again, and especially in light of this new information on Mr Rahmann.'

'Yes sir, I understand.'

They then questioned Cary at length about that day, about his run on the beach, and about his discovery of the body. They asked him to describe the body in as much detail as he could recall—skin, hair, clothing, position on the sand, even wave action around the remains. They also questioned him closely regarding his actions following the discovery before the arrival of the gardaí and ambulance crew.

Finally they took a break. Cary stepped outside and tried to calm his queasy stomach. When he came back into the interview room, Sergeant Farrell was there.

'How you holdin' up?'

Cary shook his head. 'Barely.'

Just then the superintendents and Ms McClintock re-entered and Chief Superintendent Morris resumed the interview.

'Now, I have in my report from Superintendent Lewis the information that you photographed the deceased with your mobile. Is that correct?'

Cary cringed. 'Yes sir, I did.'

'Why did you do that, Mr McGurk?'

'I don't know, I guess because I'm a journalist and I thought, well, that it might be useful. But as soon as I did, I felt bad about it. Like it violated the dignity of the deceased.'

'And why did you decide not to tell Sergeant Farrell about the photo?'

'To be honest, sir, I forgot. I mean, I was upset. I'd just found a dead body. I just forgot about the photo. But then I remembered it later in the day and I deleted it.'

'And why did you do that, sir?'

'Like I said, I felt bad about it. And I knew the gardaí would be taking lots of photographs, so I didn't think my picture would be of any use to them.'

'Then, a few days ago, I understand you revealed this to Garda Samuels.'

'Yes sir, I did.'

'And what was his reaction?'

'Del–I mean Garda Samuels–recovered the deleted file from my mobile. And they have it, sir,' he added, looking at Superintendent Lewis. 'The Glenkerry gardaí have the photo.'

'You should know, Mr McGurk, that photographing a victim of a serious crime is prohibited under Irish law. As you said, out of concern for privacy, but also to protect the details of the deceased and of the crime scene. Only a garda or someone authorised by the gardaí is allowed to photograph a deceased person.'

'Yes sir, I understand.'

Lewis went on as if lecturing to a class of gardaí recruits. 'It is often vitally important that the details of a crime scene are not made public. Even if those details seem of little consequence, they can be useful. For example, we can test the reliability of a witness by asking about those details, things that only a real witness would know. And sometimes people come forward and confess to a crime. If their confession is genuine, they should be able to describe some of those details. If those details are made public, we lose a valuable tool. Do you see what I am saying, Mr McGurk?'

'Yes sir, I'm sorry, sir. It was a mistake. But sir, it's good that I took that photo. It reminded me of those tattoos. I'd forgotten about them until I saw the photo. '

'Ah, the tattoos. And you believe those are important for what reason?'

'Because devout Muslims aren't allowed to have tattoos, sir. And the Aleppo contact said Rahmann and his family were devout Muslims, sir.'

'Meaning what? That the deceased is not Kristoff Rahmann?'

'Well, maybe, maybe not, sir. It's just–peculiar.'

Superintendent Lewis then spoke up. 'I did point out to Mr McGurk the possibility that Mr Rahmann got those tattoos years later when perhaps his religious beliefs had changed–or perhaps he didn't feel bound by Muslim law once he came to Ireland.'

'Yes,' replied Chief Superintendent Morris. 'And there's another piece of information that bears on this. A family member in Beirut has confirmed the identity of the deceased as Kristoff Rahmann–from a photograph of the body.'

Cary knew this, of course–Del had told him. But he wasn't sure he should acknowledge that. 'Oh?' he replied.

'So I think the question of the identity of the deceased has been resolved.'

'I guess so, sir.'

'Nevertheless, Mr McGurk, your photo is of interest. I'll only say that it may prove valuable. So there will be no charges against you on the matter, just a warning.'

Cary sighed with relief. 'Thank you, sir, I....'

'Especially as you are now a newspaper publisher, as I am told. And by the way, I knew your father–a fine man he was.'

Cary nodded. 'Yes sir, thank you, sir–he was that.'

'One avenue of inquiry that we are following has to do with Mr Rahmann's family. I understand that you have learned that he was married to an Irish woman, is that correct?'

'Uh, yes sir. In I believe 2004, sir.'

'But you don't know her name?'

'No, sir.'

'Okay, Mr McGurk. Well, as you no doubt are aware, we have been actively gathering evidence from the beach regarding the circumstances of Mr Rahmann's death. And of course there has been a postmortem performed at Loughlinstown. But what we really need to do is speak with Mr Rahmann's family in Syria. We are hopeful that his wife or other family members may be able to shed light on the matter, to explain why he was in Ireland, to describe his mental state, and so forth.'

Cary nodded.

'We had hoped to interview that relative in Lebanon, the uncle who came forward and made a positive identification. But so far that has not happened–the man seems to have disappeared. We want to see what else we can learn from Mr Rahmann's family, especially his wife. So we need to speak directly to your friend in Lebanon.'

Cary gulped. 'Superintendent, sir, my friend is in a very dangerous part of the world. He has told me several times how the entire Middle East is full of dangerous people, people who are on the lookout for anyone who is revealing what they consider sensitive information. "The walls have ears," is what they say.'

'Well, of course, I can assure you that we will use every precaution possible to protect him. We can have someone from the Beirut police interview him.'

Cary shook his head. 'I doubt he would agree to that, sir. Even Beirut is dangerous. And he would be vulnerable. And you can be sure he'd never tell me anything more. If anything ever happened to him, I'd feel responsible.'

'So you are refusing to reveal your source?' asked Ms McClintock.

Cary swallowed again. 'Yes ma'am, I am. He's a friend. And he trusted me with the information. I can't violate that trust.'

His interrogators exchanged stern glances.

Then Cary continued. 'You have to understand, my friend never knew this Kristoff Rahmann–he never met him–he'd never even heard of him until I called him. It was his colleague in Damascus, and that other fellow in Aleppo–they're the ones that knew him. They're the ones you would need to talk to if you wanted sworn evidence for your case. All Sam–I mean all my friend in Beirut did was ask questions of his contacts.'

Chief Superintendent Morris nodded while making an entry on his notepad.

Cary continued. 'But they both live in Syria, sir. I can't imagine that Irish authorities or anyone from outside would be allowed access to them. Syria's a closed country, as I understand it. And I doubt that a member of the gardaí, or any police or government agent, could gain entry for such a purpose. So I can't see how my friend could give you any more information than what I have already provided.'

The Superintendent nodded. 'Yes, right, except for the identity of those two contacts.'

'Yes sir, but I doubt he would ever reveal those to the police in Lebanon. It would put those men in jeopardy. And, like I said, if I gave you his name, you can be sure he'd never give me any more help. I have to protect my sources, don't you see? Not just for me, but for the gardaí as well. Otherwise we'll lose his assistance.'

Again his interrogators exchanged stern glances.

'Well, we will have to weigh our options, Mr McGurk. But this is a serious matter. We may at some point need access to your mobile and other devices.'

Cary turned white and felt sick to his stomach. 'Yes sir.'

'And Mr McGurk? This might be the appropriate time for you to seek legal representation.'

An ominous silence fell over the room. Finally Ms McClintock asked the two superintendents for a private word. They left the room for several minutes, then returned.

Ms McClintock spoke up. 'Mr McGurk, suppose we respect your wishes–for now–about withholding the identity of your source. In return we will ask you to inquire further of your friend about Mr Rahmann's family–his wife, parents, siblings, children–their names, addresses, contact information.'

'I can try, ma'am, I am willing to try. As I said, no one has mentioned anything specific to me about family members, but I can ask.'

'Do that.'

With that the interview was terminated. Cary walked out of the garda station feeling weak in the knees, but also somewhat relieved. There had been a few moments during the interrogation when he had wondered whether he would be allowed to go. Now, as he walked along a sun-drenched Wicklow street, he felt he had been liberated.

* * *

Back in Glenkerry, Cary spent the remainder of the day thinking about his interview with the two superintendents and their colleague from Immigration Services. He wanted to speak to Del about it, but his garda friend was in Dublin for a training session and not expected back until Wednesday.

About five o'clock he saw Rosie pedalling her bike along the High Street. He jumped up from his chair and darted out the door, calling to her. She was already past the *Gazette* office and starting up Anglesey Lane when he caught up to her.

'Hey, how was your day?' Cary asked.

'Okay, pretty easy really. My students are working on projects they've chosen and most of them are really getting into it. I just walk around and try to help. Not bad. And you?'

Cary grimaced. 'I got a call from the Wicklow garda station this morning. I spent nearly two hours getting grilled by Chief Superintendent Morris, Superintendent Lewis, and a woman from Immigration Services.'

Cary proceeded to recount the interview as they walked together up the lane. Then they sat in the O'Malley kitchen while Rosie brewed some tea.

'Did you tell them about your stalker–in the grey Skoda?'

Cary shook his head. 'No. It didn't come up. Besides, I can't see that it has anything to do with this Kristoff Rahmann business. I guess I should be glad that they're not mad I took that photo. Chief Superintendent Morris said it was proving helpful–I'm not sure what he meant. But I got really nervous when they started quizzing me about Sam. They want his name and contact information. I told them I couldn't give it to them.'

'What did they say to that, Car?'

'That I better get a solicitor.'

Rosie groaned, reached out and held his hand. 'Well, maybe you have to tell them.'

'No, Rosie, I can't. For one thing Sam is a friend. And he said several times that it's really dangerous where he is, that everybody's nervous about who's listenin' in on their conversations. That's why he uses VoIP, yeh know?'

'Did you tell them that?'

'Yeah, and I said if he finds out I gave his name to the gardaí, he'll never want to help me again. I have to protect my sources, yeah? The Superintendent said they might have to take my mobile and all my devices. That really has me panicked, Rosie. They could find Sam's name. But then that woman from Immigration–Ms McClintock–said maybe they'd hold off on that if I will try to get more information about Kristoff Rahmann.'

Rosie was thinking. 'I bet they're just tryin' to scare you. They probably realise that you're right. Even if they could force you to name Sam, he'd probably not be willing to talk to them. I mean, can the gardaí just go to Lebanon and start interrogating people?'

'I don't know.'

'So maybe you're in a good position. They need you, Car, to do the asking. Otherwise they'll probably get nothing.'

There was a pause and Cary seemed distracted.

'What?' asked Rosie.

'Yeh know, it's kinda funny, now I think about it. I went in there expecting the guard to tell me to back off, to let them do their own business. But as it turns out they want me to do *more*. Imagine that.'

'So what are they lookin' for now?'

'They want me to find out more about Rahmann's family, names and contact information.' He looked at Rosie grim-faced.

'Well, you can try, right?'

'Yeah, I suppose I have to, yeh know? Because if I can't come up with what they want, well, either I dob on Sam or they come after my laptop–my mobile…'

He raised his eyes to Rosie's. 'Or me.'

Powerscourt Waterfall

20 SLEEPING WITH THE FISHES

Cary spent a mostly sleepless night worrying about his new situation in the Kristoff Rahmann investigation. He had in effect made a pact with the gardaí. He had agreed to pursue additional information, particularly the names and contact information of Rahmann's wife and other family members. In return the gardaí had agreed not to press him for the name of his Lebanon connection, not to undermine his credibility as a journalist who honours his sources. But if he failed to provide the required information the deal could well be off. He might be charged with withholding information from the gardaí, he might even be jailed, if he refused to divulge Sam's name.

Facing charges, possible incarceration–he couldn't handle it. There was just one alternative–he must get the information the gardaí sought, one way or another. In a curious way they had actually recruited him to assist in their investigation. He had to find out what he could about Kristoff Rahmann's family.

But how? Sam had already done so much for him. And he knew that his friend was taking a risk each time he inquired. So it was with some reluctance that Cary went once again to the well. He texted Sam and asked him to call.

* * *

Hurley spirits were low as the players assembled for practice that afternoon. But true to her mantra, Sabrina made no mention of the team's drubbing on Friday. On the whiteboard she had inscribed three words: 'Patience,' 'Awareness,' and 'Sacrifice.'

'Let's think today about our offensive game,' she began. A crooked smile crept across her face as she spoke, her voice lowered as she remembered. 'The first time I played on a team, my coach put me in at forward. He thought because I was fast I could outrun the other guys. Well, that was a mistake he wouldn't make again. I was what, twelve or thirteen? And I just wanted to get that ball and score points. It didn't matter where I was on the pitch or how many of the other team were in my face, I could not think of anything else but scorin' a goal.'

Sabrina held up a sliotar with its gleaming white leather and neat red stitching. She twirled it between her fingers as if studying it, then looked out at her players and smiled. 'It took me a long time to realise that that's not the way you play this game. And my coach gave me plenty of bench time that first year till I learned that lesson. I was just an impatient little kid is all, a kid who wanted to score, who couldn't wait to score.' She chuckled at the memory. 'What I lacked, what I really needed to learn, were three important lessons about this sport: *patience, awareness, sacrifice.*' As she spoke each word she underlined it on the whiteboard.

'Patience.' She struck the word emphatically with her marker. 'Patience is essential in the offence, do you understand? You gotta be patient. Wait for the right time, for the right moment, the right opportunity to score. Don't go striking on the goal from the midline–or from the sideline far upfield. Wait until you can move the ball closer to the goal, get a better angle, or pass it along to a teammate in a better position, yeh hear me?'

'Now you may see some All Star hurler on the telly takin' a shot on goal from the midline.' She shook her head. 'Don't even *think* of trying to score from beyond the 30-metre line. Leave those "Hail Mary" stunts to the professionals.' They all laughed.

She pointed to the next word. 'Awareness. Awareness is key, right?' She looked around as she spoke. 'You should always be lookin' around, watchin' for your mates and your opponents. Where're they at? What're their strengths? Their weaknesses? How can I use those to my advantage? To block, to dispossess, to tackle–you gotta be aware. Of course, awareness includes listenin' as well as seein', right?' she added, hands behind her ears. 'You gotta listen to your teammates, girls. Listen for them to call your name. And be ready to give up the ball, to pass it or strike it–to move it around to someone better positioned than you.'

'Part of awareness is watchin' your line, right?' She held out her arms and sighted along each. 'Forwards–half-forwards–midfielders–watch your line. Don't get ahead a your line. Okay, maybe if you have a good chance at scoring, maybe you should advance a bit beyond your line, but only for a real good chance. Otherwise, you should be in line with your teammates–so you can see them, so you can hear them, so you can play to them, and they to you.'

'Now about the goalkeeper, remember, every goalkeeper, no matter how big or how small, how fast or how slow, every goalkeeper's got a stronger side and a weaker side. So be aware of her, yeh hear me? Take a lesson from her, yeah? If she seems to favour one side, then plan your shots for the opposite side whenever possible. If she seems a little slow off the mark, you may find it easier to get the ball past her. But if she's fast, you've gotta aim for the corners, outta her reach. Okay?'

She then pointed to the next word. 'Sacrifice. You got to be prepared to sacrifice, to give up the ball to a teammate who has a better shot at a goal or points. That was the biggest lesson I had to learn when I was just a newbie–to be willing to pass off to my teammates. That's the mark of a good hurler, girls–willingness to sacrifice for the team.'

Sabrina and Rosie had set up a drill for offence. They divided the team in two, half offence and half defence, positioning them in front of one of the goals. Then they tossed out the sliotar at random locations. The object was for the offence to work the ball around until they had the best possible shot on the goal. Every three goals the players switched positions. Sabrina praised her players frequently: 'Good patience, Aoife. Way to be aware, Lily. Brilliant sacrifice, Eileen.'

* * *

The next day Cary went to Phinney's for luncheon.

'You just missed 'im,' said Liam at the bar.

Cary looked mystified.

'That guy you were askin' about last week? The one with the tattoos? He was in again. I woulda called yeh but the liquor salesman came in just then and I got tied up with 'im.'

Cary groaned.

'Yeah, he sat by the window just like before. Musta had three double shots. Just as I brought him a fourth, his mobile rang and he scarpered. What's the deal with 'im anyway?'

Cary shook his head. 'I have no idea.'

He ordered a latte. Just then a familiar face greeted him. It was Kevin Leahy, pint in hand.

'Well, faith and begorrah, if it isn't Ciaran McGurk, Editor and Publisher of the *Glenkerry Gazette*,' said Kevin, shaking Cary's handed vigorously. 'How 're yeh, lad?'

Kevin Leahy was a familiar figure to all in Glenkerry–to all in County Wicklow, for that matter. He was a member of the County Council, a paunchy man with a round red face, a broad smile, and a twinkle in his eye for all he met.

'Hey, Kevin, I been meaning to call you.'

'And how are things in the newspaper world, son? Is it still *"All the news that's fit to print"*?'

'Yeah, well, more like *"All the news we can fit between the adverts,"'* replied Cary with an ironic grin.

'And yer sainted mother, Catherine? Is she well?'

'Yes, yup. She's doing okay.'

'Say, that story about those folks from Ukraine was excellent, young man. Very touching, and also timely. We need to be reminded of the hardships so many folks face in these times.'

'Yes, well, I hope so.'

'And the response from your readers was favourable, I trust?'

'Yes, uh-huh, for the most part. I think a lot of them feel very sympathetic, especially considering all the Irish people have been through over the centuries.'

'Quite so, lad, quite so.'

'Do you have a few minutes, Kevin? I have a few questions I thought you might be able to answer for me.'

'For you, son, absolutely.'

Just then Cary's latte was placed on the bar before him. He could see that Kevin's pint was nearly drained. 'Can I get you another?'

'Nay, nay, but thanks. I gotta drive up to Kilmacanogue shortly, yeh know.'

'Well, coffee, or tea?'

'I wouldn't say no to a cuppa tea, thank you.'

Soon they were seated at a table in one corner, well away from other patrons.

'Well, what can I be doin' fer yeh, lad?'

'Well, it's about the housing situation.'

Kevin nodded. 'Aye.'

'As sympathetic as most folks are to refugees and asylum seekers, I'm hearing some comments about the housing shortage–locally and nationally. People are asking if we can afford to provide shelter for so many foreigners when we don't have proper accommodations for some of our own citizens.'

Kevin nodded. 'Perfectly true, we have a housing shortage. Both in County Wicklow and across the Republic.'

'My first question is why, Kevin–why this shortage?'

Kevin leaned back and sighed. 'Very good question, lad, very good question.'

He took a sip of his tea. 'Like so many things it comes down to economics, Cary–*the almighty Euro*. Construction costs, for new construction as well as for renovations, are sky high these days. Developers and contractors just can't lay out the cash needed, yeh see. Plus interest rates are high so ordinary folks have a hard time getting financing for a home. And of course labour costs are rising fast as well. And even builders have difficulty getting the cash or credit they need to start a project.'

'So what's the solution?'

'Well, so far the main push has been for government subsidies–for new home construction as well as for renovation of older housing stock. Subsidies to builders and developers mainly, but also to counties and municipalities to provide adequate public housing for low and moderate income people.'

'And is that going to happen?'

Kevin shook his head. 'Yeh know what they say in America, don't yeh? "There's no such thing as a free lunch." That is, no matter how you do it, it's gonna cost, right? Government subsidies would have to be funded in one of two ways, either by tax rises, or by cutting public services.'

Cary nodded.

Kevin inhaled, then met Cary's gaze. 'And believe me, Ciaran, most folks around Wicklow are fed up to here with higher taxes and service cuts–cuts to schools, gardaí, roads, and all.' He held his right hand against his forehead to emphasise the point.

'So that's it? No one wants to bear the cost of relieving the housing shortage?'

'That's the bottom line, son.'

'It sounds hopeless.'

'Well, there are a couple of possibilities. In recent years the EU has talked about providing funds for housing for certain purposes.' Kevin paused, clasping his hands. 'Now, as we know, Brussels has a few problems of its own these days.' Cary nodded. 'But there is a possibility of something on the order of 50 million euro for housing next year, to be awarded on a merit basis across the EU. As we speak there's a committee working on Ireland's proposal in the *Dáil*,' he explained, referring to the Irish legislature.

'Wow, that sounds promising.'

Kevin's eyes lit up. 'Possibly–hopefully–yes. And yeh know, the efforts Ireland has made to accommodate refugees in the last decade will be a strong arguing point for our application. It shows we aren't just looking out for ourselves, yeh see? That we've been willing to do our part.'

'And then there's the surplus, yeh know? With all the tax revenues Ireland has been receiving from foreign corporations, we're sittin' on a tremendous surplus in the state's coffers.'

'Can't some of that go to housing?'

'Sure it could, absolutely. But you know that a decision on how to use those funds will not be made any time soon. It could be years, lad–years.'

Cary shook his head in amazement. 'Another thing, my mother's involved with the Glenkerry Citizens for Justice.'

Kevin nodded.

'And they're trying to raise money for refugee housing.'

Kevin's eyes grew wide. 'Brilliant. Yes, yes, absolutely smashing. You've hit on another very good possibility, getting charitable organisations involved, church-affiliated and others. They have a lot to offer. And they'd be going after donations from wealthy folks, from corporations, from foundations, sources that are not often available to government.'

Cary had many more questions for Councillor Leahy, but soon Kevin had to excuse himself.

'Thanks for the tea, Ciaran. I'm afraid I must be on my way.'

* * *

Sam called a few hours later. Cary began by describing his interrogation in Wicklow. But he reassured him that he had respected his insistence on anonymity and would continue to do so. And he told his friend of the new development in the case, the appearance of Rahmann's uncle in Lebanon and the confirmation of the identification of the body.

'How did they locate him, Car, do you know?'

'They told me the guy came forward on his own, that he saw the story in *Al Jazeera* and went to the Beirut police. They showed him a photo they had received from Phoenix Park, the headquarters of *An Garda Síochána* in Dublin. He confirmed that it was Kristoff Rahmann, his nephew.'

'Wow, well, that's important, I suppose, having that assurance that it was really Rahmann.'

'Yeah, it is. But now they're leaning on me to find out more about Rahmann's wife and family–names, addresses, contact information.'

Sam hesitated, thinking. 'That uncle should have been able to help them with additional family information, wouldn't you think?'

'Yeah, well, apparently the Beirut police didn't ask anything more of him. He showed up, identified the body from the photo, then left. When the gardaí learned of this they asked the Beirut police to pursue the man for the additional information, but he was nowhere to be found. So that's why they're asking me to see what else I can learn. Especially about his wife, yeh know? She must know what he was doing in Ireland, what his state of mind was, whether anyone had it in for him. Any chance you could find out about her?'

'I'll see what I can do, Cary.'

They were about to ring off when Sam said, 'Hey Car, have you heard from Siobhan lately? I texted her twice last week and never heard back.' Cary hadn't heard from her in a while either but promised he would get through to her and tell her Sam was asking after her.

Cary left a message on Del's voice mail asking him to call round as soon as possible. Several hours later he was working on a story on a family from Afghanistan when Del appeared at his door.

'Hey, mate,' he began. 'I just got back from Dublin and found your message. How'd your interview in Wicklow go?'

Cary brought his friend up to date about the interrogation with Chief Superintendent Morris and the others.

'I'm worried, Del. Worried that they'll try to force me to name my contacts in Lebanon and Syria. The only name I know is that uni friend I told you about.'

'But they haven't asked you yet?'

'Well, yes, they did. But I told them if I gave them his name, we'd lose him. He would never talk to me again. And his life might even be in danger, yeh know? The way he tells it, Lebanon is as dangerous as Syria itself. Assad has people all over the place and they aren't nice people.'

'Do you think Chief Superintendent Morris understands that?'

'I guess so. There was this woman there from Iveagh House, Ms McClintock. She suggested that maybe I could ask my contact for more information, that if I can get more information for them, maybe they won't need to talk to him directly.'

'Yeah, well, and you can bet they're thinking about the cost of getting someone from the gardaí or Immigration to Lebanon, then bringing in your friend who would probably not be too cooperative. I'd say they're better off working with you, Car, and allowing you to respect your sources.'

Cary nodded. 'Okay, yeah, that's what I was thinkin'. But Del, they also threatened to take my mobile and laptop.'

Del looked at Cary in disbelief. 'They what?' Del shook his head. 'I'd say you got nothin' to worry about–they're just messin' with you, mate.'

'I don't know, Del. They seemed pretty serious.'

'Trust me, Car. If they warned you that they might do something like that, you have no worries.'

'Huh?'

'Think about it. They would never give someone advance warning if they really expected to search their home or seize their computer, man. Don't you see? The computer would just end up sleeping with the fishes–at the bottom of the Irish Sea.'

Cary chuckled. 'I suppose so, Del. I guess that makes sense.'

Then Del lowered his voice. 'But Car? Just to be safe, if I were you, I'd go to Costcutter and get a prepay mobile. And keep it somewhere safe, somewhere away from here. Right? Especially if you want to stay in touch with your friend in Lebanon.'

'Yeah, okay, right.'

They sat in silence for several minutes.

'That guy, the one in the grey Skoda, he was around again today–at Phinney's. I'm worried about him, Del–I'm more than worried–I'm scared. What's he want from me, anyway? I've no idea–not a clue.' He looked at Del. 'Can't the guard stake out my place–just for a couple of days?'

Del shook his head. 'I wish I could say yes, mate, I really do. But we barely got the personnel to answer the phone these days. Just sit tight is my advice. And call me, anytime, day or night. I'll pick up–I promise.'

'But I don't want to just sit and wait–it's driving me crazy, Del. I need to do something–to face him once and for all.'

'Eh, Car, I'm not sure that's such a good plan. Listen to me, mate. Just keep your eyes and ears open, yeah? And like I say, call if you see him again.'

With that Del departed and Cary sat pondering his predicament. Gardaí on his case, a stalker on his tail, and a newspaper to publish. He had a few days till his next deadline. He had to take some action, either on the Kristoff Rahmann business or the stalker.

Something's gotta give, mate, he thought to himself.

Fugitive from Injustice

21 THE TRAP

Cary spent a mostly sleepless night tossing and turning, worrying himself over his stalker–what he wanted, what he might do, how the whole business could play out. During his few brief periods of sleep he was tormented by a recurring nightmare–dark figures lurking in the shadows, lunging out at him, chasing him down endless corridors and tunnels. Several times he woke in a cold sweat, his heart racing.

Over coffee the next morning he made a decision–he would set a trap for his nemesis, try to corner him, at least long enough to call Del.

He had business to attend to in Hollywood, some thirty kilometres away through the mountains. As he prepared to leave his flat, he looked out the front window onto the High Street. There it was, the grey Skoda, parked across the street, its occupant barely visible. Cary's heart pumped as he turned his bike onto the High Street, then started out on the road to Laragh. Sure enough, the Skoda followed at a distance.

* * *

Cary's mind is racing. He's trying to think ahead, to visualise the road ahead. He wants to lead his pursuer down a cul-de-sac, a side road with no outlet. But he suspects the guy will not turn into a suspicious looking farm lane, some winding boreen, not if he senses a trap.

As he approaches the rugged terrain of the Wicklow Mountains, Cary is recalling a trail he had once walked with his parents and brother in the area north of Lugnaquilla, the highest summit in the Wicklow Mountains. The trailhead is located at the end of a narrow lane off the highway. The way is paved at the start, with some new homes on either side. Then, as he recalls, it turns to gravel before ending at a turnaround where the trail begins.

That might just do the trick, he thinks. He hopes his stalker will be enticed to follow him down the paved lane, then onto the gravel way, where Cary will take cover to spy on his pursuer. At that point if the guy wants out, he'll have to either stop and reverse or make a turn at the car park. Either way, Cary thinks, he should be able to get a glimpse of him, see his registration number, maybe even take a photo.

The Skoda is still behind him several minutes later as he approaches the turning, though well back. He slows, indicates, and, when he is certain his pursuer can see him, turns into the lane. He immediately accelerates, racing as quickly as he can to the end of the pavement, then onto the gravel, hoping to have a few seconds to park his bike and hide at the end of the cul-de-sac before the Skoda appears.

The unpaved way is smooth at first and he proceeds swiftly. Then, just at a sharp turn, a large puddle spans the road. He has no time to slow his bike down and skirt the water. His rear wheel spins in the mud and slips, then regains solid ground–the bike lurches forward. Cary is catapulted onto the gravel roadbed, the bike continuing for a few feet before tumbling into the dust with a loud crash.

Dazed, Cary groans as he lifts himself cautiously onto one elbow. He scrambles into a tangle of gorse out of sight.

At that moment the Skoda appears around the corner. It runs directly into the water, sinks into the muck right up to the axles, then comes to a halt with a loud thud. The driver immediately revs the engine, trying to drive the vehicle forward again, but to no avail–the wheels merely spin and muddy water sprays in all directions. He reverses and revs again with similar results. This goes on for several minutes. Still concealed, Cary reaches into his pocket, withdraws his mobile, and starts filming.

Finally the car's engine stalls. The driver pulls a knitted hat over his face, opens the door, and emerges. Cary continues filming.

'What the hell do you want with me?' shouts Cary. The man offers no reply, turns, and flees back down the lane toward the highway.

His nemesis now gone, Cary lies breathing heavily. Then with a groan he climbs to his feet, shaking dust and grime from his trousers. He briefly considers following the man, then thinks better of it. He approaches the abandoned car and peers in the windows. Then he calls Del.

* * *

Nearly a half hour later two Garda cars arrived. Del Samuels was in the first, two garda from the Hollywood garda station in the second.

'Did you see anyone on the highway?' He had given Del a brief description of his pursuer hoping he would be sighted walking along the road, probably toward Glenkerry, the direction he had come from.

'No, Car, no one. But another patrol car is on its way from Kilcullen–I've given them the description you gave me. We'll see what they come up with.' He looked at his friend. 'Our first priority is you, mate. Are you okay?'

'Yeah, I'm fine. As you can see, I laid over my bike–and went flying. But I'm okay, Del. The bike's got a dent in one fender. But it'll be okay.'

'Well, then, let's have a look here,' said Del, nodding toward the Skoda. 'Did you touch anything?'

Cary assured him he had not touched the car. Del donned gloves, then opened the passenger door carefully, leaned down and peered around. There was a large coffee cup in the cupholder and a hoodie on the seat. Under the hoodie were several newspapers.

'Whatta ya see, Del?'

'A hoodie and some newspapers. Whatta yeh know, Car, the *Glenkerry Gazette*. A whole stack. This guy must be one of your loyal subscribers.'

Just then an ambulance appeared.

'Geez, Del, you didn't have to…'

'Just routine, Car. They'll check you out, make sure you're all right.'

'But I'm fine.'

'Just let 'em look yeh over, okay? It'll only take a few minutes.'

The examination took more than a few minutes including answering a long series of questions. When the EMTs were certain that the patient needed no care, Cary was allowed to go. He walked back to the Skoda.

'Any news on the driver?'

'Nah, nothing, Car, I'm afraid. But these guys will dust the car for prints and bag up the contents. Then the car will be towed to a garda garage in Dublin. We already traced the plates. It was nicked in Arklow over a week ago.' He looked at his friend. 'I told you not to do anything stupid, Car, didn't I?'

Cary nodded. 'Yeah. But I had to do something, Del. And anyway, at least you got the car.' Then he held up his mobile. 'And this. I filmed it–the car–the guy–everything.'

'Send it to me, yeah?'

'Already done, mate. It's in your inbox.'

Cary called to reschedule his appointment in Hollywood, then returned to Glenkerry.

* * *

Back in his flat, Cary made himself a cup of tea and tried to calm his jangled nerves. He had already received several emails and texts, all positive, about his article on the Osman family that had appeared in the new issue of the *Gazette*. The 'Contact Us' inbox included a number of comments, as well, mostly praising the story. But as with the article on the Gorayas, there were several comments about the housing shortage and whether Ireland should be diverting resources to folks from distant lands when they were unable to provide for their own citizens.

Cary watched the short video clip of his stalker for several minutes on his mobile, then sent it to his laptop where he could get a better look. There was the Skoda, sunk up to its chassis in mud, the driver gunning the engine fruitlessly. Unfortunately the man's face was obscured by a reflection on the windscreen. Then he pulled that hat over his face, emerged, and turned away from the camera. Not much to see, certainly not enough to make any kind of positive identification of the man if it came to that. But on careful examination at slow speed, there was one detail, one small detail, that caught Cary's eye.

Just then Del appeared at the door.

'How yeh doin', mate?'

'Look, Del, watch this.'

He replayed the short video for Del, first at normal speed, then slow.

'See, just as he's getting out of the car–his left arm–right–there.' He froze the video and zoomed in on the man's arm.

'What's that, mate, a tattoo?'

'Yeah. Look at it–some kind of grid–brightly coloured boxes in rows–see?'

'Uh-huh,' replied Del flatly.

'I've seen that design before, Del.'

'Oh?'

'At Travelhawk Beach–it's a lot like the ones on the dead man's arms.'

'Are you sure?'

'Yeah, pretty sure.'

'So, whatta you thinkin'?'

Cary looked into his friend's eyes. 'Del, I'm beginning to think maybe there *is* a connection between this guy–my stalker–and Kristoff Rahmann after all.'

* * *

Sam called back the next morning.

'I've got a little more information on Rahmann's family, Car. Not sure whether it'll be helpful. That chap in Aleppo, the newspaper publisher? My friend in Damascus talked to him again. He said Rahmann got married while he was in Aleppo and working for the newspaper. He never met his wife. But like I told you before, she was Irish–Ellen or Eileen was all he remembered.'

'So they would have been married in, what, 2003 or 2004?'

'Yeah, something like that. They had an Islamic wedding ceremony in Aleppo–this guy attended.'

'What about contact information? A phone number or email?'

'Yeah, no, nothing. They left Aleppo abruptly in 2012 when things got dangerous. He lost touch with them entirely after that.'

'And children?'

'He couldn't recall whether they had children. And he knew no other family members. So that's all I got, Car. Sorry.'

'No, Sam, that's okay. I'll pass this along to the gardaí right away. Thanks a lot.'

Cary immediately went to the garda station to talk to Del.

'Rahmann was married in Syria around 2004. And she was Irish. Her first name was Ellen or Eileen, according to that guy. He didn't know if they had children. And he didn't know of any other family members. And he says Rahmann and his wife disappeared in 2012. They might have left Syria–he never knew and never heard from them again.'

'That's it? That's all you got?'

'It's not much, Del, I know. But it's something. Maybe it'll help convince them that I'm trying, yeah?'

'Okay, well, let's write this up.' He pulled a form out of his desk drawer. 'I'll give my super a copy, and I'll fax a copy to Chief Superintendent Morris.'

'I sure hope this will satisfy them, Del. '

Del sighed. 'Yeah, me too.'

'I just don't know what more I can find out, yeh know?'

'You've already done a lot, Car, maybe more than you realise. I just saw an internal memo on the case. From what I can tell, it seems the gardaí are now leaning toward the possibility that Rahmann was murdered, possibly assassinated by foreign agents, for his work with the Syrian underground. Something about some physical evidence pointing to that.' Del looked his friend in the eye. 'You may have been right about that after all.'

'So, whatta you and your significant other up to this weekend?' asked Del.

'Rosie's headed to Galway. I'm dropping her at Heuston Station on Friday.'

'Oh, her ma, eh?'

'Yeah, she hasn't seen her since her dad's funeral back in July. They'll have lots of catching up to do. What about you?'

'Me and Sabrina might go into the city, yeah? Meet some friends of hers along Temple Bar.'

22   MICHAELMAS

By mid-week word had spread that Isla once again would not be playing on Friday. Sabrina was expecting this and knew she had to shake things up a bit. Before practice on Thursday, she spoke with her three most experienced players, Gráinne, Eileen, and Lily.

'You three are key to this team. You're the oldest, the most experienced. The younger girls look up to you and respect you. I need you to build them up, give them confidence, in practice and in Friday's match. Praise them, every one of them. Encourage them. Show them you trust them by feeding them the ball whenever possible. When Isla's in a match it makes sense to build plays around her, to get the ball to her. But when she's not there, you gotta trust some of the younger players to do the job.'

'I especially need you to keep them strong when the tide turns against them. Last week they just collapsed every time Arklow scored. Keep them moving, keep them positive, okay? Can I rely on you guys?'

Her three veterans came through beautifully for Sabrina in Thursday's practice. They rallied their younger teammates, encouraged them at every turn, and praised them constantly. By the end of Thursday's practice the team seemed to be working well and the memories of last week's debacle had faded away.

Friday's match was against St Barnabas School. Almost from the start it was clear that this team was weak. They were young and inexperienced. This was their first match of the season, Sabrina had learned, and it showed.

The Hurleys scored early and spirits soared. Sabrina watched with satisfaction as Gráinne, Eileen, and Lily did just what she had asked, calling out their younger teammates, praising them, making them part of every play. A light rain started to fall midway through the second period, but the Hurleys were undeterred. In the end they won, 6-2.

'Wow, you girls were brilliant today,' said a beaming Sabrina. 'Just brilliant.' And quietly she thanked the three eldest team-members afterwards for their central role.

Rosie had been dispirited since the loss of the previous week. But she was filled with admiration both for the team and for Sabrina and the way she encouraged them.

* * *

After the match Cary drove Rosie to Dublin in his mother's car. He planned to see her off at Heuston Station for the train to Galway where she would spend Michaelmas weekend with her mother and Gerry.

'My ma's family always made a big thing of Michaelmas when she was young,' said Rosie as they drove the N11 north from Glenkerry. 'I want her to tell me about those days if we have a chance.'

'Well, I hope she and Gerry are doing well, Rose. And say hello to them for me.'

'Yeah, for sure. What're yeh up to, then?'

Cary sighed. 'I have to do some serious research, see if I can find anything more about Kristoff Rahmann's wife and family. Anything. But I don't really know where to begin.'

'What about Professor Jurgenson? Maybe he can help you again?'

'Yeah, I doubt it. I don't think he has any connections in the Middle East.'

At Heuston they kissed and Rosie climbed aboard the train while Cary waved from the platform.

* * *

Back home Cary sat at his laptop surfing the web for more information on Syria. But he was getting nowhere. Then he remembered Rosie's suggestion. He placed a call to Professor Jurgenson and left a message on his voice mail: 'It's Ciaran McGurk again. I wondered if you'd have a chance to give me a call. I need some more advice.'

He must have sounded desperate. Within a half hour the professor called back.

'Thanks so much for returning my call, Professor. It's about that Syrian man, Kristoff Rahmann. The one I found on the beach at Wicklow.'

He proceeded to explain his situation. He reviewed what he already knew about Rahmann–Syrian native, educated in Beirut, probably in the 1990s, employed by a newspaper in Aleppo, married in Damascus in 2004, dropped out of sight about 2012.

'Well, it sounds like the gardaí are turning over the investigation to you, Ciaran,' the professor said with a chuckle.

'Yes, well, they're threatening to make me name my sources if I can't provide more information. It's got me worried. I mean, they could put me in jail.'

'You have to do what you think is right, Ciaran. That's a journalist's duty.' He paused. 'So you want to locate Mr Rahmann's wife. And you think she's still in Syria?'

'Yes sir. I mean, if she's in Ireland, Immigration Services would be able to locate her, wouldn't you think?'

'Yes, that's probably true. Unless of course she's here illegally. Although if as you say she's an Irish citizen, why would she risk entering the country illegally?'

'Right. So I'm guessing that she's still in Syria, or maybe one of the neighbouring countries. But I don't know her first name. And I know that Rahmann is a pretty common Syrian surname.'

'Well, how about the print media, Ciaran? Maybe you can search the archives of some Syrian newspapers for the name Kristoff Rahmann, possibly a marriage announcement.'

'That's a thought. But won't those all be in Arabic?' asked Cary.

'Well, most of them, true. But not all of them. At one time there were a few English-language newspapers in the Middle East. I'm not sure how many have survived, especially in a place like Syria the way it is today. Wait, did you say your friend is in Lebanon?'

'Yes, Beirut.'

'Well, there are a number of English language newspapers in Lebanon. Professor Mansour here at DCU worked for one of them for a time, I believe.' He hesitated. 'The *Daily Star*, yup, that was it. Remember that database of newspapers and news services we talked about in class? Why don't you search it for news publications or outlets based in and around Syria? See if any of them date back to 2004 and are accessible online. Search for "Kristoff Rahmann" in that time period and see what comes up. Of course, if he was a journalist, you'll no doubt find articles written by him. But who knows, you might stumble across a personal item, like a marriage announcement.'

'I'll do that, Professor. I'll do that right away.'

'Grand. And in the meantime I'll be thinking of any other online sources where personal information like marriages and births might appear. I'll call or text if I have any thoughts.'

Cary thanked the professor, then rang off. He made himself a cup of tea. Then he sat cross-legged on his couch with the laptop on the table in front of him and began typing.

A search for English language newspapers in the Middle East produced a long list, mostly newspapers that thrived in the days when the region was overrun with western petroleum industry personnel: the *Jordan Times*, the *Jerusalem Post*, the *Tehran Times*, the *Daily Star*, and more. Many were long gone, but the *Daily Star* maintained an archive that appeared to go back to 2000 or thereabouts.

The interface was awkward, but when he finally figured out how to search the archive for the name 'Kristoff Rahmann' in 2004, he was excited to find several dozen hits. They were all, as Professor Jurgenson had predicted, stories Rahmann himself had authored. Nevertheless Cary read several and downloaded one or two that offered some insight into the man, his writing style, his interests. But still he found nothing even close to a news item about Rahmann, his wife or family.

Somehow two hours went by in a flash as Cary dug deeper and deeper into the archives of the *Daily Star* and several other Middle Eastern English language newspapers. He wondered as he searched whether anyone in the gardaí had the time to do similar grunt work. He doubted it.

It was nearly eleven in the evening and Cary was exhausted and about to give up. Then his mobile buzzed. It was a text from Professor Jurgenson.

'How about the Alumni Association of American University of Beirut?'

Cary sat staring at the short message. 'Brilliant,' he said to himself. And suddenly he had a new burst of energy. Fortunately the university had a user-friendly web site with an extensive archive of back issues of their alumni newsletter. He found several hits for 'Kristoff Rahmann' going back to his first few years out of university when he held several internships in Beirut. But suddenly one item seemed to jump right off the screen:

Married.
Kristoff Rahmann ('97) and Evelyn O'Donnell ('98),
Damascus, Syria, April 14, 2004.

* * *

The next morning Cary visited the Glenkerry garda station. Neither Del nor Superintendent Lewis was in. The garda on duty suggested he write a short note to Lewis informing him of the name of Kristoff Rahmann's wife. He was about to explain how he had come by the name but then decided not to offer any details–let them assume the information came from his Lebanon contact, he thought.

Feeling some relief that he had made good on his promise to the gardaí, Cary turned his attention to other *Gazette* matters. He sent out several dozen subscription invoices, looked over a stack of bills that needed to be paid, then dove into his story on the housing situation and its bearing on refugees in Ireland.

Late in the day he walked up Anglesey Lane to his mother's house. Catherine had invited him to supper, knowing that Rosie was away for the weekend. Back in his flat that evening, he brooded on the marriage of Kristoff Rahmann and Evelyn O'Donnell and how he might be able to find contact information for Evelyn Rahmann, assuming that was her married name, in Syria. He sent a text to Sam with the new information, although he hesitated to ask his friend for yet another favour.

* * *

Cary met Rosie at Heuston Station on Sunday afternoon. She was exuberant about her time in Galway.

'Ma is fine, Car. Really. I never realised how sad she always used to be–with my da, I mean. I guess I took it fer granted, yeh know? But now, with her new life, she's really happy.'

'And Gerry?'

'Yeah, he's good, too. They're goin' to Spain in December for a week, can you imagine? And Gerry thinks he might retire from teaching in another couple of years. Then they can do a lot of travelling.'

'Did you and your Ma get caught up?'

'Oh, yeah, Car. On Saturday morning we went into town and spent a few hours in the shops together. She wanted me to help her pick out clothes for their holiday. Oh, and I found those drawing pens I been searching for in an art supply shop. I'm gonna finish the new *Gazette* masthead this week, I promise.'

'That'll be grand, Rosie.'

'When we got home we sat out in the garden, had tea, and talked about Ma's school days. And about her family. She goes to Roscommon every couple weeks to visit Aunt Marguerite and Aunt Elizabeth so she told me about them. Elizabeth is goin' downhill fast, I'm afraid.' Her aunt Elizabeth was suffering from dementia and had been in a care home for several years.

'Oh, I'm sorry, Rosie. That's a shame.' Cary had met Elizabeth a few months earlier.

'And I got to ask Ma about Marguerite's children, my Finley cousins. Patrick and his wife live in Dublin and they have two kids, a boy and a girl. And Megan and her husband are in Limerick. He's Pakistani. They met when he was a uni student in Dublin. They have three kids now–the oldest is like twelve. And then there's Martha–she's in banking in London–and Paul–he still lives around Roscommon.'

'Ma was talkin' about her parents and her grandparents. I never knew any of 'em. And she also told me what she knew about my da's family. After my teaching job ends, I'll have more time, and I was thinkin' I'd like to research my family tree, yeh know?'

'Oh, yeah, there's so much you can do online now. My ma's done some of that herself, for her people and for the McGurks.'

'What about you? Any success in your research on Kristoff Rahmann?'

Cary proudly told her about the marriage announcement he had uncovered. 'Her name was Evelyn O'Donnell.' Then he explained how he had found that out. 'It was Professor Jurgenson who suggested I try the alumni news of the American University in Beirut. Thanks to him. And thanks to you for suggesting I call him.'

Arriving at the O'Malley house, Rosie thanked Cary for picking her up and driving her home.

'One more thing, Car. I got a call from Maura Ahearn while I was at Ma and Gerry's. Sophie's havin' her surgery–tomorrow.'

* * *

Around midday on Monday Cary received a call from Del.

'So, d'you and Sabrina have a good time in Dublin the other night?'

'Oh, yeah, epic, Car, epic. And your sweetie got back from Galway okay?'

'Yeah, uh-huh. I picked her up at Heuston Station late yesterday. Hey, any news on the Skoda guy?'

'No joy, mate. They put out a bulletin on him with your photo and description. And the Arklow station is on the lookout especially, but nothing.'

Then Cary told Del about the new information he had obtained on Kristoff Rahmann's wife.

'Evelyn O'Donnell, huh? Well unfortunately there's gotta be hundreds of them in Ireland in the last forty or so years. And if she left Ireland in the nineties to attend university there's probably nothing in our database for her. It would help if we had a date of birth, name of parents, that sort of information. Let me talk to some of the others in the office here, and Sabrina.'

'Yeah, that would be grand, Del.'

'So, over the weekend a couple Wicklow guards went over CCTV footage from the night Rahmann died at Black Castle. Like I told you the camera up on Castle Field wasn't of much use–the lighting was bad and the carnival rides were in the way. But they looked at footage from Main Street and the quay.'

'Uh-huh.'

'Quite a few cars came down Main Street toward the castle between eleven and midnight. The ones they could pick up registration plates from turned out to be residents of the area. They're interviewing them today. They're not likely suspects, but someone from the neighbourhood might a seen something–or somebody–out of the ordinary at that hour.'

'But one of the cameras on South Quay showed two men getting into a skiff a little before midnight. They put in from North Quay, then rowed in the direction of the sailing club. We lost them there, but that's another approach to Black Castle, yeh know?'

'Any details on the men?'

'Yeah, they got a look at one of them. The lighting isn't great and the resolution is grainy. But you can see his face. And he walked with a slight limp. They're circulating a copy, a POI notice, to all garda stations nationwide and in the north. I'll send you a copy.'

'Anything else? What about the car?'

'The angle was wrong so they couldn't see the plates. They sent the footage up to Phoenix Park to see if they could at least get make and model information.'

* * *

At midday Cary had an appointment with Mr Forster at *Coláiste Gaeilge.* There had been a good deal of pushback among students as well as some parents regarding the school's new mobile policy and Cary wanted to write something on the subject for an upcoming edition of the *Gazette*.

After the interview he went looking for Rosie. She had just finished a class and was tidying up when he looked in her door.

'Hi, Rose.'

She looked up and smiled briefly. But her face was flushed.

'What's the matter, Rosie?'

She looked glum. 'I still haven't heard from Maura. Sophie's surgery shoulda been over by now. And she promised to call me right away.'

'Maura's probably with Sophie's parents, don't you imagine? Maybe they just got in to see Sophie in the–whatta yeh call it– recovery room–post-op or whatever?'

Rosie bit her lip and nodded. 'I just texted Maura. I can't stand this. I been tied up in knots all morning.'

Cary took her in his arms. 'I know, it was like this with my da. Yeh feel so helpless.'

Rosie nodded. 'I know she's not family or anything, but I feel– if anything went wrong, I'd never be able to live with that.'

Just then Rosie's mobile buzzed. Cary watched as Rosie answered the call. It was Maura. He could tell there was something amiss. Rosie was grimacing, tears streaming down both cheeks.

'Okay, ta.' She looked up at Cary. 'Sophie was in post-op, everything seemed to be fine, then her blood pressure started to drop. They've taken her back to surgery.'

'That happens, Rose, sometimes, yeh know? Maybe a suture broke–maybe they just need to do a little more stitching.'

Rosie was shaking. She sat down, her face in her hands.

'Spin me home, Car? I got just my form class at half two–I'll ask Mr Forster if he can get someone to cover fer me.'

* * *

Cary knew he had work to do in his office, but he wasn't willing to leave Rosie alone under the circumstances. So he sat with her and they drank tea together in the O'Malley kitchen. Finally Rosie lay on her bed and fell asleep. Cary walked in the garden, then sat at his laptop in the kitchen working on revisions to a story about an Afghan refugee he had interviewed by phone over the weekend.

Nearly an hour later he heard Rosie's voice from the bedroom. She was talking on her mobile. Finally he heard, 'Thanks, Maura.'

Rosie appeared at the bedroom door smiling weakly. 'Sophie's out of surgery, again. She's in post-op. And she's stable. They think she's gonna be okay, Car.' With that she leaned against Cary sobbing.

23 BLOCKING AND HOOKING

With their victory over St Barnabas still fresh in everyone's mind, the Hurleys were in high spirits. They had done what they failed to do the previous week, to hold it together without Isla, to organise themselves in her absence. And the older players deserved a lot of the credit, thought Rosie, for leading the team, for encouraging the younger girls. Now Isla was back, apparently in good health. Could the Hurleys continue their one-game winning streak?

Sabrina began the practice. 'Okay, Hurleys. Today we focus on three key tackles in camogie–clashing, blocking, and hooking. These are the basic defensive moves of the sport, moves that everyone needs to be proficient at, whatever your position.'

'Now a clash is when two players fight shoulder-to-shoulder for possession of the sliotar. It's essential for the safety of both players that they are close together, within the arc of the two hurleys. Watch me and Ms O'Malley.'

Sabrina and Rosie walked side-by-side, matching strides, swinging their hurleys in short arcs, slapping them together at the bottom of each arc.

'See how we strike when our inside legs are closest to the ball? And we use short, quick swings. A quicker swing will ensure that you contact the ball first. But of course, a shorter swing will result in a less forceful strike. You can take a longer swing if you wish, but your opponent might get to the ball first and win the clash.'

She then drilled the team on clashing. With players lined up in pairs, she positioned the bas–the enlarged tip of her hurley–on the ground in front of her facing the first pair. As they approached, the players had to time their swings so they contacted the bas simultaneously. She watched carefully to see that each player had her inside leg extended at the moment of contact.

Then they moved on to blocking. 'Blocking is preventing a player from striking the ball in the air. To block you need to be facing your opponent. Grip your hurley with both hands together, thumbs pointing upward, like this. My eyes are on the ball, right? And my forward leg is bent. I'm reaching forward with my hurley held up at an angle. Notice that I'm not chopping down on the ball–I'm holding my hurley steady–like this. My goal is to sandwich the ball between the bas of my hurley and my opponent's hurley.' She and Rosie demonstrated blocking several times. Then she drilled the team on blocking. Lined up in pairs, one player executed ground strikes on an imaginary ball while the other tried to block each swing. After several minutes she had the team spread out and repeat the drill, this time with a ball.

'Finally there's hooking. You use the hook from behind to block another player from striking the ball. You must be trailing your opponent by about a metre. Extend your hurley just above the ground with one hand like this. See how far you can reach if your balance is right.'

With her long arms and legs, Sabrina was able to extend her hurley far in front of her.

'Then as your opponent swings, deflect her hurley upwards. If you're lucky, she'll miss the ball and you can then take possession.'

She had the players line up in pairs, first walking slowly through the steps of the hook, then more quickly, and finally running. Three of the taller players, Isla, Eileen, and Lily, seemed to be struggling.

Sabrina elbowed Rosie: 'The bigger kids have a hard time with this, notice? There's something about their centre of gravity that makes it more difficult for them to extend the hurley properly and still keep their balance.'

Then it was Molly's turn with Kelly.

'Watch Molly,' whispered Sabrina to Rosie.

Molly leaned forward on one foot, extending her hurley far ahead of her. Then with a twist of her wrist, she deftly blocked Kelly's swing, the ball dropped to the ground, and she struck it away, all in one smooth motion.

'Hold up, everyone. I want you all to see something. Molly, can you show that to us again with Kelly?'

Once again Molly performed a perfect hook, seeming to extend her hurley precariously but then almost effortlessly regaining her balance while knocking the sliotar away.

'Beautifully done, Molly. Everyone, try it again, will you?'

At Thursday's practice Sabrina had the team repeat those three tackling drills, clashing, blocking, and hooking, watching the players closely, correcting mistakes when necessary, praising good form when she saw it. Near the end of practice she gathered her players around her.

'One more thing, Hurleys. When you're hooking or blocking or clashing, you are going after the ball, not the player. So be very careful. Never use your hurley aggressively against another player at any time. And never strike your opponent with your hands or your hurley. If you do, you're guaranteed to get hit with a yellow card. Hear me?'

As the practice ended, Rosie sensed that the team was gaining in skill and confidence. She hoped they could harness that progress and at the least make a good showing in their next match.

* * *

The new issue of the *Gazette* included Cary's story about an Afghan man and his family who were granted asylum in Ireland in 2016.

ONE AFGHAN FAMILY FINDS REFUGE IN IRELAND, OTHERS ARE NOT SO FORTUNATE

Ciaran McGurk, Editor, Glenkerry Gazette

Wali spoke to me recently from his home in Carlow. He asked to be identified only by his first name.

A native of Afghanistan, Wali had been working as a driver for Irish troops for six years when the last Irish soldiers departed from his country in 2016. At that time he applied for and was granted asylum for himself and his family in Ireland.

'It would have been very dangerous for me and my family to remain in Afghanistan,' explained Wali. 'We were very fortunate to be granted asylum in Ireland. Many of my countrymen were not so fortunate.'

In 2021 the Taliban took over Kabul, Afghanistan's capital and largest city. They imprisoned or killed many Afghans who had worked for the UN peacekeeping forces. They placed severe restrictions on Afghan women, prohibiting them from working or going to school.

In 2022 the Department of Justice announced a new initiative to process applications for asylum for refugees from Afghanistan. They received over 500 applications, but at last report only a handful of those applications had been processed.

For the few Afghans who have been admitted since 2021, housing has been an acute problem. And while government funds are available to those providing housing for Ukrainian refugees, there are no such funds available for refugees from Afghanistan. It's been called a 'two-tier system.' Some Afghans have been allowed temporary visas in Ireland, but their families are still in Afghanistan with little hope of being admitted.

Wali and his family feel at home in Carlow. His children attend a local primary school.

'At first we felt uncomfortable. My wife and the children spoke very little English. But the children quickly made friends in school. And we were surprised to find other Afghan expatriates nearby. We feel very comfortable and safe here. It is a good feeling.'

* * *

On Friday the Hurleys faced off against *Coláiste Kloughnarra*. With a string of four victories to their credit this season, this team would be the toughest the Hurleys had yet to meet.

As the first period unfolded, Rosie was encouraged by what she saw. The Hurleys passed the sliotar around much more than previously. The forwards succeeded in moving the ball forward and to the centre again and again, then managed to get off many shots on the goal, although none scored.

But what was most apparent was the way the team functioned defensively. They clashed, blocked, and hooked much more often than before and with frequent success, again and again dispossessing their opponents. The *Kloughnarra* team's forwards were obviously frustrated by those repeated dispossessions and their inability to score. At the end of the first period the match stood at a scoreless tie.

At the interval Sabrina praised her team. 'You guys are outstanding today, yeah? Especially those defensive moves. Keep it up–keep it up. Don't worry about scoring. The points will come, the opportunities will be there, so long as you keep the pressure on these guys. I promise.'

Sure enough, the Hurleys continued to harass their opponents in the second period. The *Kloughnarra* offensive players seemed to be trying harder and harder to evade the blocks and hooks of the Hurleys, but to no avail. With several minutes left the scoreless tie remained. Then, with less than a minute to go, Gráinne captured a ball from her opponent, then passed it to Eileen who in turn passed it to Isla. Isla wasted no time in striking it toward the goal. But it missed by inches. Just then the whistle blew ending the second half.

The match would now go to extra time. Sabrina gathered her team once again. 'Listen, Hurleys, whatever happens, you guys have been brilliant. I'm so proud of what you've been able to do against a tough team.' She took one deep breath. 'Just stay calm, Hurleys, stay calm and focus. You'll be fine.'

Only two minutes into extra time Robyn blocked her opponent, retrieved the ball, then carried it to within the 20-metre line. She turned and struck it through the uprights, giving the Hurleys a 1-0 lead. The players all jumped for joy.

'Heads up,' cried Sabrina, worried that the opposition would take advantage of the spontaneous celebration. And sure enough, one of the *Kloughnarra* forwards dispossessed Gráinne at midfield, then soloed toward the goal. She had a clear shot on the goal and was about to strike the ball when out of nowhere Molly appeared and hooked her opponent. Then the whistle blew. The Hurleys won, 1-0.

After the match Sabrina again praised the team. 'All of you were brilliant. See what a good defence can do? And Molly, we owe you big time, kid.'

Everyone cheered and patted Molly on the back.

* * *

It was Tuesday and as usual Cary found himself overwhelmed with work in preparation for the looming deadline for the new issue of the *Gazette*. He was swamped with dozens of last-minute submissions, adverts, and events, and had to make many alterations to the layouts of several of the interior pages. Then about half four he got an email from Eileen Keough with another story on the Hurleys. It had lots of details of the team's next match scheduled for Friday, so he was anxious to use it. He gave the piece a quick scan, then turned to the task of working it in on the sport page.

Cary's nerves were on edge. Besides all those last-minute tasks that needed his attention, he also had money worries. The printer would be expecting a cheque on Wednesday–but his cash situation was perilous. He removed some petty cash from an envelope in his desk, took it to the bank and deposited it. It wasn't much, but it increased the balance in his account just enough to cover the printing of this week's *Gazette*.

Meanwhile at the other end of the High Street, the Hurleys were beginning practice. This week's match pitted them against another strong team, this one from the Montkilleen National School. The team was unbeaten thus far this season and had already qualified for the County League Semi-finals just over a week away. The Hurleys needed one more victory to be eligible for that tournament, a fact that the players were well aware of.

Sabrina, however, made no mention of the tournament. All week long she held fast to her creed, focusing not on winning or losing but on those camogie fundamentals she had been drilling her team on every day. The last thing she wanted was for her team to be unnerved by the stakes of this particular match.

* * *

After practice on Thursday, Rosie helped Sabrina put away equipment, then pushed her bike through the school gate onto the High Street.

'Hey, Ms O.,' said Molly who was waiting on a bench.

'Good practice, Molly.'

'Yeah, pretty good.' Molly smiled. 'Thanks for yer help.'

Rosie shrugged. 'Yer ma pickin' you up?'

'She said she would, but she had to go to Rathdrum on an errand. Mind if I walk with you?'

'Not at all.'

She hoisted her hold-all to her shoulder, Rosie pushed her bike, and the pair started along the High Street footpath together.

'So how'd you ever learn to hook like that, Molly? You're amazing.'

Molly shrugged. 'Mostly just foolin' about in the schoolyard in Cork. One of the teachers showed me some tricks. And we had a team for a while.'

'Well, all the Hurleys are trying to copy your moves.' Molly smiled shyly and blushed.

They passed Phinney's, the newsagent shop, and the *Gazette* office on the corner, then started up Anglesey Lane.

'So how are you likin' *Coláiste Gaeilge*?' asked Rosie.

'Yeah, it's pretty good.' Again a small smile crept across Molly's face. 'Especially art–and the Hurleys.'

'Well, you've got special talents in both. And what about English, and Irish Language, and maths, and science?'

'Yeah, they're okay.'

'And your brother? How's he likin' it?'

She shrugged. 'Okay, I guess.'

'And you've made some friends.'

'Yeah, a course the team, but especially Gráinne and Eileen. And Timmy, too.'

'That's great, Molly, they're all good kids. So, are yer parents comin' to the match tomorrow?'

'My dad can't, he's got to work. And my mom's got a meeting on Zoom, but she said she'd try to come to the match as soon as her meeting is over.'

They stopped at the O'Malley drive and Rosie started to speak: 'Yeh know, I promised your ma a carton of eggs. How about…'

At that moment a small white panel van moved slowly up the hill. They both stepped off the lane to let the van pass.

Rosie watched the van with curiosity. 'That guy must be lost.'

Molly nodded. 'Yeah, he was parked in front of the school during practice. What were yeh sayin' about eggs?'

'Oh, yeah, the eggs. How about you come to the barn while I fetch 'em?'

Molly nodded. They walked up the drive past the barn to the henhouse at the rear. They stood watching Rosie's flock of hens clucking and scratching about in the pen.

'I love chickens,' said Molly.

'Really? Well, I'd be happy to give you a few if you'd like to have 'em,' replied Rosie. 'I remember the folks that used to live in your house had a coop out back. Is it still there?'

Molly nodded. 'Yeah, but the roof needs some work.'

'Well, if your parents are okay with it and you can fix up the coop, I can spare six or eight pullets.'

Molly smiled. 'Yeah, I'll ask. Thanks.'

They emerged from the henhouse and Molly noticed a rough path leading into the forest beyond.

'That's the trail to Lough Beag,' said Rosie. 'Do you know about it?'

'Oh, yeah,' replied Molly. 'There's a trail from our house, too, right down to the shore. I love that place. It's so peaceful.'

Rosie smiled. 'Yeah. Cary and I used to walk down there when we were your age.'

Molly smiled. 'Was he your boyfriend back then?'

Rosie chuckled. 'Well, off and on. You know how those things go.' Their eyes met in agreement.

'Okay, Moll, well, see ya tomorrow in class.'

'Thanks, Ms O.'

Rosie watched as Molly started back down the drive, the carton of eggs in one hand, her hold-all in the other. Rosie was about to turn and go into the house when the white van passed by once again, this time headed back down the lane toward the town centre. It was moving very slowly. Maybe one of those grocery delivery services, Rosie was thinking. She suddenly felt impelled to stand and watch as Molly ambled up the lane a short distance, then turned into her drive. Rosie stood for several minutes thinking and feeling a bit uneasy.

* * *

Over her morning tea Catherine McGurk opened the new edition of the *Glenkerry Gazette.* She sat smiling as she read her son's editorial on immigration in Ireland.

FUGITIVES FROM INJUSTICE:
IMMIGRATION IN IRELAND TODAY

Ciaran McGurk, Editor, Glenkerry Gazette

Over the last month I have had the privilege of meeting and speaking with a number of recent arrivals to Ireland from Ukraine, Syria, and Afghanistan. I have listened to their stories—stories of fear and sadness—of courage and conviction—of hope and joy. I have shared those experiences in several recent issues of the Glenkerry Gazette. The response has been heartening. It is clear that the great majority of readers are pleased that Ireland has been able to provide assistance to refugees and asylum-seekers arriving in Ireland from war-torn regions around the world.

We can all be proud of our country's response to the humanitarian crisis in Ukraine resulting from the February 2022 invasion by Russia. From the start Ukrainians fleeing that conflict have been welcomed in Ireland. Immigration Services has implemented fast-track processing of these people while the Department of Justice and Equality has rushed to identify housing for them. Most Ukrainians have received financial support, medical care, assistance in job-hunting for adults, and school placement for children.

The problem of housing has been the greatest challenge in that effort. Ireland already finds itself unable to provide sufficient housing for its own citizens. How then to provide adequate housing for newly-arrived Ukrainians? And how, of course, to pay for all this?

Even as debate on the housing issue was going forward in the Dáil, around Ireland dozens of community groups were organising, searching for potential housing, then soliciting funds for purchase, renovation, and furnishing for those homes. In County Wicklow alone at least a dozen such groups have been at work. Among them is the Glenkerry Citizens for Justice whose goal it is to have six housing units available soon, three for Irish citizens and three for noncitizens.

According to the United Nations Commissioner for Refugees, Ireland has admitted 91,300 persons from Ukraine since the war began. That amounts to 1.8% of the population of Ireland, placing Ireland first among all the nations of western Europe. Only Germany is even close with 1.3%. By comparison the UK has accepted 0.3%.

The record of our nation regarding immigration has not always been so laudable. When war broke out in Syria and in Afghanistan, refugees and asylum-seekers were often housed in inadequate facilities, in some cases languishing for several years.

Many were forced to dine in canteens with little choice of food—some adults were prohibited from working—many children were placed in inadequate educational facilities. By all indications those lapses have been corrected. The Irish government assures us that all refugees in Ireland, from wherever they hail, are being treated humanely and respectfully.

There is a double benefit for Ireland when we welcome refugees, asylum-seekers, and others from distant lands. In addition to providing humanitarian assistance in their time of need, we also enrich ourselves as we get to know people with different languages and cultures. We benefit ourselves by getting to know them, live with them, share with them.

In To Kill a Mockingbird, that towering classic of racial prejudice, Atticus Finch, attorney for a black man wrongly accused of rape, says to his daughter, Scout, 'You never really understand a person until you consider things from his point of view—until you climb into his skin and walk around in it.'

Our ancestors of course endured similar hardships, the famines, the long war against the British, then the Troubles. Many Irish became refugees in those times, leaving Ireland, often with little more than the clothes on their backs, emigrating to England, America, Canada, Australia, New Zealand. With that history, we of all people should feel empathy for the refugees and asylum-seekers in our midst today. Their plight was once Ireland's—their struggle was the struggle of many Irish, at home and around the world.

In 2002, my father, Patrick L. McGurk, founder of the Gazette, wrote of the plight of the peoples of Afghanistan: 'Let us open our hearts and our homeland to these victims of war, to these fugitives from injustice.'

That evening Catherine McGurk was busy in her kitchen preparing a meal for Cary and Rosie. When Cary arrived she was peeling and deveining prawns. She looked up at him and smiled.

'That was a fine editorial, Car. Beautifully written and to the point. And the timing couldn't be better for the Citizens for Justice.'

She wiped her hands on her apron, then hugged him. 'And thanks for bringin' your da in at the end, so.'

Cary nodded. 'Well, a while back you were the one who told me to choose my battles carefully when it comes to editorials, remember?'

She smiled. 'Yup. Just like my Paddy always did.'

Just then Rosie appeared. Catherine hadn't seen her since her trip to Galway and she was anxious to know about Rosie's mother. Over dinner she asked about her recent visit with her mother and Gerry.

'So your ma is doin' well in Galway, love?'

Rosie smiled. 'Yeah, she is. I was tellin' Cary I've never seen her so happy. Gerry seems devoted to her. And they're planning a trip to Ibiza in December.'

Catherine knew too well how hard Mary O'Malley's life had been with Harry. 'I'm glad to hear it, love. Please tell her I was asking after 'er, so. And Buddy?'

'Yeah, he and Danielle are doin' fine. Still in Shankill.'

Catherine served up their meal, starting with a fresh prawn salad.

'So Aiden and Tom? Any news from New Zealand?' inquired Rosie.

'Tom is still recoverin' from Covid,' explained Catherine. 'He was pretty sick for some time. I Skyped with them the other day and he looked better. But he lost his job, he was sick for so long. So he's looking around now. But Aiden has a good job with a stock brokerage in Auckland, and they're about to buy a house.'

'Oh, Mrs M., that's wonderful.'

'Yes. I do hope Tom's health improves.'

Catherine served the main course, a seafood paella of her own creation. Paired with a white zinfandel.

'This is delicious,' offered Rosie.

Cary nodded. 'Yeah. Whatever's in this sauce, it's deadly, Ma.'

'Well, thank you. So Car tells me you've been doing some work on your family tree, Rosie?'

'Yeah, well, my ma and I stayed up late one night just talking about her Malone people. Mostly from Wexford and Waterford. Gerry was tellin' us about all these genealogy resources on the web these days and I thought I'd see what I can learn.'

'Oh, that would be interesting. Perhaps you could help me to look up some of the McGurks and Flanagans one day?'

'I'd love to, Mrs M. Any time. It's really fascinating.'

After their meal, Cary walked Rosie home.

'I gotta go to Wexford in the morning,' he explained before they said goodnight. 'But I'll be back in time for your match, I promise.'

24 SHOWDOWN

Classes ended at 1:30 on Friday and Rosie used the time before the match to rearrange her room, pulling buckets and boxes of clay, plasticene, and papier-mâché out of the storage closet. Just then Gráinne appeared at the classroom door.

'So what's all this for?' she asked.

'Gettin' ready fer next week. We'll be doing pottery and sculpture.'

'Oh, yeah? That'll be cool. Need help?'

'Thanks, Gran, but I'm pretty much done here.'

Gráinne sat in a chair. 'Can I talk to yeh, Ms O.?'

'Yeah, sure, what's up?' replied Rosie, still busy stacking art materials in banquettes.

'I got a problem–with a boy–Brendan–you know, Brendan–from Visual Arts?'

'Uh-huh. What about 'im?'

'He texts me–constantly.'

'Oh?'

'At first I played along and may have said a few things that were, uh, maybe inappropriate.'

'Oh?'

'And now he's sendin' me pictures. I want him to stop. They're gross.'

'Well, have yeh tol' yer dad?'

'Obviously not–that'd be embarrassing.'

'Show me,' said Rosie.

'But we're not supposed to use our mobiles on school property.'

'Never mind–just show me.'

Gráinne shook her head. 'You don't wanna…'

'Show me just one, okay?'

Gráinne drew her mobile from her backpack, turned it on, and swiped the screen several times. Then she handed it to Rosie. It was a selfie of Brendan shirtless.

Gráinne blushed. 'They get worse.'

'Gran, that's harassment, yeh know? What are yeh, sixteen?'

'Almost. But I don't want to make a big deal of it. He's okay. And maybe I'm a little responsible, yeh know?'

'What do yeh mean? Did you send him some pictures?'

'No, no, I swear–nothin' like that. But maybe he thought I was flirtin' or something, yeh know, leadin' him on.'

'Okay. Listen to me.' Rosie sat down facing Gráinne. 'First thing to do is tell him to stop. Yeah? And tell him if he doesn't stop, you'll report him. If he's smart, he'll pay attention to that. They tell you about this stuff, don't they, in SPHE?' she said, referring to Social, Personal, and Health Education, a required class for all *Coláiste* students.

Gráinne nodded. Meanwhile a contact list had popped up on Gráinne's mobile. Something caught Rosie's eye.

'Gran–who's Mikhail? Mikhail-R?' she asked, pointing to one name on the list.

'Oh, that's Mike–Mike Boyle. That's his username. His parents won't let him have a mobile. So he sends email messages.'

'Like Brendan's?'

'Oh, no, he's nothin' like Brendan. He's really cool.'

'Hmm. So you and Mike Boyle, eh?'

Gráinne blushed, then shook her head. 'We're strictly in the friend zone–honest. We hang out, is all. Timmy 'n me go up to theirs sometimes. And Mike 'n Molly came to ours last weekend and we had a little kickabout in the yard. Mike's really good at footie. Timmy likes Molly a bit, I think. And she seems to like him.' She shook her head. 'I can't imagine why.'

Gráinne took the mobile and tapped it a few times, then showed Rosie an email message from Mike. 'Him and Timmy play Fortnite on weekends with this friend of Mike's from his old school–Rashid. Last week Mike emailed me to see if I wanted to play.' Gráinne shook her head and chuckled. 'I passed. I just don't get it, yeh know?'

'Yeah, well, boys, eh? If Mike likes football I'm kinda surprised he's not playin' sports at *Coláiste*.'

'He's not allowed to play contact sports–at least that's what he told Timmy. He said he has that post-stress thingy.'

'You mean PTSD? Post-traumatic stress disorder?'

Gráinne nodded. 'He told Timmy there was an explosion in his grammar school once.'

'An explosion? You mean in Cork where they lived?'

'I guess. I dunno.'

Now Rosie was trying hard to act nonchalant as she finished her cleanup. 'So have you ever met Molly and Mike's father?'

'Yeah. His name's Chris.'

'I've met Mrs Boyle–Anna–a few times, but never Chris.'

'He seems nice, but Molly says he works 24/7 in his home office–he like never goes out. Plus he's Muslim so he observes all these holy days and does his prayers. Molly said he couldn't go with her and Mike and their ma to see Ashling Thompson play in Cork because it was some big Muslim holiday.'

Gráinne stood up. 'Well, I gotta bounce.'

'Be sure to tell Brendan to stop, Gran. You have to. And Gran, don't ever send him pictures of you–ever. You hear me?'

Gráinne nodded. 'Thanks, Rosie. I mean Ms O. Without my ma, I got no one ta talk to about this stuff, yeh know?' Gráinne's mother, Nancy Phinney, had died of cancer three years ago.

Rosie nodded. 'Any time.'

Gráinne nodded. 'See you at the match.'

After Gráinne left, Rosie stood looking out her classroom window, thinking over what she had just learned, not sure what to make of it. She drew out her mobile and tried to call Cary–she reached his voice mail.

'Hey, it's me. Listen, I gotta talk with you, about Molly–and the Boyles. There's something not right there, I'm not sure what, but I got this feeling maybe they're hiding from something, or someone, that maybe they're in danger. Could you…'

Just then her mobile went dead–a flat battery. Match time was fast approaching. Finally she locked up her room, changed into her assistant coach kit, and headed out to the GAA grounds across the High Street.

* * *

With the shrill sound of the referee's whistle the match began and both teams wasted no time joining the fray. Camogie is a non-contact sport, but anyone who knew the Hurleys could tell they were more charged up, more aggressive, than usual.

The Hurley offence controlled the sliotar much of the time in the early minutes, carrying play upfield again and again. Robyn scored a goal, putting the Hurleys ahead, 3-0. But after that the Montkilleen defence presented a solid wall and the few shots that Isla, Katie, and Ava were able to get off went wide of the goal. The Montkilleen goalkeeper impressed with her puck-outs that she struck long and accurately to her teammates beyond midfield.

Midway through the period the momentum seemed to shift to the Montkilleen team as they scored two goals barely a minute apart–the Hurleys trailed, 3-6. Now the pressure was on and the next time the Hurleys brought the ball upfield, Isla was there, front and centre, as usual, ready to receive the ball. But suddenly she had three defenders clustered about her like bees around their queen. Isla attempted to strike the ball but was blocked. Ava retrieved it, then passed it back to Isla who was blocked yet again. Her frustration now showing, Isla swung wildly for the sliotar but missed it, instead striking one of the Montkilleen players on the shin. The referee issued a warning to Isla.

In the closing minutes of the first period Gráinne and Eileen ran the ball along the sideline, deftly exchanging it again and again around their defenders. Then Eileen passed the ball to Isla. A cluster of defenders surrounded Isla, dispossessing her once again. A few seconds later the ball came to Katie who spun around and struck the ball straight toward the goal. The goalkeeper was there and about to block the ball when Gráinne struck it in midflight, sending it just beyond the goalkeeper's reach and into the net. Less than a minute later Eileen struck the ball through the uprights for another point. The Hurleys were in the lead, 7-6, as the first period ended.

Most of the team were exuberant as they headed to the sideline, but Isla was red-faced and uncharacteristically glum. Sabrina gathered them around her.

'All right, girls, a cracker first period–good defence, grand offence. Keep it up now. The pressure is on Montkilleen to keep the play at their end. Bank of six, be strong, okay? And everyone be ready to tackle–make life miserable for 'em.' The Hurleys broke from their huddle with a loud cheer. But Sabrina could see that Isla was not sharing the joy.

'Isla, a word?' she said. The girl could be surly and independent, but she also respected her coach's authority and knowledge of the sport. She seemed to be listening to what Sabrina had to say.

'They're all over you, Isla, I know. They're double- and triple-teaming you. I think their coach is under the mistaken impression that if they can keep you in check, the rest of the team won't be much of a threat.'

Sabrina's strategy for the second period was this: any time Isla saw the Montkilleen team shifting their defence her way, she was to move toward the sideline, away from the action, taking several defending players with her.

'If you do that,' explained Sabrina, 'I think they'll be in for a surprise from the rest of our offence. Do you see what I mean?'

In other words, Sabrina was asking Isla to be prepared to sacrifice herself, to relinquish her central role in the offence, when necessary for the good of the team.

Isla nodded but would not look Sabrina in the eye. She walked away without a word.

Sabrina told Rosie of her strategy as they watched the team taking the pitch for the second period.

'I know Isla likes to be at the centre of the action. But she also wants to win. And she's smart enough to see that too much of a focus by Montkilleen on defending against her could give the Hurleys an advantage.'

Rosie understood. 'Yeah, I get that. Our guys have come a long way since that match against Arklow when Isla was out sick, haven't they?'

Sabrina nodded. 'You know, I was really worried that day,' she said in a hushed voice. 'But now I'm beginning to think that Isla's absence for those two matches was actually good for the team. It forced the younger players to be more assertive–it gave them more confidence. Yeah, you're right, Rosie, they're now the "new and improved Hurleys." '

At that moment Rosie saw Cary on the sideline and waved to him. She wanted to speak to him, to tell him of her concerns about Molly and the Boyles. But then the whistle blew and the second period began.

As Sabrina had predicted, the Montkilleen offence came back strong right from the throw-out, carrying the play up to the goal several times. But the Hurleys' defence were ready with blocks and clashes. Molly and Kelly each managed to hook their opponents' shots. But finally the Montkilleen left corner-forward struck the ball through the uprights. The match was tied, 7-7.

The Hurleys quickly recovered, moving the ball upfield. Eileen passed it to Isla who once again found herself with three defenders crowding her on all sides. She tried to strike the ball through the uprights, but her hurley was blocked by one of the defenders. She recovered the ball, then attempted to strike it off to Ava. In the process Isla's elbow struck the girl in the ribs.

'Rough play, number 7.' He held up a yellow card.

'Isla,' shouted Sabrina. The girl did not respond. Again Sabrina called to her. No response. A minute later the Hurley defence had done their job, moving the ball up the pitch yet again. Molly received a pass, pivoted, and passed it to Isla. But once again there was a crowd of defenders around her, one of whom knocked the ball down right in front of her. In the scrum that followed Isla threw herself at the girl, knocking her to the ground. The girl lay motionless for a moment. Then a whistle blew. The referee pointed to Isla.

'Pushing, number 7,' he called. Then he held up a red card. Isla had been expelled from the match. She stalked off the pitch at the far end.

Sabrina groaned.

Montkilleen took a free, carrying the ball well down the pitch, but Megan intercepted it, dribbled along the sideline, then struck it to Gráinne. Gráinne slapped the ball back to Allegra, the right half-forward, who in turn passed it to Katie near the goal. Katie struck the ball through the uprights, putting the Hurleys ahead by a point.

'Way to go, Katie, Allegra,' shouted Sabrina. Rosie shook her head in amazement at what had just happened.

A few minutes later a free by Ava was received by Sofia who struck it through the uprights for another point. The Hurleys now led by two points 9-7.

In the last two minutes of play the Montkilleen offence once again dominated and managed to score a goal, taking the lead, 9-10.

The Hurleys now took control as Willow and Ava carried the ball along the left sideline. Ava took a shot on the goal that went far wide. The Montkilleen goalkeeper pucked the ball well beyond midfield but it was intercepted by Ella who passed it off to Gráinne. Gráinne passed it to Sofia who passed the ball to Katie who was all alone. Katie quickly turned and struck the ball into the net. The Hurleys had regained the lead by two points. Before the Montkilleen team could get a chance at another score, the whistle blew. Final score, 12-10. The Hurleys had prevailed.

* * *

The players were boisterous as they walked together across the High Street to Kelly's for a celebratory ice cream cone. But Isla was nowhere to be found.

'Yeh done yerselves proud–and Glenkerry, too,' declared Jim Kelly, the proprietor, as the girls approached his stand. 'Free cones for the lot of yeh!' Everyone, the team as well as onlookers, cheered wildly. Horns blared from passing cars–it seems word of the Hurleys' victory had already spread around the town.

Back at the GAA grounds, Cary was helping Rosie and Sabrina return equipment to the storage shed.

'Those guys were brilliant, Sabrina,' offered Cary. 'Just brilliant.'

'Well, I'd have to say I agree. They did things today I never saw them do before. They were really on it, every minute. They must have dispossessed Montkilleen a dozen times in the second period. And practically every one of their shots scored.'

Rosie spoke to Cary. 'Did yeh get my message, Car?' He shook his head.

'I had a strange conversation with Gráinne,' she began. 'It's got me worried…'

But just then Del appeared.

'By the looks on your faces, I'm guessing the Hurleys won, yeah?' said Del.

'Oh, Del, they were unbelievable,' replied Sabrina.

The four walked through the gates and into the car park together, then crossed the street to join the ice cream celebration. Gráinne and Mike were seated on a bench enjoying their cones as were Timmy and Molly who were standing a bit awkwardly nearby.

At that moment Seamus, Bart, and Mike, the house band at Phinney's (band name: 'Seamus, Bart, and Mike') emerged from the bar, instruments in hand, and joined the celebration, playing a rousing rendition of 'Come On Eileen.' Several of the Hurleys joined in the chorus, then launched into a hilarious dance to the tune as bystanders clapped along.

Finally the crowd began to disperse. Molly finished her cone and spoke to her brother. Then she and Timmy started walking along the High Street together, Timmy carrying Molly's hold-all over one shoulder, Molly carrying her hurley. Rosie nudged Cary and nodded toward the pair.

* * *

Cary turns and sees Tim and Molly shambling side-by-side along the footpath past a row of parked cars, the last of which is a white delivery van. As Cary watches, the van starts moving slowly in the same direction as the pair. Suddenly a man with a dark hoodie drawn down over his face jumps out of the van, leaving the sliding door open. He grabs Molly's arm and pulls her toward the open van door. Molly screams.

'Del! Sabrina!' shouts Cary. And in an instant the three are racing down the street toward the van with Rosie only a few steps behind.

In those few seconds the hooded figure forces Molly through the sliding door, struggling to wrest the hurley from her with one hand while trying to slide the door shut with the other. But at that moment Del throws himself into the gap, then lunges at the driver, pulling his hands from the steering wheel just as the van accelerates. Tyres squeal, the vehicle lurches, then smashes into a parked car and comes to a halt. Molly's attacker is thrown to the floor of the van by the impact and Molly seizes the opportunity to jam the hurley hard into his gut, then leaps out of the van. Sabrina draws her onto the footpath where Timmy and Gráinne gather around her in disbelief.

Meanwhile the driver has pushed his door open and is about to make a run for it only to find Cary and Jim Kelly standing in his way. They throw him to the pavement, pinning him down until Del cuffs him. By then the man with the hoodie has jumped out of the passenger door and is racing away down the High Street.

Sabrina sees him fleeing but hesitates. 'You okay, Molly?' she asks.

Rosie is now holding Molly's arms trying to reassure her. 'We got her, Sabrina, go ahead,' she shouts, gesturing toward the runner who is already a half dozen storefronts away.

With Molly in good hands, Sabrina takes off down the street in pursuit of the runner, all the while talking into her radio. With lightning speed she manages to overtake him right in front of the *Gazette* office. Throwing him to the pavement, she pins him with an arm lock and a knee in the back.

In less than a minute two gardaí from the Glenkerry station come running up the street followed seconds later by two garda patrol cars.

An eerie silence falls over the scene as the half dozen gardaí load the pair into patrol cars, make U turns, then proceed slowly down the High Street past the team members and other bystanders. As they pass, the crowd cheers the gardaí and offers some rude gestures toward the perpetrators.

* * *

Bewildered by what had just taken place, the entire team encircled Molly. She appeared to be calm through the mayhem while her brother was looking pale and unsteady. Rosie nodded to Cary who took Mike's arm, then they led brother and sister into Phinney's and sat them in comfortable chairs by the fireplace. Mike sat with his head between his knees.

Just then Sabrina appeared. 'I've got their mom's mobile number. I'll try to reach her.' And she walked a few steps away to make the call.

'Who were those guys?' Rosie asked Cary. 'Do you have any idea?'

Cary was still shaking but he nodded. 'I don't know who the driver was, but that other guy was the one in the grey Skoda–I'm sure of it. I saw that tattoo on his arm just as he took off up the street.'

'I saw that van drive up the lane yesterday, going real slow,' replied Rosie. 'I had this eerie feeling about it. They must've been watching Molly and me. So they wanted to take Molly?'

Cary nodded. 'Yeah, I think so. That must have been why he was tailing me. But I don't know why they wanted Molly. I don't get it.'

'I think maybe I do,' said Rosie.

25 STILL PROCESSING

nna Boyle arrived on the scene quickly accompanied by a tall man with dark hair, both looking ashen and grim-faced. They hugged Molly and Mike, reassuring themselves that they were uninjured. Then Anna turned to Rosie.

'Ms O'Malley, this is my husband, Chris.'

Rosie smiled. 'I'm so sorry about all this.'

Chris spoke. 'Thank you for taking care of our kids, you and the guards.' He nodded toward Del and Sabrina who were standing apart talking.

'This is Cary McGurk, a friend,' said Rosie. 'He tackled one of those men, right on the street.'

'Well, thank you, Cary,' responded Anna. 'We don't understand what happened here.'

Just then Sabrina approached them. 'This must be your husband,' she said to Anna.

'Yes. Chris, this is Coach Selkirk–she's also Garda Selkirk.' She turned to Sabrina and Rosie. 'We should've been here. Perhaps none of this would have happened if…' She shook her head while hugging her daughter.

Sabrina urged them to go home, that a garda would visit them the next morning for a debriefing. As the four Boyles walked away toward their car, Cary was watching them closely. What was it about Chris that seemed vaguely familiar to him?

Soon the black Range Rover was pulling away. Sabrina was now talking into her radio while Del was engaged with Garda Keough.

Rosie caught Sabrina's eye. 'We're goin' along, Coach. Let me know if we can do anything, yeah?'

Sabrina nodded, still listening to someone on the radio.

* * *

Rosie and Cary walked the short distance to 1 Upton Road, both still shaken by the events they had witnessed. They sat in Cary's kitchen sipping tea.

'You okay?' asked Cary.

'Gettin' there,' replied Rosie. 'You?'

'Yeah, but I still don't understand what that was all about,' he admitted.

'Well, I have a guess,' replied Rosie as she sipped her tea. Gráinne came to see me after class today, before the match. She was upset about this boy who's been sexting her.'

'Really.'

'Yeah, I just gave her some, yeh know, sisterly advice.'

'Not about how to take better selfies, I hope.'

Rosie cast him a sly look. 'No, a course not. But she told me some things about the Boyles that got me to wonderin'. That's what I was tryin' to tell you when my mobile died.'

She recounted her conversation with Gráinne, about Mike and his username, about his friend Rashid, and his PTSD. Then she repeated what Gráinne had said about Mike and Molly's father.

'Plus Sabrina discovered that the school never received Molly's records from Cork.'

'What are you thinkin', Rose?'

'The Boyles, Car, there's something about them–I think maybe they're hiding from something–or someone.'

She took another sip of her tea.

'I'm thinkin' they aren't Irish–that they entered Ireland illegally–maybe from the Middle East. That would explain Mike's username, Mikhail, his friend Rashid. And the PTSD? Maybe they were in a war zone somewhere.'

'Like Syria?'

'Maybe.'

Now Cary was gazing out the window, momentarily distracted. 'Yeh know Chris?' he began. Rosie nodded. 'He looked familiar somehow. Something about him…'

Cary looked at Rosie with a startled expression. He went to his laptop, opened his email, and showed Rosie a photo.

'Del just sent me this. It's from CCTV the night Kristoff Rahmann was killed.'

'Yeah?'

'That's him, Rosie, I swear, that's Chris Boyle. At least the hair and the shape of his head look about the same. Plus Del said on the CCTV you could see that he walked with a limp. I saw that, as he walked to their car just now–that's what rang a bell.'

'What are you sayin', Car? That Chris Boyle is the guy on the CCTV? The one the gardaí are looking for?'

'Maybe–possibly.'

'But Car–how can that be? It doesn't make sense. Look, he's a husband–a father.' Rosie shook her head. 'A murderer? I can't believe it.'

'Well, I know what yeh mean, Rose, but it looks like he was there, headed for the Black Castle, just a few minutes before midnight. With that other guy. If the medical examiner's report is correct, Kristoff Rahmann died right about that time.'

'If what you say is true, then the Boyles are in trouble, aren't they?' asked Rosie. 'Unless we, yeh know, keep it to ourselves.'

'Yep, right. But if the gardaí find out that we knew, that could be very bad for me. I've already been warned about withholding information. I could be charged–I could go to jail, Rose.'

Rosie took his hand and drew him down onto the couch. She looked into his eyes. 'Yeah, I get that, Car, I do. We have to tell the gardai–a course. But let's just think about this a bit, yeah?'

She took a deep breath.

'Yeh know, the minute we tell them what we know, there'll be a parade of garda cars headin' up the lane. Can you imagine if Molly and Mike had to watch their father bein' collared and cuffed?'

'So what should we do, then. Just sit on this?' he asked.

Rosie was looking out the window onto the High Street. 'I don't know, I just don't feel right about turning this over to the gardaí, not quite yet.' She sighed. 'I know Anna Boyle a bit, mainly through the Hurleys. She seems nice, and I think she trusts me. How about if I talk to her, maybe go to the house and see her?'

'And do what, Rose? Tell her we're grassing on her husband?'

'I don't know, Car. But let's just think on it for a while.'

Cary made them supper, reheating some of Catherine's paella from the previous evening. They were cleaning up when Rosie's mobile rang.

'Anna, yes. No, this is fine. Is everything okay? How are Molly and Mike?'

She listened.

'Good, yup, we were worried.'

Anna continued.

'Well, I guess. Can you wait a minute?'

She turned to Cary. 'Anna and Chris Boyle would like to talk to us, in the morning, early. Okay?'

Cary nodded.

'Yes, Anna, we'll be there. Uh-huh. Yep. No problem. See you about eight.'

The call ended, Rosie slumped onto the couch. Cary sat next to her.

'Anna and Chris are planning to go to the garda station tomorrow morning. To turn themselves in. She says they are both in Ireland illegally.'

Cary nodded.

'She said they realised that if the gardaí come to their house to ask about yesterday, they'll figure it out soon enough. And it might be better for them to turn themselves in first.'

'Yeah, I guess so. So what do they want with us?'

'They want us to stay with Molly and Mike and keep them occupied. She says they'll tell them what they're doing before they go.'

Rosie grimaced. 'But what if they arrest Anna and Chris? They wouldn't just leave the kids with us, would they?'

'I can't imagine they would do that. I suppose they'd get someone from Social Services to come until another family member could be contacted.'

'I can't stand the thought of those kids being separated from their parents, Car.'

'If it's just an immigration violation, I should think Anna and her husband would be released until they have to appear in court.'

'Yeah, I hope so. But Car, there might be more to this, lots more.'

'What do you mean, Rose?'

'Anna and Chris Boyle–those aren't their real names.'

'Oh?'

'Remember how I said that my cousin, Megan, and her husband from Pakistan were married twice? Once in Pakistan and once in Ireland?'

'Yeah. Okay.'

Rosie then described her discovery. As surprising as the events of this day had already been, this was even more surprising.

26 'THERE MUST BE SOME MISTAKE!'

Early the next morning Rosie and Cary walked together up Anglesey Lane, then turned in the drive to the house they both had known as the O'Donnell farm. They walked down the long winding way through a grove of tall Norway spruce until finally the farmhouse came into view.

A grim-faced Anna Boyle stepped out onto the front walk.

'Rosie, Cary, come through, please.' She led them into the cool interior. 'Please, have a seat,' she said as they entered the sitting room. Just then Chris Boyle appeared in the doorway. He smiled and extended his hand to each.

'So, Anna tells me you're Molly's art teacher,' he said to Rosie. 'She loves art.'

'She's very talented, I can tell you that.'

Chris smiled. 'I'm afraid I can't take any credit for that. I'm hopeless when it comes to art.'

'Well, I've enjoyed getting to know her, both in Visual Arts and with the Hurleys. I'm the assistant coach–uh, the *unofficial* assistant coach.'

'Yes, with Garda Selkirk. At first we were uneasy about Molly having a member of the guard as a coach. But Molly loves the game–and she adores you and Ms Selkirk.'

'And I've met Mike once or twice. He's gonna be as tall as his father one of these days I bet.'

'Yes, he will be,' responded Chris with a smile. 'I already miss the days when I could pick him up and toss him in the air.'

They all laughed. Then Chris's smile faded.

'Thank you, both of you, for all you did yesterday. Molly tells us that Cary single-handedly stopped the driver and pinned him down until the guard arrived.'

Cary shook his head. 'Jim Kelly, too. I couldn't have done it alone.'

'And you two stayed with Molly and Mike until we arrived. That was very kind of you both.'

'Of course, they're great kids. And Gardas Samuels and Selkirk were both busy.'

Chris then spoke. 'So, as Anna told you on the phone, we've decided not to wait for the gardaí to come to interview us about yesterday. We're going to them. It seems best, especially for the kids. We've told them what we plan to do. But we assured them we'd only be gone an hour or two–I wish we could be sure of that.'

Anna spoke to Cary. 'As I told Rosie on the phone, we're in Ireland illegally. So we've decided to turn ourselves in to the gardaí and to Immigration Services. And Chris's brother Kamal has agreed to do the same.'

Rosie and Cary exchanged surprised glances. A brother, Kamal?

'We've decided that we have to throw ourselves on the mercy of the Irish authorities. We think it would be better if we go to them rather than wait for them to come here. I'd hate for them to arrive and make a scene in front of the children.'

Rosie winced. 'Of course.'

Then Chris spoke. 'As Anna said, we're in Ireland illegally–we have been for nearly ten years. We have no choice–we've got to turn ourselves in.'

'What–what's likely to happen?' asked Rosie nervously.

'We don't know. We just don't know. And we're worried sick about the children. I mean, they could end up in care,' said Anna, a look of dread in her eyes. 'But maybe if we turn ourselves in, maybe that will weigh in our favour.'

'You two apparently know your way around Glenkerry,' said Chris. 'Maybe you can suggest who we should talk to.'

'Well, there's Garda Selkirk of course,' said Rosie.

'And we know Garda Samuels, too,' added Cary. 'But if you approach either of them, I'm sure they'll have to turn the matter over very quickly to their superiors. I also know Superintendent Lewis a little. He's right here in Glenkerry. He's a reasonable man and I believe he'll give you a fair hearing. But no doubt he'll have to refer this to his Chief Superintendent in Wicklow, or to Immigration Services.'

'Okay,' said Chris, 'well maybe we should start with Superintendent Lewis. And we won't mention your names. We'll simply say that we're tired of being on the run, of living a lie.'

Anna sighed. 'That's why we asked if you two could be here. Just to keep Molly and Mike company and reassure them. I'm an Irish citizen, so we're hoping that they will take that into consideration.'

Cary's brow was knit. 'If you're an Irish citizen, then you're not here illegally, are you?'

'Yes, I'm afraid so. You see, Anna and Chris Boyle are not our real names. But it's a long story. We'd best tell it first to the gardaí.' Rosie nodded. She'd already figured that out.

Just then Molly and Mike appeared.

'Are you sure you don't mind staying with these two?' asked Chris. 'They can be a handful, yeh know,' he added with a grin as he tousled Mike's hair.

'No, not at all.'

* * *

Rosie and Cary spent several hours with Molly and Mike awaiting the return of Anna and Chris Boyle. First the four went outside and kicked a football around. Later inside Molly served tea and scones with Rosie's help. Then Mike challenged Cary to a video game while Molly showed Rosie her room and some of her artwork. Again Rosie was struck by how calm Molly appeared, considering what she had been through yesterday and what was going on at the garda station barely a kilometre away.

Finally the Range Rover returned. Anna got out. Molly ran to her and hugged her while Mike looked on uneasily.

'Your father's still being questioned,' she said. 'It could take a while.'

'Are they gonna let him come home?' asked Mike, looking very worried.

'I don't know, hon, I really don't know. They need to talk to your Uncle Kamal, too–he's coming from Dublin with a solicitor. And Garda Samuels and Garda Keough will be calling round to ask you two about yesterday. They'll be here soon.' She looked at Rosie and Cary. 'They may want to speak to Ms O'Malley and Mr McGurk as well.'

Anna wrapped her arms around Molly and Mike and kissed them each. 'Go, have a kickabout, eh?'

She led Rosie and Cary inside. They sat in the sitting room and Anna began to speak. But she was having difficulty keeping her emotions in check. After several minutes she looked up.

'Superintendent Lewis was very nice, as you said. He listened to our story very patiently. And he seemed to understand the situation with Syrian refugees in Ireland. You see, Chris is Syrian.'

Rosie nodded.

'The Superintendent admitted that the treatment of Syrians in those reception centres was disgraceful.'

She swallowed hard, then continued. 'He said they would have to refer the matter to Immigration Services. But he assured us that we would get fair treatment. It's out of his hands, he said. But he doesn't believe anyone is being deported to Syria these days, in light of the situation there.'

She sighed. 'I don't know where it will end. But after yesterday it seems like our only hope, like I said, is to throw ourselves on the mercy of the folks at Immigration Services. I'm of course an Irish citizen. Which is probably why they released me. Whether Chris will be allowed to go, I don't know.'

She started to cry. Rosie sat next to her and took her hand.

'I'm sorry. It's just–we–we've been living in fear for so long, first in Syria, then in Ireland. And it's been hard–on us all. I'm sure you've sensed that the kids have suffered. Chris and I feel very guilty about that.'

She sighed deeply.

'But honestly, I'm glad that we're doing this. We couldn't go on the way we've been. We just couldn't.'

Rosie spoke softly. 'Well, whatever happens, Anna, we–Cary and me–and I bet everyone in Glenkerry–will be wanting to help however we can.'

'Thank you. Yes, as soon as we moved to Glenkerry, we felt–or imagined we felt–safe and secure. Until yesterday, anyway.'

'Did you grow up here, in Glenkerry?'

'Well, not exactly, no. In Dublin. But I spent several summers here–with my grandparents.'

'I remember them, Anna. My ma knew them both. She'd have them over for tea now and then.'

'So you can imagine that this house, this town, all feel very comfortable to me.'

Just then a garda car appeared in the drive. Anna immediately went to the door, followed by Cary and Rosie. Molly and Mike soon appeared as well, anxious to see their father. But it was Del Samuels and Garda Riley from the Glenkerry station.

'Where is my husband?' asked Anna fearfully.

Del smiled at her and spoke softly. 'Ma'am, Mr Boyle is still being questioned at the station. I saw him just before we left. He asked me to tell you that he's okay, that everything will be okay.'

'When will they let him come home?'

'Well, it depends, ma'am. They can hold them–Mr Boyle and his brother–for up to twenty-four hours without charging them. We're here to talk to your daughter and son–and to Cary and Rosie–about yesterday. Just routine stuff–just to be sure we understand what happened.'

Just then three more garda cars arrived.

'But Mrs Boyle, Superintendent Lewis has a warrant to search your home,' explained Del.

'What?'

'So we're gonna need you all to remain outside, all right?'

'But why?'

'It's just a routine part of the investigation.'

'Is it really necessary, Garda Samuels?'

'Yes ma'am. It's, yeh know, an investigation of a suspicious death, a possible murder.'

'What? Who died?' said Anna with alarm.

'Why, ma'am, I thought you knew. Kristoff Rahmann.'

Anna looked at him incredulously.

'Your husband is being questioned,' continued Del, 'regarding his role in the death of Kristoff Rahmann.'

'But officer,' replied Anna, a look of desperation in her eyes, 'there must be some mistake.'

27 MARRIAGE RITES

Del and Garda Walsh sat in the garden talking to Molly and Mike about the events of the previous day while Anna looked on. Had they seen that van previously? he asked. Had they seen either of the men before? Had anything unusual occurred in recent days that might have any connection to the event? Had either of the kids engaged in any online activities lately that might have been connected? Neither Molly nor Mike could offer any clues. Their mother sat quietly, looking uneasy.

The other four gardaí spent nearly an hour searching the farmhouse. Then they departed, taking with them two bags containing items they had collected in the search. That included two laptops, two mobiles, and a pair of boots.

After they left, Del concluded his conversation with the young Boyles. He promised Anna he would be in touch as soon as he knew anything about the status of her husband and his brother.

'By the way,' added Del. 'Those two goons in the white van have been charged with attempted kidnapping and a number of other offences. If convicted they'll probably go to prison–for a long time.'

Before he departed Del spoke to Cary and Rosie.

'We'll need to talk to you guys, too, maybe tomorrow? I'll be in touch. No worries, yeah? Just routine.'

Rosie spoke up. 'Listen, Del, Anna's right–the gardaí are making a mistake. Look.'

She showed him an image on her mobile.

'What's that?'

'It's a marriage certificate, in Dublin, April, 2004. The bride's name was Evelyn O'Donnell. This is Evelyn's grandparents' house. Remember, the O'Donnells who lived here?'

Del was struggling to take in all this information.

'So what are you sayin', Rosie?'

'Evelyn O'Donnell–that's Anna Boyle, Del. And that's her husband.' She pointed to the groom's name. 'Kristoff Rahmann. Chris Boyle *is* Kristoff Rahmann.'

Del stood motionless, staring at Rosie in disbelief.

'Run that by me again, Rosie.'

'The Boyles are the Rahmanns–Evelyn and Kristoff Rahmann.'

'Where'd you find this?' he asked, bewildered, squinting into the screen of her mobile.

'From the Civil Registration Service database. It's public information, yeh know?'

He turned to Cary. 'I thought you said the Rahmanns were married in Syria.'

'They were,' replied Cary. 'But Rosie discovered that they were also married in Dublin a few weeks later.'

'So the husband and the kids would be eligible for Irish citizenship,' explained Rosie.

Del was still looking confused. 'Okay, let's just say for a moment that you're right. If that's true, if Kristoff Rahmann is the man being questioned at the station right now, then who was that guy Cary found on Travelhawk Beach? And why did he have Kristoff's identification card on his person?'

'We don't know, Del. But I'm guessing Anna and Chris will be able to shed some light on that.'

Del spoke privately to Anna. They could see her nodding, as if confirming what he was saying. Finally Del and Garda Keough departed.

Anna looked wearily at Rosie and Cary.

'How did you know?'

Rosie showed her the marriage certificate on her mobile.

'Well, I should have been up front with you and told you the full truth before asking you to come this morning. We had been hoping to avoid telling the gardaí our real names.'

Rosie shook her head. 'I still don't understand why you entered Ireland illegally under assumed names, Anna. Not that it's any of my business.'

Cary spoke up. 'It must have something to do with Syria, right?'

Anna nodded. 'I'll explain it all, I promise. Once Chris is back home safe and sound. You folks should go along now. We'll be okay, I think.'

Cary nodded to Rosie.

'Call me, Anna, if you need anything,' said Rosie as they departed.

* * *

Rosie and Cary sat in the O'Malley kitchen sipping tea.

'Well, Rosie, you were right. You sussed it, before me, even before the gardai.'

'Like I told you last night, it was Gráinne's mobile that tipped me off. Mike's username–and his friend named Rashid–that's when I started to put the pieces together. That maybe Mike and Molly were born in Syria–that it must have been in Syria that Mike's school was bombed. That maybe Anna and Chris decided they had to leave. That they emigrated to Ireland, Anna's home–under assumed identities.'

Cary took up the narrative. 'Right. They were afraid someone would come after them, some Syrian operatives or something. And maybe that's just what happened yesterday.'

Rosie nodded. 'Yeah, and it was my ma's stories about my cousin Megan that was my next clue. Megan, in Limerick? I told you about her, right?'

'The one who married a Pakistani man?'

'Yeah. My ma was telling me they had two weddings. First in Pakistan, then, a few weeks later, they came to Ireland and were married in a church in Dublin. Maybe in part because her parents wanted them to have a Catholic wedding. But Ma said there was another reason. They wanted to be legally married in Ireland–that way her husband and their children could apply for Irish citizenship one day. Which they did a few years later.'

'Uh-huh. And Anna and Chris must have done the same.'

'Right.'

Last evening, while Cary watched, Rosie started tapping on her mobile, searching for the names Christopher and Anna Boyle in the Civil Registration Service database in Dublin thinking it might explain the Syrian connection. No joy. But suddenly it occurred to her to search for the name Kristoff Rahmann. Within minutes she had downloaded a copy of Kristoff's marriage certificate from Dublin in 2004.

'And of course, as soon as I saw Kristoff's wife's parents and grandparents, I made the connection to Glenkerry.' Anna–Evelyn

O'Donnell–was the daughter of Herbert and Eileen O'Donnell. Those names weren't familiar. But the witnesses shown on the marriage certificate were Daniel and Maura O'Donnell of Glenkerry, the O'Donnells who lived just up the lane. I remember that they had several grandchildren who visited from time to time, although I never met them. Maura O'Donnell, Anna's grandmother, passed away just a year or so ago.'

'Then it hit me. The Boyles were the Rahmanns, living in Anna's grandparents' house two minutes' walk from here. So Kristoff Rahmann is the husband of Anna Boyle and the father of Molly and Mike.'

'So what happened to Molly yesterday?' wondered Cary.

Rosie nodded. 'Those guys were trying to kidnap Molly. Why, I don't know–but I'm betting it has something to do with her father. Maybe they hoped to use her to get at him.'

'So if Chris Boyle is Kristoff Rahmann, then who was that guy I found at Black Castle?' asked Cary. At that moment he was looking at his *Gazette* inbox. A new message had just appeared and he was reading it intently.

'What's that, Car?'

He didn't respond for several seconds. Finally he looked up at Rosie.

'It's a press release from the gardaí.' He read it to her.

'A body found on a beach in Wicklow town on the morning of Monday 4 September has been identified as Viktor Koslov, a 35-year-old male and Belarus national. An investigation into the circumstances of the death is ongoing and further details will be released when available. Any persons having information on the death are asked to contact the Wicklow gardaí station.'

'So you were right, Car, all along. About that guy. Remember, the tattoos?'

'Yeah, I guess I was. Yeh know, I saw that guy's tattoos when they were putting him in the garda car yesterday–they were similar to those on the body. Maybe that guy and Viktor Koslov were partners–hitmen, human traffickers, whatever?'

'But we still don't know how this Viktor Koslov died, or who killed him.'

Rosie was staring into her tea. 'I hated to leave them, Car–Anna, Molly, and Mike–not knowing what's happening with Chris. I just hope they don't decide to put him in jail right away. What do they call that?'

'On remand,' replied Cary. 'It means holding someone pending a trial. Yeah, I don't know, I suppose if the offence is serious enough, or if they think he'll scarper, yeh know?'

They sat at the kitchen table with some vegetable soup and brown bread, deep in their own thoughts.

'Maybe I'll head back to mine, okay? I got some work to do. But call me if you hear from Anna. You comin' down later?'

Rosie nodded and smiled.

Nearly an hour later as he worked at his desk, Cary saw two garda cars pass his door and head up Anglesey Lane. In just a few moments his mobile buzzed. It was Del.

'Hey, mate. Good news–well at least I think it's good. They just took Chris and his brother back to the Boyles.'

'Yeah? Oh, that's a relief. So, what's the deal?'

'Well, they've been released on their own recognizance. They have to stay in Wicklow or Dublin until their hearings. They'll appear before an immigration court first–the two of them and

Anna. For being in Ireland illegally. And for presenting false documentation to immigration.'

'Well, what do you think?'

'I don't know, Car. And please don't pass any of this on to the Boyles–I don't want to be givin' 'em false hope. But Mrs Boyle is an Irish citizen. And I kind of doubt they'd deport Chris and Kamal back to Syria, yeh know? But whether they'll have to serve time, or receive suspended sentences, or probation, who knows?'

'Okay. And the death? Of Viktor Koslov?'

'Yeah, well, that's a long story. I probably shouldn't tell you. And I wasn't in on most of it. But Car–for now they're being charged only with failure to report a death.'

Cary exhaled.

'For now, mate, for now. Well, I betta ring off.'

'Thanks Del.'

He was about to call Rosie when he decided he wanted to speak to her in person. At the O'Malley farmhouse Rosie was trying to busy herself in the herb garden. When she looked up he was smiling.

'Tell me Chris is out. I just saw the garda cars go by. I been prayin'.'

'He's out. He and his brother.'

At that moment Rosie's mobile buzzed. It was Anna.

'We just heard, Anna, about Chris and his brother. That's great news.'

'What?'

'When?'

'We'll be right there.'

She looked up at Cary with a panicked expression. 'Now Molly's disappeared.'

* * *

In minutes Cary and Rosie were back at the Boyle's. Anna, Chris, and Mike were standing in the front yard looking desperate.

'She was right here, I swear, not twenty minutes ago," said Anna. "I know she was worried about her dad. I was talking to my father in Dublin, bringing him up to date–she went into the house. And then when Superintendent Lewis called to say that Chris and Kamal had been released and would be here in a few minutes, Mike and I suddenly realised she was gone. I just–I can't imagine where...'

Just then two more garda cars appeared in the drive. Del jumped out of the first car and talked to Anna, Chris, and Kamal.

Rosie was whispering to Cary. 'She looked so calm on the outside, but I could tell she was in knots about her dad. I think she was thinking she was responsible for his arrest, somehow.'

'Well, where do you think she would have gone, Rosie?' asked Cary.

'I bet I know,' she replied. Just then Sabrina arrived and Rosie spoke to her.

'We've got a pretty good idea where she might be,' Rosie said to Cary.

'Lough Beag?'

'Yeah.'

'Let's go–the path is back here,' he said, gesturing to the rear of the barn.

'Better let me and Sabrina go, Car. That kid's like a frightened deer. We don't want to scare her away with a whole search party.'

Rosie and Sabrina took off down the path to Lough Beag.

A few minutes later they could see the lough's waters glistening through a stand of spruce. As they drew nearer they caught a glimpse of a figure sitting on a boulder close to the water's edge.

'You go ahead, I'll let the gardaí know we found her,' said Sabrina, grasping her radio.

Rosie approached Molly slowly, trying to gauge the girl's state of mind. She could hear her sobbing.

'Molly, hey, it's me, Ms O'Malley.'

Molly sat immobile, looking out across the quiet waters.

'I thought I might find you here.'

No reply.

'I just thought you might want to know that your dad and uncle are back home.'

Now Molly looked up at Rosie.

'Don't you wanna go back and see them?'

Molly shook her head. 'Everyone will be mad at me. It's all my fault.'

Rosie sat on the ledge next to Molly. 'Whatta yeh mean?'

'I wanted to play on the Hurleys. That's how those guys found us. They were after my dad, I'm sure of it. And I led them to him.'

'Listen, Mol. You shouldn't blame yerself. They would probably have found him one way or another. Besides, your ma and da don't expect you to give up everything, to live like a hermit, yeh know? You and Mike, you need to be able to do things, go to school, play sport, hang out, like the rest of the kids of Glenkerry, without worryin'.'

Molly looked up at Rosie.

'Anyway, that's all done with now. Those guys are in jail and they're gonna be there a long, long time. And you, Mike, and your parents, you'll be safe in Glenkerry. Everyone watches out for everyone in this town, maybe you noticed. No one stays a stranger for long. And no one can keep a secret for long.'

Molly nodded.

'Your da and your Uncle Kamal–I know they'll be wantin' to see yeh.'

Sabrina approached and knelt in front of the girl.

'Hey, Mol. You okay?'

Molly shrugged.

'I told her about her dad and uncle.'

'Let's go back, huh?'

The trio started up the path together. Back at the house there was a happy reunion of the four Boyles and Chris's brother, Kamal Rahmann. The gardai all had departed except Sabrina and Del who were standing apart talking quietly.

Rosie noticed Molly looking at them. Molly turned and spoke softly to Rosie.

'So what's the deal with Coach Selkirk and that garda?'

Rosie smiled. 'Those two? No deal, they're just friends.'

Molly cracked a slight smile. 'So how come I saw her giving 'im the shift the other day behind the storage shed after practice?'

Rosie chuckled. 'Good friends,' she said with a wink. '*Real* good friends.' And Rosie and Molly exchanged glances. 'Like I said, there are no secrets in Glenkerry.'

28 THE WHOLE TRUTH

The next morning Anna and Chris Boyle sat in Rosie's garden talking to her and Cary.

'We'd been in Ireland nearly ten years and thought we were safe at last,' began Chris. 'But this spring I received an email from someone named Viktor. He said he worked with this man in Turkey, Hasim was his name–the guy who arranged our transport to Ireland. He said we still owed Hasim 15,000 euro and he was in Ireland to collect it.'

'We had paid in full before we left Syria. That we knew for sure,' interjected Anna.

'I told him as much, but he persisted,' added Chris. 'And he warned that there would be consequences if we didn't pay him within ten days. I wasn't sure what he was saying at first, but when we didn't pay up, he repeated his warning. And then he told me he would report us to Immigration Services in Ireland, that he had copies of our passports and other papers that he would turn over.'

'I contacted my friend in Lebanon who had told us about Hasim. He talked to Hasim and confirmed that we owed him nothing.'

'For a time I doubted that this Viktor would actually follow through on his threat. I figured if he actually turned us in, he'd never get anything, yeh know?'

'But then he made some vague threats about my family and I got worried. Kamal came to Ireland shortly after we did and has been living with a Syrian friend in Tallaght. He and I had been talking about this business and agreed that maybe I better pay the guy and hope that would put an end to it. I didn't tell Anna or the kids about this. I didn't want to worry them.'

'So finally I emailed Viktor and said I would pay him, in cash. And I told him I would meet him at the Black Castle in Wicklow at midnight on the fourth of September. I had 5000 euro with me–that was as much as I would pay him, I'd decided. I told Anna we were going to a football match in Dublin.'

'Kamal had his friend's car and he picked me up in Glenkerry and drove us to Wicklow town. We'd already been there in daylight and planned it all. We parked on the North Quay, then rowed a small dingy across the harbour to the sailing club, near the lighthouse. It was very dark and we had to use torches to find our way.'

'As we approached the Black Castle, we split up. Kamal moved along the edge of the cliff just out of sight while I walked straight to the castle. Viktor was there, alone. There was just enough moonlight to see. We exchanged a few words. He took the money but wanted more. I was about to walk away when he pulled a gun on me.'

' "Let's go for a little stroll on the beach, Mr Rahmann," he said.'

'At that moment Kamal came at the guy from behind, trying to wrestle the gun out of his hand. The gun went flying. Viktor's back was now to me. So I lunged at him and sent him flying. He disappeared into the darkness over the cliff below the castle without a sound.'

'We climbed down the stairs to the beach and found the guy on the sand. He was already dead.'

'We went through his pockets. We took the money I'd just paid him and the contents of his wallet including his documents. He had a copy of my old Syrian ID that must have been used in forging my documents. It was a bad photocopy and it was Kamal who suggested that it looked a bit like me, that we should leave it on the body–as though I was the dead man. Neither of us was sure that it would work, but if it did, if it convinced the gardaí, the traffickers, the forgers, and the Syrian government that Kristoff Rahmann was dead, well, that would be fine. After all, I was now Chris Boyle.'

'The next day Kamal and I spent hours talking it over. We had to let our parents and friends know that I was alive and well on the possibility that the death of Kristoff Rahmann would be reported back home. I talked to my Uncle Aziz in Lebanon. He agreed to go to the Beirut police and confirm my death from a photograph sent by the gardaí.'

'When we read the story in *Al Jazeera* we thought we had succeeded in fooling the gardaí, Interpol, and the media, into thinking I was dead.'

'So what did this Dymitri guy have to do with all of this?' asked Cary.

'Dymitri Sokal was Viktor Koslov's partner in crime. They were both from Belarus–I guess they were in some kind of gang or fraternity–that's why the distinctive tattoos. It turns out they had rented a boat in Arklow that day and cruised up the coast at night. Dymitri stayed with the boat, waiting for Viktor to collect his fee. When Viktor never returned to their meeting point, Dymitri must have figured out that things had ended badly for him.'

'So Dymitri went searching for you?'

'Yes. Maybe he thought he could still get money from me, or maybe he just wanted revenge for the death of his partner. I suppose he guessed that I lived somewhere in Wicklow. He must have seen those stories about refugees in your newspaper, Cary.'

Cary blanched at the thought. 'That's why he was stalking me. I wrote that I was doing a story on Syrian refugees in County Wicklow. He thought I would lead him to you.'

'Yep, I think that's right.'

'And Molly,' began Rosie.

'Yeah, he must have seen her name in that story about the camogie team. We were careful not to allow any photographs of the kids, but we hadn't expected Molly's name to appear in your paper.'

Cary looked at Rosie. 'Eileen's article on the Hurleys. She listed the team members and their numbers.'

'I'm afraid so. That's the only way we can figure that he found her,' replied Chris.

'I'm so sorry,' responded Cary, looking first at Kristoff, then at Anna.

'Don't be too hard on yourself, son. It's really down to us. We brought those kids to Ireland illegally and forced them to live a lie. The truth was bound to come out eventually.' Chris reached out and touched Anna's hand.

'Did you two meet in Syria?' asked Rosie.

'Actually, we met in Beirut, in Lebanon,' replied Anna. 'My father worked for the Foreign Service. He used to tell us about his travels to exotic places all around the world. And I always dreamed that one day I would travel, too. So when it came time for university, I decided to go to the American University in Beirut. That's where we met.'

She smiled at Chris and took his hand. Then she continued. 'We married in Lebanon in 2004. A few weeks later, as you figured out, we travelled to Dublin and had a ceremony there as well. We'd been advised that we ought to have a legal marriage in Ireland, for ourselves and for our children. In 2005 we moved to a suburb of Damascus. That's where Mikhail and Malina were born. We really loved it there, despite all the troubles of that country. But in 2011 war broke out. We moved to a small town farther out in the countryside that seemed safer and we lived there for almost two years.'

'The Syrian underground had always existed but with the outbreak of war and crackdowns by Assad's government, the resistance movement geared up. Chris started writing for an underground journal. He wrote very detailed accounts of corruption in the Syrian government. Friends started telling us it was getting too dangerous and we should get out, but we refused to believe them at first.'

'Then a bomb went off in Mike's school–several students were injured. Mike wasn't hurt physically, but it took a toll on him emotionally, a huge toll we came to realise. We started thinking about leaving. Our first thought was to return to Lebanon, but Chris's colleagues said it was almost as dangerous there, that the Syrian secret police had a lot of influence in and around Beirut. So we started thinking about Europe.'

'We thought we probably could get Irish citizenship for Chris and the children. But we were worried about what would happen if we applied for refugee status. We had heard stories about those reception centres that many Syrian refugees were placed in–they sounded more like prisons. They were supposed to be just temporary housing until families could be settled, but many Syrian and Afghan families were detained for years. And the schooling provided for the children was barely adequate. We didn't want that for our children, or ourselves.'

'One of Chris's friends in Beirut got us in touch with Hasim who agreed to arrange our transport–and supply us with papers–for a fee, of course. In April 2013 we sailed on a small chartered boat to Cyprus, then aboard a large freighter to Southampton.'

'Our new documents, Irish IDs and passports, listed us as Christopher and Anna Boyle,' explained Anna. 'Mikhail became Michael, Malina became Molly. We hated the thought of the kids having to pretend to be someone they weren't, but at the time it seemed our best option.'

'We finally travelled by a small private vessel to Cork. Our documents must've been pretty good because we moved through Irish immigration very easily. Luckily for us they had not yet started to include any biometric information like eye scans or facial recognition on passports.'

'Some friends from Beirut found us an apartment in Cork City and we lived there for over seven years. Chris did some writing and consulting for international relief organisations–the kids attended a local grammar school. I taught piano at a community music school in Cobh. Then Covid came along. We were all at home in that little apartment. We home-schooled the kids as best we could. And we started thinking about finding a place out in the country, maybe in West Cork.'

'But in October of last year Chris learned that there had been a number of assassinations or attempted assassinations of Syrian resistance workers in Italy, Germany, and France. We were told that the Assad government had hired a dozen hitmen to track down and kill dissidents who had fled Syria. We knew that if they were on the Continent, they probably could get to the UK and Ireland. We suddenly got very nervous again.'

Anna continued. 'So we talked to an old friend in Dublin who had some connections in County Wicklow, family and coworkers. One of them, Declan Murphy, agreed to find us a place in Wicklow. It had to be out in the country and not visible from any public road. Declan spent a weekend looking at properties in Enniskerry, Roundwood, Aughrim, and Glenkerry. He didn't talk to estate agents, but he looked in their office windows at property listing, then drove around scouting them, contacting the owners directly.'

'We were about to purchase a house in Aughrim. But then my grandmother passed. She and my grandfather had lived in this house for more than thirty years. My parents offered it to us. I of course already knew this property. It seemed ideal, at the end of a long, narrow drive, surrounded by trees, completely invisible from the road. One extra plus for this property was access to the forestland to the north.'

'Yeah, that's the Lough Beag demesne,' said Cary.

'We liked the idea of having a second route out of our property. That's how worried we've been,' said Anna. 'So we made the move to Glenkerry in July. At first I was the only one that went to town, to the shops. But once I knew my way around, I let the kids have more freedom. I was able to get a driver's licence while we were in Cork. Chris never tried. Even as Chris Boyle he wanted to be pretty invisible. And our only credit cards are in my name.'

Chris smiled. 'We just hoped that no one in Syria would be able to connect Kristoff Rahmann of Damascus with Christopher Boyle of Ireland.'

'We wanted Molly and Mike to go back to school in September,' said Anna. 'So I took them to *Coláiste Gaeilge*. They wanted their school records from Cork. Back in 2014 when we arrived in Cork, we told the grammar school that we had just come from Lebanon and the kids' school records were not available. They accepted that, but the principal at *Coláiste Gaeilge*, Mr Forster, wanted some kind of documentation from Lebanon. I've been promising him that it was coming. I don't know how long that can go on.'

'Then about the middle of August we had a visitor, Chris's brother Kamal. He came to Ireland a year or so after us. He's been living in Dublin. He told us there were agents working for Syria in the UK and we needed to be very careful, to stay low. We were frightened for Chris, for me, and for the kids. And of course what happened yesterday in Glenkerry—well, our worst fears came true.'

'So what happens next?' asked Cary. 'I mean, with the gardaí.'

'Well, we are scheduled for an immigration hearing in a couple of weeks,' explained Chris. 'Our solicitor has had some experience with Syrian refugees—he seems pretty confident that we'll get fined, nothing more.'

Chris exhaled loudly, his eyes meeting Anna's. 'But then there's the Black Castle business. They're keeping us, Kamal and me, in the dark about that. We're not really sure what's going on. But it's making us very nervous. I'm not sure that they believe our story. If we'd reported it right away it would have looked better for us. But we felt trapped. If we went to the guard to report a death, they would have pretty quickly figured out our immigration status. And I was worried that that would implicate Anna, even the kids. We, Kamal, and I, just couldn't take that risk.'

Anna spoke up. 'So we are living day to day, waiting on the immigration decision and the Viktor Koslov case. But for the sake of the kids we're trying to maintain calm. We keep reassuring them that everything will be all right. I wish we knew that for sure.'

'We'll do whatever we can,' replied Rosie. 'And you can be sure that at least for the coming week Molly's mind will be on the Hurleys and their next match. She's a real natural, you know.'

Anna smiled proudly. 'And thanks to you and Sabrina she's made a number of good friends on the Hurleys, Gráinne Phinney and Eileen Keough in particular. But even that girl Isla seems to have taken her under her wing.' They all laughed at the thought of Isla and Molly, best buddies.

* * *

That evening Cary texted Sameed to let him know of all the recent developments in the matter of Kristoff Rahmann. Around noon the next day Sam called Cary.

'You're not going to believe this, Sam, but you were right, that wasn't Kristoff Rahmann who died. In fact Rahmann is alive and living right here in Glenkerry.'

Cary went on to tell Sam about the Rahmanns' story, their arrangement with Hasim, departure from Syria, arrival in Ireland under assumed names, and all. Then he told Sam about the attempt to extort money from Rahmann.

'I've heard about that, Cary–about this international network of document forgers. Many of them are based in Montenegro and Belarus where they seem to be invisible to the authorities. So they make a double living. They get paid by people like Hasim to forge documents for his clients. But then after they reach their destination, usually in Europe or America, these guys try to blackmail those folks by threatening to turn them in.'

'What an awful way to make a living, yeah? Prey on people who have already suffered so much.'

'Yeah, for sure,' replied Sam. 'I've heard that these guys make more money by blackmail than by producing the fake papers in the first place.'

Cary was curious. 'So, then, it wasn't Assad and his thugs who were after Rahmann.'

'I guess not,' replied Sam. 'Not that that guy's an angel, not by any means. And these traffickers, like that Hasim fellow, they're in on this, too. They'll claim they are in the business for humanitarian reasons. But then they allow their clients to be victimised all over again once they've reached their destination.'

'Yeah, well, this time the bad guys lost,' said Cary. 'Viktor Koslov is dead and Dymitri Sokal has been charged with attempted kidnapping and two counts of auto theft.'

'So how did this all come out, Cary?'

'Wow, it's a long story. Very long.' He told Sam about his personal involvement in the death at the Black Castle, about the photograph he took, then deleted. And he described how Dymitri stalked him for days before the attempted kidnapping. 'Your question about the tattoos on the body was really what convinced me that the dead man was not Kristoff Rahmann. But the gardaí were slow to come around to the idea. In the end it was the fingerprints from the dead man that convinced them, but it took over a month to find a match. It turns out the guy had a police record in Turkey—that's where the prints were finally matched.'

Cary paused. 'And then when you found out that Kristoff married an Irish woman, that was key, too. You were a huge help, Sam. I'm just really grateful for all you did. Especially knowing the risks.'

'Yeah, well like I said, in the Middle East, the walls have ears.'

They both laughed.

'Hey, Sam, I talked to Siobhan a couple times this last week. She's really loving her job. I think she's in London to stay, I really do. She'll be a CEO before long, I bet.'

'That's great, Car, really great. She'll do well, wherever she is, I have no doubt. I wish I could interest her in international affairs, you know? One night we were Skyping and we'd both had a little too much to drink, I guess. Anyway, she was talking like she wanted me to move to London and share a flat with her. I'll admit I was tempted.' He chuckled. 'In more ways than one.'

'I get that, Sam. Uh-huh. But you're in the NGO world, right?'

Sam sighed. 'Yup. And I probably will never get that kind of offer again. Oh, well.'

* * *

Around midday Del stopped by the *Gazelle* office. He looked knackered as he slumped into a chair.

'Well, I think Chief Superintendent Morris and Superintendent Lewis have wrapped up the Black Castle case.'

'Really, Del? Please tell me Chris Boyle and his brother aren't going to be charged with murder.'

Del smiled and shook his head. 'Relax, mate, it's all good–or well, maybe good isn't quite the right word for a death.'

'So tell me.'

Del shook his head. 'I can't, really, not until they have their day in court.'

'Come on, Del. Just a bit, yeah? I'm dying, and so is Rosie.'

'Okay, but you can't pass this along to anyone, understand?'

'I swear to God, not a word.'

'First I need tea, yeah?'

A few minutes later they were in Cary's small sitting room, each with a cup of tea.

'Those guys are lucky, Car, just plain lucky. The gardaí were this close to filing murder charges against them both, this close,' said Del with a grin, holding up his index finger and thumb. 'But they brought it on themselves by not telling the truth from the start. First they claimed they weren't there that night. Then when they were shown the CCTV footage, they admitted they were there but claimed they just paid off Koslov and left. Then when they were told about the boot print, well, then they had to admit they were involved in Koslov's death.'

'The boot print?'

'Oh, yeah, they didn't tell you? That was what convinced the gardaí that it wasn't an accident or suicide. Your photo of the body–on your mobile–there was a boot print in the sand right next to the body. It showed there must've been someone there before you, possibly the murderer–or someone who witnessed the death.'

'But I didn't see any boot print. Neither did you, right?' asked Cary.

'Yeah, well, the lab people did. They altered the lighting–yeh know, the brightness, the contrast–just enough to reveal the print. It was a very distinctive tread. They found the boots when they searched the Boyles' house.'

Cary was gobsmacked. 'I remember the waves were washing right up to the body. Those waves probably washed away the print before the gardaí took their photos.'

'Yeah, probably.'

'So then Kamal and Chris told the full story. They claimed Koslov had a gun and threatened Kristoff with it–that Kamal had been hiding and came up behind Koslov trying to disarm him–that in the scuffle the gun went over the edge and so did Koslov. They admitted they found the body on the beach below and removed the contents of the guy's pockets–including the ransom money they had just paid him–but left the Kristoff Rahmann ID. They said that was not a plan–it just occurred to them at that moment when they found it in Koslov's pocket and it looked something like the dead man.'

'Honestly, at that point I think Chief Superintendent Morris was ready to charge them, either with manslaughter or murder. But they decided to do a search for the gun. They called in a special assault unit from Dublin to scale the rockface and the water below. And they found the gun, a Russian revolver, wedged in the rocks. It even had Koslov's prints on it, not in very good condition but good enough to make the match.'

'So that gave support to their claim of, what, self-defence?'

Del nodded. 'So as things stand right now, the only charge against the two is failure to report a death. They go before a judge in early November.'

'Well, I'm really glad to hear it, Del. Of course, I can see why they didn't report it. If they had, Chris's immigration status, those fake documents, would probably have been discovered.'

'Yeah, you're right. It all goes back to the way Syrian refugees were treated, yeh know? Not that what the Boyles did wasn't wrong, but you can understand it, a family not wanting to be held indefinitely in one of those reception centres.'

'And you and Rosie and your mate in Lebanon deserve a lot of credit. You convinced them that the dead man was not Kristoff Rahmann and you sorted he was married to Anna Boyle. You took the photo that reminded you of the tattoos, right? And you two were right there when those two guys tried to snatch Molly Boyle.'

'Yeah, Rosie had a feeling something was about to go down. And she tried to warn me about her conversation with Gráinne.'

'But Del, you saw how Sabrina took off after Dymitri–that was incredible. She should get some kind of award for that.'

'All in a day's work for members of the gardaí, Car,' said Del with a swagger of pride. 'All in a day's work.'

William Butler Yeats

29 CÉAD MÍLE FÁILTE ROMHAT

Father Desmond of St Brigid's, the Roman Catholic Church in Glenkerry, Reverend O'Ryan of St Mark's, the town's Church of Ireland parish, and Kevin Leahy of the Wicklow County Council stood proudly before a block of modest brick townhomes on the Arklow road on Monday morning. Before them were gathered several dozen onlookers including the members of Glenkerry's chapter of St Vincent de Paul, the Glenkerry Citizens for Justice, as well as several representatives of the local media. Also present were Mr Archbold and Ms Bryan, TDs representing County Wicklow in the *Dáil*, and building contractor Jim Henderson.

Reverend O'Ryan spoke to the group. 'Today we celebrate the conclusion of nearly a year-and-a-half's work by many of you. It is truly a dream come true–and a prayer come true–the official opening of these six homes. They are empty right now, but within days they will be filled with life, and joy, and hope for the future, as six families move in.'

He continued. 'It was nearly two years ago, just before the war in Ukraine broke out, that Father Desmond and I sat in his study discussing the housing problems in this town and in County Wicklow. We knew that the *Dáil* was already debating the matter of Ireland's growing housing shortage. Little did we know that another war was just around the corner, putting still greater pressure on our country's housing situation.'

'In both our parishes we found strong interest in taking action of some sort. Even as debate was taking place in the *Dáil* in Dublin, these folks began working. With the aid of Gloria Hennessy...' He nodded to Gloria who smiled and waved her acknowledgement. 'With her assistance potential housing was identified. This block was at the top of her list. Construction had begun back during the days of the Celtic Tiger. They were to be part of a development of some thirty units. But that project failed, like so many in that time, and these buildings stood unfinished for nearly a decade. They suffered from deterioration, as you can imagine. One unit burned in a fire some five years ago.'

'In June of last year that group approached Jim Henderson of Carlow, a well-known contractor and lifelong resident of that town. He agreed to begin renovations even though the funds for the project were still mostly wishful thinking at that point.'

'That's when the fund-raising phase really got going. We received pledges totalling 60,000 euro from over 1000 individuals in the next six months, then received matching funds from the Hibernian Fund. We owe a tremendous debt of gratitude to that foundation and all those individual donors. When construction costs began to exceed projections, the County Council appropriated another 10,000 euro for the project. Many thanks to *Comhairleoir* Leahy and the other members of the council for their assistance.' He nodded to Kevin.

'Meanwhile another committee was preparing to receive applicants for tenancy. They were flooded with responses as you can imagine. From the start it was agreed that refugees from war zones such as Ukraine and Syria would receive first priority for three units but the other three would be designated for citizens of Ireland. I am pleased to announce today that we have tenants for all six units, the first of whom are expected to arrive within the week. The committee is now busy seeking furnishings for each unit and planning a welcome event for the families.'

He paused and looked around him, smiling.

'I would be remiss if I did not extend our group's special thanks to the newspapers and television stations in Wicklow and in Dublin who gave this project the attention it deserved. We are of course especially grateful to our own *Glenkerry Gazette* and its editor, Ciaran McGurk, for his series of articles on refugees and the housing crisis in Ireland.'

Cary smiled and nodded.

'I would just like to say that it gives me, Father Desmond, Mr Leahy here, and all the members of the Citizens for Justice great pride to think that so many folks in this town, in this county, in this country, care so deeply about our fellow countrymen and women and about those who have come to Ireland seeking refuge in time of war. Ireland has been on the receiving end of such kindness from others so often in the past, and we are only too happy to be able to return the favour in kind.'

'And lastly let me add that Ireland today welcomes new neighbours, new friends, and new ways. This project is just one small symbol of that openness that we all prize in our country. And we say to the new occupants of these homes, to these new residents of Glenkerry, *Céad Míle Fáilte Romhat*–a hundred thousand welcomes. As Ireland's beloved son, poet William Butler Yeats, once wrote, "There are no strangers here, only friends you haven't met yet." '

A group of students from Glenkerry's grammar school and *Coláiste Gaeilge* were poised to cut the ribbon with a giant pair of cardboard scissors. The group consisted of natives of Morocco, Nigeria, Pakistan, Ukraine, and Syria, including Molly and Mike Boyle. It took several tries, but they finally succeeded in actually cutting the ribbon with those giant scissors, to the amusement of all. Cheers then rose from all in attendance.

Father Desmond offered a brief benediction, thanking God for this occasion and praying for the health and happiness of those who would soon occupy those new homes.

Finally everyone was invited to tour one of the completed units.

Catherine was beside herself at the completion of the project she and her friends had been working on for so long.

'Congratulations, Ma, you did it,' said Cary.

'With yer 'elp, love, with yer 'elp.'

'And Dad's, too, yeh know?' he added.

Catherine hugged her son.

30 REUNION

The Wicklow County League Semi-finals Tournament was scheduled for the coming Saturday on the GAA grounds in Wicklow town. Still on a high from their stunning upset over the Montkilleen National School just a few days earlier, the Hurleys threw themselves into practice, convinced that they could do it again–they were scheduled for a rematch with the Montkilleen team in this, the first round of the semi-finals. If they lost that match, they would be eliminated; if they won, they would go on to the County Finals the following week.

But Isla MacDonald was not at practice. Sabrina had not heard from her since she stormed off the pitch after being red-carded. After practice Sabrina texted her. No reply.

'I'm worried, Rosie, I really am,' said Sabrina to Rosie in a phone call that evening. 'I think she's quit the Hurleys.'

Rosie could hardly believe this. 'Oh, I'm sure that's not so, Sabrina. Nobody wants to play this sport more than Isla–and nobody wants to win more than her.'

Then Rosie had an idea. She ran it past Sabrina first, then sent a text to Gráinne and Eileen.

On her way home she stopped at 1 Upton Road. Cary was not around so she left the *Gazette* masthead, the final version she had been working on for weeks, on his desk. At home she looked through some photographs she had taken during practice, photos of Coach Selkirk in action. She chose one that she especially liked and sent it to Cary.

* * *

The next morning Rosie went to the canteen to get a cup of coffee before the first lesson. At a table in the corner sat Gráinne, Eileen, Molly, and Isla. Isla looked glum.

But at practice that afternoon, there was Isla. Sabrina took her aside and had a chat while the rest of the team did their stretches and laps.

Again Sabrina tried to lower the tension by focusing her team, as usual, on the fundamentals. They drilled long and hard on swinging, ground striking, passing, dribbling, blocking, hooking, and clashing. No talk about strategies or tactics, just the fundamentals.

Rosie admired her friend's allegiance to that principle, but she could tell that Coach Selkirk was a bundle of nerves all week long. Rosie was beginning to suspect that, despite her lectures to her team, winning *was* a big deal for Sabrina—a very big deal.

Rosie was amazed at the confidence exuded by the Hurleys as they approached the biggest challenge of the season. She just hoped that their 3-1-1 record including three consecutive wins and advancement to the semi-finals wouldn't make them overconfident. But the way they worked during practice suggested that they were not taking Saturday's match for granted in the least.

That evening Rosie walked into Phinney's. She didn't really want a meal or a drink, not on a school night. But she sat at a table by the window, sipping tea, waiting. Soon Gráinne appeared.

'Whatever you did, you and Eileen and Molly, thanks.'

Gráinne shook her head. 'And I used ta think Molly was a high maintenance friend. But Isla…'

They shared a laugh.

'So, what did you do?'

'We just told her how much we needed her, yeh know? But that she had to listen to Coach Selkirk. She knows she nearly cost us that match, getting red-carded. I think it was partly out of embarrassment that she stayed away. She couldn't face us.'

'Yeah, Gran, I bet yer right there.'

* * *

Rosie stopped at the *Gazette* office after school. She hadn't seen Cary in two days and had received only a very short text message the previous evening. She sensed something was wrong.

'Car?' she called as she stepped through the door. A pile of mail protruded through the slot in the door. The words 'FINAL NOTICE' were stamped in big letters on one envelope.

'Car?' she repeated. Still there was no response and not a sound from above.

She piled the mail on the desk, then climbed the stairway. The bedroom door was shut. She rapped lightly.

'Cary?'

Finally she heard a grunt and the creak of a bedspring.

'Rosie?'

She pushed the door open. It was dark inside, the shades drawn. And it smelled foul, like a sickroom. 'You okay, Car?'

Another grunt. All she could make out was a pile of blankets and a coverlet on the bed. She sat on the edge of the bed, one hand on the heap of blankets. In the rubbish bin she could see several empty beer bottles.

'You sick, Car?'

Slowly the covers were withdrawn and she could see his face in the dim light. He looked like death warmed over–several days' growth on his chin, matted hair, bloodshot eyes.

'What's the matter? You hibernatin' or something?'

He sighed, then boosted himself up onto one elbow.

'I suppose. I'm–I'm not doin' so well, Rose.'

'Why? What's wrong?'

He sat up, planted his feet on the floor, then sank his face into his hands.

'I screwed up, Rosie. Royally.'

'Whatta yeh mean?'

'The cheque, for the printing of last week's *Gazette*? It bounced. It was returned to Mr Hadley by the bank–due to insufficient funds.'

'Oh, Car, I'm sorry. What happened?'

He was nearly in tears. 'I thought I had it covered, I really did. Just barely, but I thought I was okay. But I forgot about the insurance payment that hit the account on Friday.'

'So what happens?'

'Mr Hadley called me. He was nice enough about it. He knew my dad, yeh know? But he wants the cash, right away, for last week's paper and for tomorrow's.' He paused. 'It's over, Rosie, finished. The *Gazette*'s done. And I'm done.'

'Well, what about your ma? Can't she help–I mean, to tide you over?'

'She just found out she needs a new roof. That's a huge job. Thousands. Tens of thousands probably. I can't ask her to bail me out anymore.'

'Well, I could 'elp. I got a little saved away.'

Cary shook his head. His hair looked greasy and tangled, as if it hadn't been washed in a week.

'Well, thank you, Rosie.' He took her hand. 'But I could never ask you to do that. I'd be draggin' you down with me.'

He started to sob. Rosie wrapped her arm around him, then kissed him on the forehead.

'Let's think this through, Car, yeah? There must be something you can do. What about a bank loan? I mean, I don't know much about business, but don't nearly all companies have to take out loans to get them started?'

'I'd be a bad risk, Rosie, let's face it. I got no business experience, I'm trying to restart a newspaper that already failed once. What bank would want to lend to me?'

She knelt in front of him, then took both his hands in hers. 'You should ask, anyway, shouldn't you? What about Mr Sullivan at the credit union? He's a nice guy, and he was a friend of your dad's, wasn't he?'

'That's just it, Rosie. Everybody in this town knew my dad. And nearly everybody knows me. And how humiliating is it gonna be when I have to tell them the paper is done, after just, what, eight issues?'

He looked as forlorn as she had ever seen him. He sat shaking his head. 'I shoulda gone to London.'

'What?'

'Yeah, I shoulda taken Siobhan up on her offer. I'd be in a place where if I screwed up, nobody'd know me, yeh know? Instead of here, in this fishbowl–on public display.'

'Do you really mean that, Car?'

He shrugged. 'I don't know. Maybe I do.'

'So, the hell with Glenkerry?' she asked sharply. 'The hell with the *Gazette*–the hell with us?'

Cary was startled by her tone. 'No, Rosie, I didn't mean that.'

Rosie's face was suddenly red, her jaw set.

'You better make up yer mind, Ciaran McGurk. If you're that close to leavin'–you better say so, yeh know?' Her lips started to quiver. She stood up abruptly.

'Do whatever yeh want, yeah? If you decide you're leavin', just let me know, huh?'

She started to turn away, then turned back. 'If you decide to stay, you gotta tell me, understand? You gotta commit, yeh know what I mean? I need to know you're committed, that's what I need. I don't wanna be your…' She hesitated. 'Your–your dirty stop-out until something–or someone better comes along.'

Cary looked up at her confused.

'I'm goin'. You know where to find me when you decide.' Just as she was about to start down the stairway she paused.

'Oh, and there's a whole pile of mail on yer desk downstairs. Maybe you should check it out before you decide.'

This was it, Rosie said to herself as she climbed the hill. This was the heart of the problem and it had been all along between them. Cary was never committed to the *Gazette*, or to her. He was just buying time. And as soon as things turned against him, he'd be gone, gone to London, to Siobhan. The hell with Ireland–with Glenkerry–with me.

Catherine was kneeling in her garden as Rosie passed.

'Hello, Rosie, how are you?' Rosie waved but kept on walking.

'Everything all right, love? Something happen at school?'

Rosie didn't look back.

* * *

During her luncheon break the next day, Thursday, Rosie went to the school office to drop off her attendance record. There on the counter was a copy of the *Glenkerry Gazette*. On the front page was a photo of Coach Selkirk talking to her players, one Rosie had snapped just two days ago. It caught Sabrina perfectly, a twinkle in her eye, a dazzling smile on her lips, the girls' attention fixed on her. Below the photo was a profile of Sabrina, written by Cary. And above, across the top, was that new masthead she had worked so hard to perfect. Below the fold was Cary's story about the dedication of the new houses.

Minutes later she received a text from Cary with an embedded link to the digital edition of the new *Gazette*. It said simply, 'Thanks.'

After practice she was putting all the camogie kit in the storage shed when Cary appeared.

'The *Gazette* looks great,' she said. She looked at him blankly.

'Yeah, it does, thanks to you. That photo of Sabrina, everyone loves it. And the new masthead, it's perfect.'

'So what happened with Mr Hadley?'

'I paid him, for last week's and this week's. I drove to Arklow with the cash last night.'

'Your ma help yeh?'

He shook his head. 'Nope. Did it myself. That stack of mail? It was all subscription payments. And then I checked the bank account–nearly a hundred more, all within the last three days. I had stopped looking I was so discouraged. But there they were.'

'So your subscribers came through. I told you they would.'

'Yeah, you were right.'

She nodded, her expression still a blank.

He took her arm. 'Listen, Rosie, I'm sorry–about what I said yesterday. I didn't mean it, I swear. I was down in the dumps is all.'

She looked up into his eyes. 'It hurt.'

'I know, and I'm sorry. That's all I can say. I owe you so much. You're the reason I decided to stay in Glenkerry, yeh know. Not the *Gazette*, not my ma, not Del pestering me. You. You told me I could do it. And you were right. And your photos, your artwork, they're making a big difference. It makes the paper look better.' He paused. 'It makes *me* look better, yeh know?'

Rosie's mask began to soften.

'And I am committed, Rosie, to Glenkerry, to the *Gazette*, to us.'

* * *

At home over tea Rosie read Cary's profile of Sabrina:

SABRINA SELKIRK

Garda, coach, marathoner

Ciaran McGurk, Editor, Glenkerry Gazette

Sabrina Selkirk's earliest memories are of playing football with the children in her neighbourhood in Gibraltar.

'There was this little gravel pitch behind the housing estate where we lived,' she recalls. 'That's where we played. We were from all over—Spain, Italy, Morocco, Algeria, Senegal, Nigeria, Pakistan, Yemen. We had nothing in common—not language—not religion—nothing except footie. And we played morning, noon, and night.'

That's where Sabrina came to love sport, any sport—footie, soccer, rugby—so long as it required nothing more than a ball, because all they had to entertain themselves was a dusty old soccer ball.

'We must've looked like a UNICEF poster—all those smiling faces, all those different colours, and from four continents. And it was footie that brought us together.'

Sabrina was born in a small village in Senegal. Her birth father died when she was still an infant; her mother, Marieme, struggled to provide for her family. Senegal had been hit by a terrible drought that year—disease and death were everywhere. And so Marieme decided to leave her native country. She led her three children, Sabrina, Moussa, and Malik, on a harrowing journey by rail and ferry to Gibraltar in 2010. They settled in a rundown housing development far from the glitzy casinos Gibraltar is known for. There Marieme met and eventually married James Selkirk, a native of Scotland, who was working in construction.

A year later the family moved to Manchester, England. Marieme worked in a factory, James for a building contractor. The three children attended a local school. It was in her school in Manchester that Sabrina was introduced to a sport that was entirely unfamiliar to her, something called camogie. Her parents bought her a hurley and a sliotar. It was love at first sight.

'From that day on I was a hurley girl,' explains Sabrina with a grin.

Even in the UK, camogie was all the rage among young girls. Her grammar school had a team and Sabrina joined. She did well in her studies, eventually attending Manchester Metropolitan University. While at university she played on the local GAA team.

'I had the most wonderful coach at Manchester—Gerald Cronin. He was strict and very demanding, and as I've told my team at Coláiste Gaeilge, it took me a while to understand what teamwork was all about. Gerry was patient with me and in time I became a starting midfielder.'

At age eighteen Sabrina moved to Ireland where she was admitted into the Garda College in Tipperary. She completed her training with full marks and received her appointment to An Garda Síochána in 2018. She served as a garda in Dublin for two years. In 2022 she was seconded to Glenkerry as Family Liaison Officer. Since April 2023 she has been FLO in Wicklow town.

'I love my work,' she says. 'Especially being involved with families, trying to help them and support them through difficult times.'

In September 2023 Sabrina took up her duties as coach of the newly established camogie team at Coláiste Gaeilge, supported by Chief Superintendent James Morris.

'We need our young people to be comfortable with the gardaí, to trust us, to feel they can come to us when they are in trouble,' says Morris. 'So I was pleased to authorise Garda Selkirk to take on her coaching duties in Glenkerry.'

Of her camogie team, the Hurley Girlies, Sabrina says, 'I can't say enough for those girls. They are brilliant. They went all *the way to the County Semi-finals this fall, quite a feat for a new team.'*

Many of the residents of Wicklow town and Glenkerry know Sabrina as Coach Selkirk and Garda Selkirk. But they may not know that she is also a marathoner. She placed first in the Belfast Marathon in 2022. She is currently training to compete in that event in 2024.

'Sport can do so much for a young person, especially girls. They learn teamwork, patience, discipline, and they build strong bonds with their teammates.'

'I know what camogie did for me. I believe it can do the same for anyone who is willing to commit to the game.'

I asked Sabrina how she liked Ireland. Was it a difficult adjustment, after living in Senegal, in Gibraltar, and in Manchester?

She shakes her head. 'Not at all.' Then she laughs, her eyes wide. 'Well, except for the language—and the food.'

* * *

The Hurleys were exuberant on the bus ride to Wicklow town, cheering and periodically breaking into song. They arrived just in time to see the second period of another semi-final match, this between Arklow and a team from Bray. Arklow won narrowly, 7-6, but the level of play for both teams was impressive. Rosie wondered if some of the Hurleys were thinking they were out of their league.

Just as the players were about to take the pitch, Rosie saw three familiar faces approaching along the sideline, Fiona, Roger, and

Sophie. Fiona waved and Rosie walked toward them. Sophie was beaming.

'Oh, my god, Sophie,' said Rosie, shaking her head in disbelief at that smiling face, full of colour. It had been barely a month since she had seen her at Mercy Hospital, but she looked like a different girl, at least a stone heavier and standing tall. Rosie wasn't sure if she should hug her, but just then Sophie stepped forward and gave Rosie a hug.

Rosie took both the girl's hands in hers. 'Oh, Sophie–you look–wonderful. I am so glad to see you.'

Sophie smiled at Rosie but stood speechless for a moment. Then she exchanged glances with her parents.

'Maura called your school and found out about today's match,' began Fiona. 'Sophie wanted to surprise you.'

'Well, you have done,' replied Rosie, her eyes shining with delight.

Just then the whistle blew for the start of the match.

'I gotta go. But can yeh stay? I'd love it if you could.'

Once again the Montkilleen team jumped out to an early lead on the strength of two shots between the uprights. But the Hurleys seemed undismayed. When their opponents launched another attack on their goal, the Hurley defenders were ready, blocking several shots on the net in quick succession. Then Frya, the Hurley's goalkeeper, got off a strong puck-out that reached well upfield. Robyn brought the ball close to the net, passed it to Molly who then passed it to Isla.

It was like déjà vu. Suddenly a wall of three defenders rose up around Isla. Sabrina and Rosie watched anxiously. For a moment it looked as though there would be a repeat of last week's debacle, as Isla and one of her defenders fought for possession of the sliotar.

But suddenly Isla pivoted away toward the far sideline. Her three defenders followed her. And in that moment Molly was there, lifted the ball, and struck it into the net. The Hurleys were ahead, 3-2.

With the Montkilleen offence again on the move, the Hurley defence hung tight, Saoirse and Hannah repeatedly blocking and hooking their opponents. With but a minute remaining in the first period, the Montkilleen offence scored a goal. At the interval Montkilleen held a 5-3 lead.

Sabrina gave the team her usual peptalk, urging them to stay calm and focus on defence, suspecting that the Hurleys' newfound skill in blocking and hooking had a dual benefit, discouraging their opponents while at the same time energising their own offence.

'Stay cool, Hurleys, and focus. Bank of six, keep it up. You can do this.'

She looked at Isla. 'Way to go, Is. Way to go.' The girl smiled at Sabrina—she actually smiled.

Just as the second period started a cold rain began to fall and the pitch became very slippery. Isla received a pass from Katie. She was encircled with defenders as usual. This time she passed it backwards to Allegra, then spun away toward the sideline. The three defenders followed. Allegra seized the opportunity and dribbled the ball to the centre of the pitch, then struck it over the uprights. The Hurleys now trailed by just one point, 5-4.

A few minutes later as Isla spun to take a shot, she slipped and fell in the mud. The Montkilleen defence wrested the sliotar from her and moved it toward their goal. Despite a strong effort to deflect by the Hurleys' defence, they scored a point. The pitch was getting increasingly treacherous, and Rosie wondered if the referee would halt the match. But it continued. In the last moments of the second period, Allegra passed the ball to Katie who struck it toward the net. But it missed, still passing between the uprights. Then the final whistle blew. Montkilleen had prevailed, 6-5.

The Hurleys were glum, but Sabrina praised them.

'Hey, that was tough going out there, girls. Give yourselves a lot of credit. You did just fine.' Everyone began to pack up to leave.

Just then Cary appeared.

'Hey, congratulations, you lot,' he said to Rosie and Sabrina and the several players nearby.

Rosie thanked him. 'Can you put the kit away in those duffels fer me? I wanna talk to these folks.' She gestured toward the three. 'That's Sophie–and her parents.'

Cary took over equipment duties and Rosie returned to Sophie, Fiona, and Roger. Sophie was very excited about the match and had a number of comments on the Hurleys and their play.

'I'm sorry your team didn't win, Rosie.'

'Oh, well, they did themselves and Glenkerry proud. And there's always next season, right?'

'So, what's new with you?' asked Rosie, her face glowing.

Sophie smiled broadly. 'I'm back at school–half days for a while. And I'm helping out the camogie team for now. Maybe next spring I'll be able to play. We'll see.'

'And you're feeling okay?'

Sophie nodded. 'Yeah, one hundred percent. I got a special nurse who comes to see me every few days,' she said. Then her voice dropped: 'Yeh know, ostomy stuff. But I'm doin' okay with that, I won't need her much longer.'

Fiona and Roger were watching with delight as Rosie and Sophie talked. Just then Rosie caught sight of Cary and beckoned to him.

'Sophie, Fiona, Roger, I'd like you to meet Ciaran McGurk.'

Cary smiled and shook hands with all three.

'Cary's the editor and publisher of the *Glenkerry Gazette*.'

'Editor and publisher, wow,' noted Fiona. 'That's quite an accomplishment for someone so young, I'd say. Congratulations.'

'Well, thank you. It's still a work in progress, but I got lots of support in Glenkerry.' With that he looked appreciatively at Rosie and put his arm around her. 'Including this lass.'

'She's something else, isn't she?' offered Fiona.

'She is that,' replied Cary.

Roger spoke directly to Cary. 'We owe Rosie everything.' Then his eyes met Cary's as he repeated that word: 'Everything.'

'Rosie, Maura tells us you're thinking about going to school in medical social work,' said Fiona. This was news to Cary.

Rosie looked hesitant. 'Well, it's a thought, anyway. We'll see. She's invited me to attend a couple of group sessions with her patients at Mercy next weekend. I agreed, but honestly, I'm a little on edge about it, yeh know?'

Fiona took her arm. 'You'll do fine, Rosie, I'm sure of it,' she said, nodding toward Sophie.

Before they departed, Sophie took Rosie aside and spoke privately to her.

'Thanks again for all your help. I'm sorry if I didn't, well, maybe seem that grateful in the hospital that day. I just…'

Rosie shook her head. 'Don't apologise, Sophie. I been there–I can appreciate what you were dealin' with. I'm just glad you made the decision to have the surgery. Obviously it was the right decision, yeah?'

Sophie nodded, tears welling in her eyes. 'Yeah, it was.' She hesitated. 'Well, thanks again.' And again she hugged Rosie.

The Glenkerry Gazette

Established 1987   Issue 9   19 October 2023

GLENKERRY CAMOGIE TEAM
ADVANCES TO SEMI-FINALS

In their first season *Coláiste Gaeilge*'s camogie team, the Hurley Girlies, has earned a spot in the County Semi-Finals. They are scheduled play the Montkilleen National School on Saturday, 21 October, on the GAA grounds in Wicklow. The team, that includes players from Glenkerry, Ballinoch, Dunbraugh, Kloughnarra, Whidfield, Rathnew, Aughrim, Laragh, Kilmacanogue, Roundwood, Bray, Enniskerry, and Wicklow town, has a record of 3 wins, 1 ties, and 1 loss.

31 BRA AND KNICKERS

'Hey, Rosie. How are you doing in Dublin?' asked Cary. It was late Saturday afternoon. He was lying on his couch munching on some crisps as he talked on his mobile.

'I'm okay, yeah. Exhausted but okay. Maura and her husband Bill picked me up at O'Connell Station–took me to their house in the Liberties. What a neat place, Car. Uh-huh. They have two little ones, a girl and a boy, six and eight–very sweet kids. Bill made us a delicious meal–a curry–we all drank way too much wine, and Maura and me stayed up late talking.'

'Sound, Rosie. I'm glad you had a good visit. And your meetings today? How did they go?'

She sighed. 'Yeah, there were about twelve participants this morning, age eighteen to about twenty-five, all with ostomies, some recent, some several years ago. Some of them seemed pretty much at ease talking about their challenges. But a few I could tell were nervous and didn't have much to say at first.'

'Were you? Nervous, I mean?'

'Yeah, I was. I really had no idea what to expect. But Maura's good, yeh know–puts everyone at ease. But she doesn't hesitate to speak up, too, when necessary. And she made sure everyone participated.'

'Did it go on all day?'

'Yeah. One morning session, two hours, then another one in the afternoon with a new group. They were young, Car, from twelve to about fifteen.'

'So what did you do?'

'Well, Maura introduced me to each group and then, part way into the meeting, she asked me to tell my story–yeh know, about my disease, my surgery, my recovery, and so on. But she especially wanted me to tell them about my life now, ten years on. I gotta say, Car, I felt like I had a lot to contribute. But it was very emotional for me. I started to feel weak midway through the afternoon session.'

'I'll bet you being there meant a lot to them, Rosie, especially the younger ones.'

'I hope so, I don't know. It's not like I have any secrets about living with an ostomy to share with them. They've probably already read it all or heard it all from Maura and others. But maybe seeing someone close to their age who's been through it, yeh know? Maybe that helps. But it was hard, hearin' their stories and seein' their faces, yeh know? Especially the younger ones. By the time that afternoon session ended I was physically and emotionally spent.'

Just then Cary's mobile beeped. 'I better take this call, Rosie. So I'll see you tomorrow, right? You sure you don't want me to come get you?'

'No, that's okay. Maura will drive me to the bus station or the nearest Luas stop. I'll be fine. I'll probably get to Glenkerry by 3 or 4.'

Cary rang off, then switched to the incoming call.

'Hey, Shiv. Wow, how're you?'

He listened, then replied. 'Yeah, good, real good, Shiv. Busy, but good.'

Again he listened. 'Well, that's a long story, Shiv. Yeah, Sam's been a big help. But it got complicated, yeh know? Very complicated.' He paused, not wanting to go into many details. 'So, how's work goin'?'

Again he listened. 'Oh, Shiv, I'm so sorry. What happened?'

He listened for nearly a minute. 'Well, did you talk to him, ask him for an explanation?'

Again there was a long pause as Siobhan talked.

'Gee, Shiv, that's awful. Aw, Shiv, don't cry. Everything'll be all right. I'm sure of it. The labour market is probably in your favour right now, especially in tech, right?'

'What? You're where?' He looked up. Parked at the kerb in front of the *Gazette* office was a small sedan. The driver was waving at him. It was Siobhan.

'What the heck?' He rose from his desk, opened the door, and stepped out onto the footpath. Siobhan was still seated, looking up at him, tears streaming down her face.

'I'm sorry, Car. I'm rubbish, total and complete rubbish.'

He crouched down, reached through the open window, and touched her on the shoulder. 'Hey, it's gonna be okay, Shiv. You'll bounce back, I know you will. And those idiots in London will be missing you–count on it.'

Siobhan was wiping her eyes. Cary opened the car door and offered his hand.

'Come through, I'll fix you a cuppa.'

Siobhan resisted. 'I don't want to burden you with my problems. That's all you need. And Rosie.'

'Listen, no worries, yeah? Rosie's above in Dublin overnight. Come on.'

He led her up to his flat and made her a cup of tea. She sat on his couch sniffling. 'I hate for you to see me like this, Car. I really do.'

He sat next to her and took her hand. She rested her head against his shoulder.

'So tell me everything, Shiv.'

Siobhan Sullivan–hard-driving, ambitious Siobhan. The last time he'd seen her she'd been headed to London for a deadly new job. And now, barely three months on, she had been laid off, made redundant. She was blindsided.

'Just the last few weeks my boss was talkin' like I was doin' great. He couldn't say enough for me. But I guess business has been slack and he got the word Monday from his boss that he had to let someone go. And well, that someone was me. Yeh know, last hired–first fired.'

She slumped forward, her face in her hands. 'I'm so humiliated, Car. I haven't even told my family. You, Ellen, and Anders are the only ones who know.'

'Anders, oh, yeah, well, I'm sure he'll be there for you, right? And his job is solid?'

'Yeah, I guess. But he's hardly ever around.'

'Whatta you mean? Where is he?'

'He's been stayin' at Freja's flat lately.'

'Freja?'

'Yeah, his girlfriend. From Sweden. She moved to London about a month ago out of the blue.'

Cary was partially stunned at this news. Partially because he was never really certain that Anders was anything more than a flatmate to Siobhan, and vice versa. This 'mate' business, this vagueness about relationships, it was an unstated rule that Cary and Siobhan had observed almost as long as they had been friends. More than once Cary found himself intimating to Rosie that Siobhan and Anders were a couple. But he was never really sure of it. It was just his way of trying to allay Rosie's lingering worries about him and Siobhan.

'Aw, Shiv, I'm sorry. So, you're moving back to Ireland...'

Siobhan bit her lip, then looked away. 'I don't know where else to go, Car. At least I've got a few friends here, I mean, at DCU–and you.'

'Oh, yeah, well, a course.'

'So I'll start job hunting right away is what I'm planning. As soon as I find a place to live...' She paused. Maybe she was waiting for a response from Cary. But after a few uncomfortable moments of silence she continued. '...in Dublin.'

'Wow, well, there's lots of flats available in the city these days, or at least that's what I've heard.'

Siobhan smiled and nodded. 'Yeah, I'm sure there are.'

'But, hey, yeh know, if yeh want to spend the night here, you can. You can have the bedroom. I'll doss on the couch. You don't want to drive like this.'

'Wow, thanks, Car, that's really sweet of you. Yer sure, now? Yeh know...' She cocked her head as if to emphasise what was unsaid, about the white elephant in the room, or rather in Dublin.

'Yeah, sure.'

They stayed up late talking about their uni days and their many mutual friends from DCU. Cary recounted with great animation that visit by Brendan Canty and Cian Mahoney back in July, their raucous evening at Phinney's and the memorable football match the following morning. And Siobhan told him about several of her girlfriends who were married, engaged, in new relationships, and/or pregnant. Siobhan had brought along several bottles of wine and they somehow managed to finish two and make a serious dent in the third.

Finally Cary helped Siobhan into his bedroom, retrieved her luggage from the car, and managed to find some clean towels for the loo. He would have apologised for the condition of the ensuite, but Siobhan was already asleep, fully dressed, in his bed. He drew some pyjama bottoms from his closet, stepped out into the hallway, and switched off the bedroom light.

* * *

Early the next morning Cary slipped out to Costcutter to purchase the ingredients for a decent breakfast for his guest. He knew Siobhan's breakfast tastes were very different to his own and he wanted to do well by her, boost her morale. When she finally rose and staggered into the kitchen, Cary was hard at work.

'Wow, streaky bacon, blood sausage, mashed peas and beans. Now I know I'm back in Ireland, Car.'

Over coffee they talked more about old university friends. Cary brought Siobhan up to date on the death at the Black Castle. And he shared with her some of his stories from interviews with the Gorayas and others. Finally they talked more about her job situation and her housing situation.

'Well, they gave me a decent redundancy package anyway, so I have a month or two to get myself settled. And Anders thinks Freja might move in with him, so I won't be leavin' him in the lurch.'

Just then Siobhan's mobile buzzed.

'Hey, Maria, yeah. You got my message.'

She was on the phone for quite a while. When she finally rang off she was beaming.

'That was Maria, from that hotel I worked at on Whitworth Road. Yeah, she says I can stay with her for a while. And they probably could use me part-time in reception, too.'

Soon Siobhan had showered, dressed, and with Cary's help hauled her two large suitcases down the narrow stairway and out to her rented car. Cary lifted the valises into her boot, then they said their goodbyes.

'Thank you, Car. For everything.' She hugged him, then leaned back and smiled. Then she kissed him. At that very moment Catherine passed by in her car, on her way to the shops.

* * *

Anxious about the story on the housing situation, Cary ignored the kitchen sink full of dirty dishes and sat at his desk working for the remainder of the morning. At midday he went for a run, across the bridge and along the river road toward Whidfield. When he returned he was surprised to see Rosie just stepping out of the door at 1 Upton Road.

'This is a surprise, Rosie. You're back early,' he said brightly.

She was red-faced and appeared on the verge of tears. She shot him a withering glare, then turned her back on him and walked away along the footpath, carrying a small valise.

'What's the matter, Rosie?' he asked, following after her. No response. He ran after her and took her arm.

'Let go of me,' she said angrily as she jerked her arm from his grasp.

He continued to follow her.

'Sod off, you dick.'

But Cary persisted. Finally she turned and faced him, tears streaming down her cheeks.

'Don't you get it? I'm done with you. Get lost.'

'But…'

She was stalking away. 'I'm away one night and you're entertaining another girl.'

'It was just Siobhan, Rosie. She came unannounced. She's been laid off. I just let her stay the night, that's all.'

But Rosie didn't look back. Cary stood watching forlornly as she ascended Anglesey Lane.

Back in the *Gazette* office he was already kicking himself. She'd surprised him–come home early–gone looking for him in his flat–found the sink full of dishes and two unfinished breakfast platters. The smell of fried breakfast meat still hung in the air, hardly Cary's typical morning fare as Rosie would have noticed. And there in the trash were two empty wine bottles and a third opened on the sideboard. He usually cleaned up after a meal, but he had been distracted, distracted by his visitor, by Siobhan. And the clues of that encounter, he quickly realised and rued, were everywhere.

Suddenly he had a sinking feeling in his stomach. In the bedroom the bed was unmade, a towel was thrown over a chair. Then he looked in the loo. Over the towel bar hung a bra and knickers–Siobhan's. She'd rinsed them in the sink, he guessed, hung them to dry, and forgotten to pack them. Rosie had found them, no doubt. She'd probably gotten off the bus and stopped at his flat to use the loo.

He slumped onto the bed, his face in his hands, his head pounding. Was this it? Was this the end for him and Rosie? Why?

Because of his own carelessness, not cleaning up the place after his visitor had departed? Or letting her stay in the first place? Or thinking he could be seeing Rosie, sleeping with her, while pretending to Siobhan that he was still available?

He was trying to see the situation from Rosie's perspective, and it did not look good. She had expressed to him more than once her worries about him and Siobhan Sullivan.

And then he thought of Siobhan. Granted she was at a low point in her life right now and had to be allowed some slack. But the thought suddenly struck him. Was it possible, was it conceivable, that Siobhan's visit, those wine bottles, those undies hanging in the loo–was it part of some intentional plan, some scurrilous subterfuge, to do damage to Cary and Rosie? It seemed absurd. But...

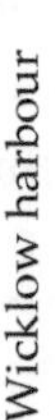

Wicklow harbour

32 STAND-DOWN

I'm not gonna take this lying down, Cary tells himself. *I'll make things right with Rosie or die trying.*

But there needs to be a stand-down period, that much is clear. Nothing can be done or attempted until the emotions of the moment have subsided, until the shock of what Rosie stumbled onto has faded, if it ever will. A day, at least.

After cleaning his flat thoroughly and carefully removing all evidence of his overnight guest, he devotes the remainder of the day to his article on the housing crisis in County Wicklow and in Ireland, even as thoughts of self-recrimination and remorse constantly intrude.

He rises early Monday morning, watching for Rosie to pass on her bicycle enroute to school. Maybe, just maybe, she'll wave and smile, even stop and tell him all is forgiven. But as she pedals past she doesn't so much as glance in the direction of 1 Upton Road. To his eye she looks wan and pasty.

But he has a plan. He will watch for her return in the afternoon. Then, a few minutes later, he'll climb Anglesey Lane and pay a visit to the O'Malley farm with some flowers in hand, flowers from his mother's garden. Except that he isn't sure that Catherine is any too pleased with him either, having witnessed that furtive kiss on the footpath.

Then at midmorning his mobile buzzes.

'Cary McGurk?'

'Yes.'

'This is Margaret Healy. I'm the nurse at *Coláiste Gaeilge*.'

'Yes.'

'I see that you are listed as Rose O'Malley's emergency contact.'

'Huh?'

'She's being taken to hospital by ambulance.'

Cary's mind is racing. 'What? When? What's wrong?'

'She came to my office around ten–she was looking poorly. And she was confused. I had her lie down and took her pulse. Her heart was racing and she was very jittery. She passed out briefly. I thought knowing her medical history we ought to get her to A&E in Wicklow right away. They're loading her in the ambulance right now.'

'Yeah, right, okay. I–I'm on my way. Can you tell them to tell Rosie I'm on my way?'

In minutes he is speeding down the road toward Wicklow town on his motorcycle, unable to think of anything except seeing Rosie, of being there for her. God forbid, he is saying to himself, anything should happen to her before he can be at her side. He can't bear the thought.

He arrives at A&E only a few minutes after the ambulance. He is instructed to have a seat in the waiting room. Feeling light-headed and vaguely nauseated, he sits bent over, his head between his knees, then lies down on the pew.

Finally, after what seems like an eternity, a nurse appears and speaks to him.

'Rose is stable, Mr McGurk. She was pretty weak when she arrived but she's on an IV and resting now.'

'What's this all about? Can you tell me?'

'She was severely dehydrated–her electrolytes were very low. She's getting all she needs intravenously now. But it would probably be best to let her sleep for a while.'

'Couldn't I just see her for a moment? Just so she knows I'm here?'

'All right. But just one minute, okay?'

He stands and takes several steps, then teeters, feeling light-headed.

'Are you okay, sir?'

'Yes ma'am.'

He follows the nurse down a long aisle of drawn curtains, trying to catch his breath and steady his racing pulse. Near the end the nurse pulls aside a curtain.

'Rose? You have a visitor,' she says softly.

Cary steps up to the side of Rosie's bed, trying his best to smile though his lips are quivering. Rosie is lying very still, her eyes closed. He takes her hand, bends over and kisses it. She opens her eyes and looks at him.

'Hi,' he says. 'How are you doing?'

'Been better,' she answers softly.

'I–the nurse says I can only stay for a minute. But I'll be outside. If you need me. And I'll come back later.'

She nods, then closes her eyes.

'Rosie? I'm sorry. Okay?'

No reaction.

* * *

Cary went back to the waiting room and sat looking idly at his mobile. He wanted to call Rosie's brother, Buddy, and her mother, but first he felt he should talk further to the nurse, so he'd know what to tell them. He caught her eye a few minutes later.

'Rose said she had a long weekend, that she was visiting friends in Dublin and had more to drink than she is accustomed to. And she said she attended a support group for ostomy patients at Mercy Hospital and it was exhausting–emotionally draining. Too much alcohol and stress can take a toll on anyone, even a healthy young person. But with her ostomy, well, dehydration is a particular risk. You know, maintaining just the right balance of electrolytes in the intestines. It can be tricky. But the doctor has seen her and believes she'll be all right. She can probably go home tomorrow if all goes well.'

Reassured, Cary called Buddy's mobile and left a message. Then he called Mary, Rosie's mother, in Galway. She was alarmed as any mother would be. Should she come straightaway?

'No, Mrs O'Malley,' insisted Cary, 'I don't think you should. Best to talk to her when she gets home, probably tomorrow. See what she says then. I promise you'll hear from her or from me in the morning.'

Mrs O'Malley lavished words of praise on Cary for his care of her daughter, words that stung.

If she only knew.

Then he called his mother and had to reassure her repeatedly that Rosie was all right, that this was just a temporary setback.

Nearly two hours passed. Buddy O'Malley arrived looking worried. He and Cary shook hands. 'How's Rosie?'

Cary reassured him. The nurse had said that Rosie was awake and having a light meal, and they could both visit with her shortly.

Rosie was sitting up in bed. She smiled at her brother. 'Oh, you shouldn't have come all that way.'

Buddy chuckled. 'It's not the other side of the moon, sis. How are you?'

'I'm okay, Bud. Gettin' better.'

'So what happened?'

Rosie shook her head. 'I just got careless, is all. I had too much to drink, and I had a stressful day with those support groups at Mercy. Sometimes I just forget that I have to be careful, yeh know?'

'Well, you look fine, Rosie.'

'Thanks. Nice stylish hospital gown, eh?' she said with a chuckle as she smoothed out the blue and white fabric with one hand. 'Plenty of ventilation, too.'

Buddy and Cary laughed.

'Thanks for comin', both a you.'

'Ma sends her love, too,' added Buddy. He turned and patted Cary on the shoulder. 'Himself called her. Good man.'

She turned then and looked directly at Cary for the first time.

'Yeah. Good man.'

Buddy stayed for nearly an hour, telling his sister about Danielle and her work, about his job, and about the Shankill GAA football team he had joined. Then, noticing that Rosie was looking sleepy, he left, promising to come by the house after she was home and offering to do chores for her.

'Well, I guess I'll be on my way, too,' began Cary.

Rosie reached out for his hand.

'Thank you, Car, for everything.'

'No worries, Rosie. After all, I am number one...' He paused. 'On your emergency contacts, that is.'

Rosie smiled.

When he returned to Glenkerry, Cary went straight to Rosie's and followed her instructions for tending to the chickens and the sheep. Then he stopped at his mother's to reassure her about Rosie, but also to try and undo the damage that scene in front of the *Gazette* office may have wrought.

First, 'Yes, Ma, that was Siobhan you saw me with yesterday.'

Then, 'No, Ma, there is nothing going on between us.'

Then, 'Yes, Ma, she kissed me.'

Then, 'No, Ma, it meant nothing.'

Then, 'Well, Ma, she's in a bad way right now.'

Then, 'Yes, Ma, she stayed overnight.'

Then, 'No, Ma, of course not. I would never–I am *not* having this conversation with my mother.'

Then, 'Yes, Rosie knows.'

Then he added, 'Everything's fine with us,' while thinking, '*If only.*'

Then, 'Enough of this third degree, Ma. I'm goin' home.'

33 NUMBER ONE

Rosie called the next morning just as Cary was preparing to email a set of nearly one hundred subscription invoices.

'They tell me I'll be discharged shortly, Car. They'll get me a taxi.'

'No way, Rosie. I'm coming to get you. No, of course I don't mean on my bike. I'll borrow Ma's car. I know she's at home, she just called. So I'll be there in say thirty. No, it's not a problem at all. Just sit tight, yeah?'

As soon as he had rung off, he got another call, from Del.

'Good news, mate. The Boyles were in immigration court this morning, Anna, Chris, and Kamal. Yeah. They got fined a thousand euro each. That's it. The judge said he was taking into consideration the difficult situation in Syria as well as the problems confronted by many Syrians who sought asylum in Ireland.'

Cary thanked Del for the call but explained that he had to be in Wicklow to pick up Rosie. 'Yeah, she's okay.'

Del knew about her sudden departure from school the previous day.

When Cary pulled up to the hospital entrance, he could see Rosie waiting inside in a wheelchair. An attendant pushed the chair out to the car and helped Rosie into the passenger seat.

'Well, you look fine, Rose. How are you feeling?'

'Pretty much normal, I guess. But I imagine I'll want to lie low for a bit. I already called Mr Forster to say I'll be out of school at least two more days.'

He inquired about how she slept, about what she had for breakfast, and what instructions she had received from the doctor.

'Rest, relaxation, plenty of fluids. And no alcohol.' She buried her face in her hands. 'I'm so embarrassed.' She nodded toward the hospital. 'They all must think I'm some kind of dipso in there. I didn't drink that much, I swear. It's just, well, yeh know, I lost track is all. I can't tell Maura–she'd feel responsible.'

Then they fell silent, both pretending to watch flocks of sheep grazing on each side of the road while struggling to find the right words.

Finally Cary spoke. 'Oh, hey, Del called just after you. Good news.' He told her about the outcome of the Boyles' immigration case.

Rosie sighed. 'Oh, what a relief. I've been so worried about them, especially what might happen to Molly and Mike if...'

At Rosie's house Cary walked her inside.

'Can I fix you a cuppa?'

'No, thank you, Car. I'll be fine. I'll just check on the chickens, shower, then take a nap.' Then she smiled. 'Oh, yeah, and drink five or ten litres of water.'

Cary chuckled. 'Good idea. And don't forget to call your ma. I promised her one of us would give her a call.'

He wanted to give Rosie a hug but wasn't sure how it would be received. He turned to go but she took his arm, stepped up to him and kissed him on the cheek.

'So, thank you, emergency contact number one, for everything.'

'I'm still number one, am I?'

'Yes, Car, you are still number one. And so you shall remain, I hope.'

'As long as you want me, Rosie, I swear.'

She gave him a hug. Then she stroked his hair and looked into his eyes. She smiled as she spoke: 'We're not finished, yeh know, with Sunday.'

Cary nodded, his eyes averted. 'Yeah, I had a feeling we weren't.'

She sighed. 'Another time, mate.'

* * *

It was Friday. Rosie seemed to be fully recovered and was back at school. She stopped by the *Gazette* office on her way home.

'You won't believe this, Rosie. I just checked the *Gazette* subscriptions account. I hadn't looked at it in a couple weeks, I was so discouraged. But the payments have been really coming in. As of today we have over a thousand paid subscribers. And quite a few for a full year.'

'Wow, that's incredible, Car.'

'Yep. I guess people liked my stories on the refugees and all.'

'Like I been tellin' you all along, they want the *Gazette* to succeed, Car, they want *you* to succeed. You have to know that by now. It should make you feel good.'

'I suppose.'

'That's your problem, Ciaran McGurk, you never give yourself enough credit. You're always second guessing yourself. With work–and other things.'

That last phrase set him back momentarily. But he rallied.

'Listen, how about we go to the Grenadine tonight, my treat? Call it an anniversary.'

'Anniversary?'

'Yes, an anniversary. It was–hmm, let's see–exactly ninety-three days ago that we had dinner there. Remember?'

'I do.'

'And then went back to my place.'

'Uh-huh.' She did remember it all–the lovely meal–the walk home in the rain–the invitation to stay the night. 'Wow, our ninety-third anniversary. Now that is a landmark. How many couples ever celebrate their ninety-third anniversary? Does this mean gifts?'

'I hope not,' said Cary with a wry smile. 'Because I have no idea what the proper gift is for a ninety-third anniversary.'

They shared a laugh.

'All right, then, the Grenadine it is,' said Rosie. 'Although maybe I'd better skip the wine.'

'Well, Ciaran, this is lovely. Shall we toast?' asked Rosie.

They raised their water glasses.

'To Cary for being there for me when I needed him.'

'To Rosie for allowing me to be her number one.'

They clinked their glasses. Then they tucked in to a sumptuous meal reminiscent of the one they had enjoyed together in July.

'So is it true what Sophie's ma said, that you been talking to Maura about studying social work?'

Rosie hesitated, biting her lip. 'I'm curious, yeh know. And Maura is all for it, a course. But I'm not sure I could do it–help other people cope with surgery, and all.'

'But look what you did for Sophie.'

Rosie nodded. 'Yeah, but that day, with Maura's support groups at Mercy–it was really hard, Car. I was a mess, watchin' those folks, especially the young ones.' Cary could see she was struggling to control her emotions. She took a sip of water. 'I see how Maura handles it. She connects, but she doesn't get too emotionally involved. She sort of walks them up to the edge, yeh know what I mean? Then she steps back. I get that, I really do. She has to, to maintain some distance, or she'd be unable to help them.' Rosie bit her lip. 'I'm just not sure I could do that. Do you see what I mean?'

'Yeah, I think I do. You're right, there's gotta be a fine line, between empathising and sympathising, maybe?'

Rosie reached out and touched his hand. 'Thanks, Car. You get me.' She looked into his eyes. 'But anyway, Mr Forster talked to me today. Maureen Brogan is not coming back from maternity leave after all. So he wants me to stay on for the whole year.'

'Wow, Rosie, what did you say?'

'I asked him if I could think it over.'

'And?'

'I wanted to talk to you about it. Whatta yeh think?'

'What do *I* think? You know what I think, Rosie. If you want to do it, you ought to.'

* * *

When it was all over they walked the short distance along the High Street to 1 Upton Road. At the door Cary hesitated, still not certain about how the evening would end.

He took both her hands. 'Roisin O'Malley, can we put Sunday behind us, please?'

'Well, Ciaran, what do you have to say for yourself?'

'I was an eejit.'

'Well, yeah, but we both knew that,' she replied with a grin. She was waiting for more.

'I should've offered to take Siobhan to my ma's.'

'Yeah, you shoulda.'

'And I should've told her about us all along, instead of trying to keep it from her, like I was protecting her or something.'

'Yeah, agreed.'

'But I wasn't unfaithful, Rosie, I swear. I slept on the couch. I still have a backache to prove it. Honest, Rosie, there's no one but you. Please believe me.'

She looked into his eyes, those puppy-like eyes that couldn't lie if they wanted to. She waited what seemed to Cary an awfully long time before she replied.

'I do, Car, I believe you. Maybe I'm naïve, but somehow I don't think you would sleep with another woman so long as we're together–even if that other woman was Siobhan Sullivan. You're too good.' She paused. 'But maybe *I'm* the eejit–thinkin' that?'

Cary shook his head. 'I would never, I swear.'

He kissed her, took her hand, and led her through the door.

'One more thing,' said Rosie as they lay in bed, arms wrapped around each other. 'I hope you don't flatter yourself that you are the reason I got sick. Because you weren't. Not at all.'

'No, of course not, I know that. It was the wine, and the long day with those support groups.'

'Right. And I was already feeling sick on the bus ride home before my surprise visit to your flat.'

She put on her most innocent expression.

'Besides, if any bloke ever did me wrong, really wrong...' She placed both hands around his neck, the twinkle in her eyes momentarily replaced by that studied teacher's glare. 'I wouldn't get sick–I'd get even.'

34 NOTHING COMPARES 2 U

A celebration for the Hurleys took place on the Glenkerry GAA grounds on Saturday. It included the families of the team members as well as a number of townspeople and school staff. True, the Hurleys had lost that match against Montkilleen National School, but all of Glenkerry was determined to show them how proud they were of their performance in this, the first season of *Coláiste Gaeilge's* own camogie team. Just reaching the semi-finals was a tremendous accomplishment and the team had comported themselves extremely well, all agreed.

An impressive feast was laid on for the occasion thanks to contributions from nearly every restaurant and market in Glenkerry including spring rolls from Paddy's Chinese Takeaway, corn and crab fritters from Siam Bistro, cod crunchies from the Glenkerry Fishmonger, and burgers and chips from Phinney's Pub. Cary's mother assisted her friend Devi Patel serving stuffed dosas, potato cakes, and naan bread at the Punjab Palace table. Jim Kelly of Kelly's Cones set up a make-your-own sundae table which was of course a big hit.

'Have you seen the Boyles?' Rosie asked Cary as the festivities got underway.

But at that very moment Molly, Mike, Anna, and Chris appeared. Molly waved enthusiastically to Rosie.

'I think you've got a new BFF, Rosie,' said Cary.

'Yeah, well, we kinda bonded that day at Lough Beag. You know what that place can do to people, right?' She winked at him.

Soon Del arrived in civilian clothes. He stood next to Sabrina gazing around in amazement, then turned to Cary with a wry smile.

'Why didn't anyone throw a party like this for us in our footie days at *Coláiste*, Car?'

'I don't know, Del, maybe because we sucked?'

'Oh, come on, we went to the county championship at least once.'

'I think that must've been in your dreams, mate.'

Just then someone turned up the music and the real fun began. It was mostly Taylor Swift, Ed Sheeran, and the like, although Cary was pleased to hear one song by Van Morrison and one by the Saw Doctors. Some wild dancing ensued with Cary, Del, Mike Boyle, Tim Phinney, and several other brothers of the team members recruited to the delight and amusement of all.

Most of the songs were lively, but the tone of things changed dramatically when the strains of 'Nothing Compares 2 U' sung by Sinéad O'Connor rang out. That Irish icon, symbol of the new Ireland for decades, described by many as the 'moral compass of Ireland,' had lived out her last days in County Wicklow and the memory of her funeral just a few months earlier was still strong for many, even those too young to have known her in her prime. Cary took Rosie's hand, she wrapped her arms around his neck, and they swayed to the music. Soon Del and Sabrina and several parents did likewise. Then some of the younger folks stepped out, even a very uncomfortable Mike with Gráinne and an awkward Tim with Molly. Many of the older folks couldn't help but tear up at the sight of so many happy young faces moved by one of Ireland's most famous songstresses.

The mood changed abruptly as once again the strains of 'Come On Eileen' reverberated and Eileen Keough, who was after all the team captain, led another performance of that raucous line dance to the delight of all. They replayed the song and repeated the dance several times until at last the entire team fell to the ground laughing.

Then Sabrina stood up to say a few words.

'Wow, Sinéad and "Come On Eileen"–those are hard acts to follow.' Everyone laughed.

She looked around at the crowd, parents, friends, well-wishers, and lastly at her team seated in front of her.

'I just want to say what a pleasure–what an honour–it has been to coach you guys this season. You were brilliant, every day, rain or shine, in victory and in defeat. And the fact that you made it to the county semi-finals, well, that was amazing. And it's all on you, Hurleys, *you* did it. So congratulate yourselves.'

Cheers and applause rose from the team and the onlookers.

'Now Mr Forster has a special surprise for you, Hurleys.'

The principal stood up and offered more words of praise for the Hurley Girlies, *Coláiste Gaeilge's* first ever camogie team. And then to everyone's surprise, he presented a gold and green t-shirt to each team member, to Coach Selkirk, and Assistant Coach O'Malley. On the front of each shirt was the school's logo. On the back was inscribed, '*A day without Camogie is like–just kidding–I HAVE NO IDEA!*'

The crowd cheered as the team members held their shirts high.

'Now we have a special guest who has a few words to say,' added Sabrina.

Kevin Leahy, never one to miss an opportunity to speak to his constituency, addressed the Hurleys and the gathered throng.

'We're all very proud of you, my dears, and what you've accomplished. And so in my capacity as a member of the County Council, I hereby declare this day Hurley Girlies day in County Wicklow.'

Another tremendous roar rose from the crowd. The players hugged each other one last time. With the music and formalities out of the way, the team crowded around the food tables intent on finishing every last morsel.

Anna and Chris Boyle spoke to Rosie and Cary.

'I don't know if you heard, but Chris and Kamal were in court yesterday in Dublin,' said Anna. 'They received suspended sentences.' Tears welled in her eyes.

'Oh, Anna, Chris, that's wonderful news,' said Rosie.

'We owe you two a lot, and Coach Selkirk. Thanks to you, we don't feel like strangers anymore.'

Just then the team assembled for parents to take pictures. They were all beaming, including Molly Boyle, front and centre, her arms wrapped around her teammates.

And again the voice of Sinéad O'Connor rose in what seemed both an anthem and fitting finale for the day, 'Nothing Compares 2 U.'

AN DEIREADH

GLOSSARY

Aoife (EE-fuh) – A common girl's name in Ireland

An Dílis – The faithful

Banger – A beat up old car

Bas (or boss) – The expanded tip of a hurley

Bewley's – A popular Irish tea

Boke – Vomit

Boot – The trunk or storage area of a car

Boreen – A narrow country road

Camogie – A traditional Gaelic women's team sport played with stick and ball

Céad Míle Fáilte Romhat – A hundred thousand welcomes

Coláiste – (coh-LAS-teh) An Irish secondary school

Comhairleoir – Councillor, mentor, also the title of an elected member of a county council in Ireland

Craic – Good times, friendly social activity

Demesne – Land associated with a manor or other large estate

Doss – To sleep rough, bed down, crash

Eejit – An idiot

Free – In camogie, an unobstructed shot awarded to one team following a foul

Footpath – A sidewalk

GAA – Gaelic Athletic Association, a sporting association in Ireland that supports Gaelic games

Gaeilge (GWAL-gah) – Gaelic, Irish

Garda (pl. gardaí) – The Irish police, also the title of an Irish police officer

Garda Síochána, An – The national police service of the Republic of Ireland

Gráinne (GRAHN-ya) – A common girl's name in Ireland

Hurley – A wooden stick with a wide, flat blade used in camogie and hurling

In donkey's years – A very long time

Isla (EYE-la) – A common girl's name in Ireland

Kit – A uniform, outfit, gear

Knackered – Tired, exhausted

Knickers – Women's underpants

Loo – Toilet

Lough – Lake

Michaelmas – The Feast of St Michael, celebrated on September 29

Pew – Bench

Puck-out – In camogie, the return of the ball to play after it crosses the endline

Quid – Old term for a pound (currency)

Red card – A card raised by a referee in camogie to indicate a serious foul

Runners – Running shoes, sneakers

Saoirse (SUR-shuh) – A common girl's name in Ireland

Shemozzle – A noisy dispute or argument

Shift – Kiss

Slán agat (SLAWN-a-gut) – Goodbye, said by the departing person

Slán leat (SLAWN-lyat) – Goodbye, said by the person staying

Sliotar (SLO-tar) – The leather ball used in camogie

Torch – A flashlight

Townland – A small geographical division within an Irish town

Yellow card – A card raised by a referee in camogie to indicate a minor foul

ACKNOWLEDGEMENTS

This book is dedicated to my great-great-grandmother, Hannah Hughes McGurk. Hannah emigrated from County Tyrone to America in 1849 with her four children, the youngest of whom was an infant at the time. Like millions of others, Hannah and her children were fleeing the famine that had wrought misery, disease, and death in Ireland for nearly a decade. Throughout the famine, the English exported Ireland's food crops by the tonne to feed their own people, leaving their Irish subjects to starve. And Hannah's husband, Bernard McGurk, was convicted of theft in an English court and sent to prison in Tasmania for seven years. According to family lore, he was caught stealing a loaf of bread to feed his family. Hannah McGurk and her children were surely 'fugitives from injustice.'

In June 2022 while visiting Wicklow town, I stood on Travelhawk Beach looking up at the Black Castle, that venerable fortress, and made the decision right then and there: book two of the series would begin with an incident on that very spot. Soon the story of *Fugitive from Injustice* began to unfold in my imagination.

Camogie is as much a part of modern Ireland as baseball is of America, but it is little known in the US. That's a shame. It is an exciting game to watch, lightning fast and demanding on its players both physically and mentally. I hope the descriptions of camogie in *Fugitive from Injustice* do justice to the game and the young women who play it with such devotion and passion.

As always, I am indebted to my wife, Susan D. Milsom, for her careful reading, editing, and comments on early versions of this book.

CREDITS

Cover, page 6. The Black Castle, from Robert O. Newenham, *Picturesque Views of the Antiquities of Ireland Vol. 1.* London: Thomas and William Boone, 1830. Artist: R. O. Newenham Engraver: J. D. Harding

Page 40. Camogie, from Pixabay.com. Photographer: Roninmd

Page 98. Cliff Walk, from Flickr.com. Photographer: Chris

Page 106. Irish cottage, from Pinterest.com.

Page 112. Lough Tay, from Pixabay.com. Photographer: Darren Quigley

Page 124. Travelhawk Beach. Photographer: Robert T. McMaster

Page 136. Great Sugar Loaf, https://www.flickr.com/photos/paulodonnell/7818352834/, CC BY 2.0, https://commons.wikimedia.org/w/index.php?curid=80325506. Photographer: Paul O'Donnell

Page 150. Dublin, from Pixabay.com. Photographer: Sean Griffin

Page 162. Lugnaquilla, Joe King, CC BY-SA 3.0, https://commons.wikimedia.org/w/index.php?curid=15786571. Photographer: Joe King

Page 174. Powerscourt Waterfall, from Pixabay.com. Photographer: Ciarán Ó Muirgheasa

Page 186. Mountain road, from Pexels.com. Photographer: Oscar Cotter

Page 222. Tralee. Photographer: Robert T. McMaster

Page 248. Ireland forest, from Pixabay.com. Photographer: H. Bieser

Page 272. William Butler Yeats, oil painting, John Singer Sargent, 1908.

Page 302. Fishing boats in Wicklow harbour, from Pixabay.com. Photographer: Ciarán Ó Muirgheasa

Page 316. Dingle landscape, from Pixabay.com.

ABOUT THE AUTHOR

Robert T. McMaster grew up in Southbridge, Massachusetts. He holds a B.A. from Clark University and graduate degrees from Boston College, Smith College, and the University of Massachusetts. He taught biology at Holyoke Community College in Massachusetts from 1994 to 2014. His parents' reminiscences of growing up in early 20th century America were the inspiration for four novels, *Trolley Days* (2012), *The Dyeing Room* (2014), *Noah's Raven* (2017), and *Darkest Before Dawn* (2022). He has also authored a biography, *All the Light Here Comes from Above: The Life and Legacy of Edward Hitchcock* (2021). *Fugitive from Injustice* is the second in his series of County Wicklow Mysteries; the first, *Rose of Glenkerry*, was published in 2022. He has at least two ancestral ties to Ireland: John and Katharine McMasters emigrated to America from County Antrim in about 1713; Hannah McGurk and her children lived in County Tyrone before making their journey to America in 1849.

ROSE OF GLENKERRY
Book 1 of the County Wicklow Mystery Series
by Robert T. McMaster

Twenty-one-year-old Ciaran McGurk has just graduated from a Dublin university and is about to set off on the adventure of a lifetime. He's planning a move to London with a classmate in hopes of landing a job in journalism, ideally for a newspaper. Writing is the work he loves, though he fears that in an era of social networking, print journalism is fast becoming the dinosaur of career paths.

But a family emergency interrupts all Cary's plans. Suddenly he finds himself back in his hometown, Glenkerry, in County Wicklow. There he reconnects with an old friend, Rosie O'Malley. Her story has always been a sad one, and now it seems history is repeating itself. Her mother has disappeared, and Rosie is desperate to find her. And Rosie's father and brothers are her biggest obstacles. So she turns to her old friend, Cary McGurk, for help. But it's complicated, with a web of secrets and lies entangling them.

Cary is torn—torn between starting a new life in London and plunging back into his old life in Glenkerry, a place full of sweet memories tinged with sorrow and regret. His head is telling him to move on, but will his heart listen?

Rose of Glenkerry—mystery, suspense, romance, all set against the backdrop of Ireland's incomparable County Wicklow. For additional information please visit

www.WicklowMysteries.com

THE TROLLEY DAYS BOOK SERIES
Novels of early 20th century America
by Robert T. McMaster

The nineteen-teens was a tumultuous era in American history. The pace of social change was dizzying: the rising tide of worker unrest, the battle for women's suffrage, the scourge of discrimination against minorities. New technologies—electricity, the telephone, the automobile—were transforming life. Meanwhile the war in Europe was drawing America inexorably into its vortex.

Author Robert T. McMaster transports his readers back in time to early 20th century America in the Trolley Days Series of historical novels. Set in a bustling New England industrial city, these books follow the lives of teenagers Jack Bernard and Tom Wellington through good times and bad, hope and despair, love and loss. Readers young and old will be captivated by the world of their grandparents and great-grandparents, an era seemingly remote that nonetheless speaks to us across the generations.

Trolley Days, *The Dyeing Room*, *Noah's Raven*, and *Darkest Before Dawn* are currently available in paperback and in several eBook formats. For additional information please visit

www.TrolleyDays.net

ALL THE LIGHT HERE COMES FROM ABOVE: The Life and Legacy of Edward Hitchcock

by Robert T. McMaster

EDWARD HITCHCOCK (1793-1864) was one of nineteenth-century America's foremost scientists. Best known for his pioneering research on the fossilised tracks of dinosaurs, he was also a geologist of international reputation, one of the first American scientists to embrace the theory of continental glaciation. A professor at Amherst College for nearly four decades, he took over the presidency in 1845 and saved that venerable institution from dissolution.

In *All the Light Here Comes from Above: The Life and Legacy of Edward Hitchcock*, Massachusetts author Robert T. McMaster brings Edward Hitchcock to life, revealing the humanity of the man with dignity, charm, and humour. Relying largely on Hitchcock's own words from his letters, notes, and other unpublished manuscripts, McMaster presents an intimate view of Edward Hitchcock, his scientific achievements, his theological writings, as well as his battles with powerful personal demons that threatened him at every turn.

For additional information please visit

www.EdwardHitchcock.com

The Dyeing Room (2014)

'…a compelling and carefully researched story.'
- Eileen Crosby, Archivist, Holyoke (MA) Public Library

Trolley Days (2012)

'…a joyful, engaging read from beginning to end…a masterful first novel.'   - Mark Ashton, *Southbridge* (MA) *Evening News*

All the Light Here Comes from Above: The Life and Legacy of Edward Hitchcock (2021)

'McMaster's biography brings Edward Hitchcock alive in all his facets…The book is eminently readable…I am confident in the scholarship of this work and recommend it to scholars as well as to anyone interested in history.'
- Joanne Bourgeois, Professor Emerita, University of Washington, review in *Earth Sciences History* 41(1) 2022

'A superb book that brings to light the person and his times.'
- Stephen George, Professor Emeritus of Biology, Amherst College

www.ingramcontent.com/pod-product-compliance
Lightning Source LLC
Chambersburg PA
CBHW060901140726
47996CB00001B/64